The Sunday Brunch Diaries

THE
Sunday Brunch
DIARIES

A Novel

Norma L. Jarrett

Broadway Books
NEW YORK

Copyright © 2008 by Norma L. Jarrett

Published in the United States by Broadway Books. an imprint of The Doubleday Publishing Group, a division of Random House, Inc., New York.
www.broadwaybooks.com

BROADWAY BOOKS and its logo, a letter B bisected on the diagonal, are trademarks of Random House, Inc.

BOOK DESIGN BY JENNIFER ANN DADDIO

Library of Congress Cataloging-in-Publication Data
Jarrett, Norma L.
The Sunday brunch diaries : a novel / Norma L. Jarrett. — 1st ed.
p. cm.
1. African American women—Fiction. 2. Female friendship—Fiction. 3. Church membership—Fiction. 4. Christian women—Fiction. I. Title.
PS3610.A77S863 2008
813'.6—dc22
2007052774

ISBN 978-0-7679-2143-5

PRINTED IN THE UNITED STATES OF AMERICA

1 3 5 7 9 10 8 6 4 2

First Edition

TO

Norman D. and Ethel Jarrett

ALWAYS & FOREVER

*"I am a little pencil in the hand of a writing God
who is sending a love letter to the world."*
—*Mother Teresa*

To God, my heavenly Father, for allowing me to be used for His glory. Lord, help me to stay strong in this literary journey. May I continue to be a good steward over Your gifts and remain faithful in what You have ordained for me to do. For only what You have purposed in my life will stand.

For my earthly father, Norman D. Jarrett, you are the ultimate fan! Your love and support is never ending. To my husband to be, Clarence K. York, our meeting was nothing less than divine intervention. Because of you, I'm able to experience unconditional love—"I have been blessed and divinely favored." As always, love, peace, and blessings to my family, Stephen Jarrett (Bro.), Paulette (Sis), Big Al, Little Stephen, Quiana, Al (II) Ashley and Ariel Jones. To extended family far and wide, especially (Quinne Ewing, Bessie Crutchfield, Leroy and Alfred Page, Arlene Jarrett, and the rest of the Jarrett-Page family). To the York family, thank you for making me feel so welcome, I feel extremely loved!

To faithful friends who are just like family: Mary Upshaw, Michele Austin, Tracy Hines, Carol Guess, and Quinella Minix.

To the Sorors of Alpha Kappa Alpha Sorority, Inc., much pink and green love. Especially Alpha Phi Chapter—Fall 86 (shouts out to Cynthia Throckmorton, Michelle Baker, Andrea Walbrook, Audra Foree, and the rest of my line). Special shout out to Soror Sheila Cash and Erica

Lowery. Always love to North Carolina A&T State University—Aggie Pride!

To literary friends: Anointed Authors on Tour (Kendra Norman-Bellamy, Vivi Monroe Congress, Tia McCollors, Vanessa Miller, Michelle Stimpson, and Shewanda Riley), Victoria Christopher Murray, Jacquelin Thomas, Trisha Thomas, Tiffany L. Warren, Reshonda Tate Billingsley, and many others. To Rawsistaz and other book clubs across the nation who have supported me. To media entities that have featured my work, including but not limited to: *Essence, Ebony, Upscale, Gospel Truth, USA Today, Houston Chronicle, Houston Defender;* Special thanks to: Majic 102, Yolanda Adams Morning Show (Don Corbett, Marcus Wiley, Larry Jones, and of course Ms. Yolanda Adams!), Madd Hatter Morning Show and many others!

To Lakewood Church and Pastor Osteen for blessing me weekly. To my favorite artists for constant inspiration: Israel Haughton and New Breed, Ce Ce Winans, Yolanda Adams, Oprah Winfrey, Tyler Perry, and others.

Lastly, special thanks to my publisher, Broadway Books at Doubleday, Janet Hill, Clarence Haynes (first editor), and Victoria Sanders. If I have forgotten anyone, charge it to my head and not my heart! Blessings . . . *Norma*

The Sunday Brunch Diaries

CHAPTER ONE

Shock and Awe

It's Monday and you're listening to the Yolanda Adams morning show with Brother Larry Jones and Marcus Wiley, "92.1 Praise!"

Jewel was starting her Monday morning after a busy weekend coordinating two major events. In the midst of listening to one of her favorite radio shows she realized the mail hadn't been checked in the past several days.

She jumped up and headed outside toward the mailbox station. As soon as she stepped outside she noticed the August heat was still in full force. She retrieved the mail, her fingers quickly sorting through envelopes as she walked back in the house. *Off 5th Annual Sale, Victoria's Secret—free pair of panties . . . I'll keep that one. Ohh . . . What's this?* Her eyebrows furrowed as she looked at the stamp and mouthed, *"Cayman Islands?"* She rushed inside, tore open the envelope, and pulled out a card. Her eyes grew bigger with each word she read. Her heart pushed and pounded as if it was about to bolt out of her chest. The breaths started coming quickly and her hands were shaking as she stared at the picture. "Nooooo!!!" she cried.

She picked up the phone and dialed frantically. *I just cannot believe this.* She dialed the first number. *No answer.* Then she dialed Capri at home. "Stan-ton residence . . . no, Mrs. Stanton *no es* home. Can I take a mess—? *Click. Got to move on.* She called Capri's cell phone. *No answer. Okay, relax.* She set the phone on the counter for a second. She paused with one hand on her hip and the other rubbing her forehead. She snatched it up again. *Angel . . . but Angel hates when I call her at work, oh well, that's never stopped me before.* Jewel's fingers danced across the phone with precision. She went through all her friend's numbers and no one answered. *This is a serious conspiracy—for real.* She took a few deep breaths. *Okay, okay, let me think here.* She rubbed her forehead and tears welled up in her eyes. She looked at the card and read it again.

> *Today I married my best friend.*
> *Please celebrate with us as we take this journey of life*
> *Together.*
> *What God has joined together, let no man put asunder . . .*
> Alexis and Chris Reynolds

The phone rang. She exhaled heavily as if holding her breath in protest for the last several minutes. *Finally.*

"Yes, Jewel, why have you been blowing up my phone?"

"Capri . . . I, I just can't believe it. Did you get something in the mail today? A wedding announcement—it's a joke, right?" Jewel's heart slowed its pace as she awaited a response.

"I don't know, Jewel." Capri's words crawled out of her mouth. Then she paused momentarily. "Girl, I haven't even checked my mail yet." Capri's words sped up. *Uh-oh. The Eagle has landed.*

"Have Consuela check for you. Never mind, we don't have that kind of time. Well, you need to brace yourself. This is big; I mean I can't believe Lexi did this to me. She promised. She promised me that I would coordinate her wedding. I mean, you saw the beautiful shower I gave her. The horse-and-buggy carriage centerpiece made of flowers, the Swarovski crystal slipper on the cake. I made *all* her dreams come true."

Why me, Jesus? "Uh-huh." *Tap, tap.* Capri kept stroking the keys on her laptop.

"Is that all you can say? You must be working. How could you focus on something else at a time like this? I know. You're doing freakin' research on the Internet. I need your complete attention, Capri!" She clapped her hands as if she were standing in front of Capri. "This is a crisis. Our best friend has eloped! Have you no sensitivity?" Jewel was yelling into the phone.

Capri leaned back in her chair and removed her hands from her computer keys. "Hmmm. Okay, Jewel. First of all, you need to calm down and stop yelling in my ear, or the only thing you will hear is a dial tone. And for the record, Jewel dear, Lexi didn't do anything *to* you. Furthermore, you gave Lexi the shower of *your* dreams, not hers. Lastly, if the girl ran away and got married in peace it's her prerogative. And I can't say I blame her!"

"What?" Jewel's nostrils flared. "Wait, a minute . . ." she paused as she bit the side of her lip. "You knew, didn't you?"

"W-e-l-l—"

"You *all* knew, didn't you?" She didn't give Capri a chance to respond. "Betrayal! This is the thanks I get for coordinating your wedding and special events for free?" Jewel started pacing back and forth.

"Girl, listen. Don't take it so personally. Lexi and Chris just wanted a private event and, well, you know how you are. Look at how you're acting now. Just once, let this be about someone else besides you. It's not about a wedding—it's about the marriage Jewel. Think about it."

Jewel sat quietly. She could feel her skin burning. Like a cartoon character, she felt crimson blood rising from her toes, about to explode out of the top of her head. *10-9-8-7-6-5-4-3-2-1.*

Father, forgive them for they know not what they do. I have to remember my event planning creed: "Not everyone will appreciate or utilize even the most experienced and exquisite event coordinators."

"Well, I just resent the fact that you all think I'm *so* controlling that you couldn't tell me. I mean y'all let me go on and on about their wedding. Even the last two weeks. That's just cruel. I feel so foolish." Jewel plopped down on the couch and poked out her bottom lip.

Capri rolled her eyes and refocused on the screen. She'd left her research site and was now on eBay. After Jewel's first few sentences Capri had partially tuned her out. The emotional drain attached to a Jewel conversation usually subsided after the first ten minutes.

". . . I mean I could have helped with something. I could have made the travel arrangements."

"Uh-huh."

Jewel stood up and began pacing again. "God knows there are some cheap, classless destination packages out there. And a cruise? Puleeze. You know I have the best travel connections and, well, never mind."

"Jewel . . ."

"What?"

"Lexi and Chris are *very* happy."

Uh, she talked to them? Jewel finally stopped pacing, then plopped down on the large fabric ottoman. "Well, I *guess* that's all that matters."

"Yeah, I would think that *is* the most important thing. What a mature way to look at this. I'm proud of you, girl," Capri said.

"Well . . ." Jewel bit her quivering lip. "I *have* grown you know. I'm—I'm happy for her, I mean them. Yes, I—I'm *very* happy, absolutely ecstatic!" she said as if deciding in midsentence how she truly felt.

"Bye, Jewel," Capri sang as she hung up, not giving her friend a chance to utter another word.

Jewel sulked a few minutes more. *You just wait until Lexi sails her little narrow behind back into the States . . .*

CHAPTER TWO

"It's Not Going to Be Pretty"

Dear Jesus:

   I finally got a moment alone. It's so peaceful, lounging here on the Royal Caribbean, as it glides upon a blue-denim ocean carpet. I never would've thought I'd elope, but it was the best thing. God, You already know I'm just about the last of my friends to get married; I always had visions of wedding grandeur. I guess over time my priorities changed.

   Well, I'm sure the bomb has dropped by now. Poor Jewel, she'll get over it. There will be a million other weddings in her lifetime to plan. I do feel a little guilty, but I'll deal with that when I get back.

   It's amazing how our lives have changed so much since law school. I miss our weekly Sunday brunch fellowship. Spouses, careers, and life in general have made connecting a challenge, but brunch once a month is better than nothing.

   Jewel's maturing—well, sort of. Who would've thought she'd

have a ready-made family and marry a blue-collar man. But Kevin has tamed her little butt (even though she doesn't want to admit it). I like Kevin, but he is a bit country and soulful at times. That boy can eat and he can work a nerve, but his heart is good.

Jermane and Rex were destined to be together from the time they locked eyes in our first year of law classes. They're still going strong, despite Jermane's close call. God, You really had her back. I guess anyone can be tempted. And Angel finally stopped tripping with Octavio; it's amazing how you can get it together if you think you're about to lose somebody. And Octavio was about to shut down their relationship. Thank You, God, for breaking through. Angel finally let You and love in. What a blessing!

Capri, the anti-diva, is adjusting to life as an NBA player's wife in that big, gorgeous new house of hers. But I'm thankful You're keeping her grounded. She's still the down-to-earth sister and "around the way girl" I've come to know and love. It'll be interesting to see how our law firm comes together. I'm a little nervous, but we plan to make our mark in Houston with the firm of Reynolds & Stanton.

Anyway, God, thank You for making this time in my life so special. We just left Ocho Rios, Jamaica. After we docked, I gazed on some of the most beautiful azure waters I've ever seen. But the island's poverty almost overshadowed the beauty of the lush vegetation, refreshing waterfalls, and tropical gardens. I still can't believe I allowed Chris to talk me into climbing up Dunn River Falls. Eighteen feet of waterfalls and I didn't fall once! God, You know I'm not the most coordinated person. But I need to get back into my Pilates routine!

I have to admit, part of me wanted my friends here. I talk about Jewel, but her mishaps led me to my husband. What a story to tell my children.

So, God, what's up for the next season? Just like me, always wanting all the answers now. I guess if I take care of today, tomorrow will take care of itself. I have to stay in the moment. Anyway, Jesus, You sure can make life interesting and unpredictable.

When I get back from my honeymoon, we'll have our first Sunday brunch in some time. I better get all the rest I can, since I'll have to deal with Jewel and all her drama over our elopement. And then the real work begins. Father, please provide the energy I need so Capri and I can get our law firm up and running.

God, it's been a long, lesson-filled journey, filled with lots of pain and disappointment. I have to believe the seeds I've sown over many years have finally yielded my due season harvest. If only I could bottle up this moment and keep it forever.

God, above anything else, I want to say I'm grateful. For all of it, even the crazy, inexplicable trying times. I'm thankful because my trials have made me the woman I am today. God, I love You and all, but I've got a sexy husband waiting back in our stateroom. Father, as always, may I—I mean we—always honor You and seek to stay inside Your will.

In Jesus's name,
Lexi

CHAPTER THREE

Welcome Home

link. All five ladies raised their crystal glasses for a toast. "To Mr. and Mrs. Chris Reynolds. May you make lots of love and have pretty babies," Capri said. "Here, here."

"I'm still not speaking to you." Jewel rolled her eyes slightly, then sipped a bit of her drink. Her mouth slowly curled into a smile. "But I'm willing to make an exception since this is your welcome back brunch and also because it's Sunday. Besides, an unforgiving Spirit is bad for the complexion."

"Jewel, nothing, not even your pouting, could spoil my mood." I placed my hand across my chest. "Because I, my sisters, have *officially* 'exhaled.' "

Jewel grabbed a chocolate-covered strawberry and waved it in my face before plopping it in her mouth.

"Yeah, yeah, we'll talk later. You owe me, sister. I was looking forward to that check *and* you deprived me of planning a wedding for my best friend," she said as she grabbed another strawberry.

"Jewel, please! Let it go. Nobody owes you a da—I mean doggone thing," Angel shouted.

"Besides, you *were* doing the wedding for free, right?" I said.

Jewel placed her index finger on her chin, "Did I say that? Oh yeah, I guess I did. Well, this is all I'm gonna say: you just missed out on another Fabulous Jewels event that . . . can you all say it with me?"

"Sparkles like diamonds." Everyone moaned.

I swear, if she says that tired old slogan one more time I'm gonna take off my pump and throw it at her. Jewel's turned into a party planning monster. Just yesterday, Jewel was a law school graduate, wandering around trying to figure out what the heck to do with that expensive degree. But after a few life-altering events, including getting canned at her last job, she finally stepped out on faith, pursuing her party planning passion. I have to admit, the girl can throw down on an event. She stays booked, so I don't know why she's complaining.

"Jewel, all I want to know is how does Kevin put up with you? Is he on meds?" Angel sliced through her shrimp and avocado frittata. She placed a forkful in her mouth and savored the flavor. "Umm, this is to die for!" she moaned.

"Please, that man worships the ground I walk on; especially since I've been doing Oprah's debt diet," Jewel said as she eyed her own San Francisco crab dish.

"Yeah, but you're still hiding handbags in the garage. You just couldn't keep that last Fendi bag to yourself, remember?" Jermane interjected. "But I can't be mad at you for that. It *was* the rainproof signature satchel," she said as she tucked her freshly blown-out hair behind her ear. Normally Jermane sported her own natural waves, but lately she was enjoying a sleeker look. She took a small sip of her café mocha.

Jewel rocked a little in her seat, rubbing her hands together. "I know, girl, I know," she said, lowering her voice as if her absent husband could hear her. "That bag was just gorgeous. It looked like the pocketbook that Kanye West's woman had on in that photo that was circulating on the Internet. She just looked so fly, I had to have that bag. Okay, so I had one setback. I've been doing well since then. I'm focusing on my hair." She snapped her head from side to side so we'd notice her precision cut bob.

"Okay, moving on. Did you guys see the game the other night? My baby's on the starting lineup." Capri's words halted Jewel's shopping saga. She moved her fork around on her plate. "Ooh, these turkey and orange butter sauce crepes are the bomb!"

"Yeah, yeah. What's up with the season tickets? You were supposed to be hooking us all up for a couples' night? Anthony finally got off the bench and we can't even be there live and in person to watch." All eyes were on Capri, awaiting her answer.

"Okay y'all, ever since Lexi got a man, she's been on this group dating thing." Angel winked her eye at Capri.

Angel is wrong for saying that, but she's right. What's a girl to do after years and years of singleness? I mean every date you could possibly take yourself on, I've done it! So, excuse me for wanting to soak up the entire couples experience.

"Who cares if Anthony plays or not? Doesn't he get a check either way? What's the big deal?" Jewel blurted out, then waved her hand at the waiter. "The food at this place is great, but the service leaves something to be desired. Anyway, what you need to be working on is some babies. Be like old girl Shaunie O'Neal, Shaq's wife—oops, then again, I'm not sure that worked out too well. Anyway, haven't you heard the phrase 'It's cheaper to keep her?' " She waved her hand again at the waiter. "I sure miss Antonio. Brunch just isn't the same without him."

"Jewel, I can't believe an intelligent woman like you is even thinking like that," I said. "But I do have to say, some of these women, even the young ones, have major game. I mean, sometimes it makes you ask why you even need a degree. But that's a lie from the enemy. It's short-term gain, for long-term pain. Anyway, I miss Antonio too. He was the best, with his nosy self, all up in our conversation every five minutes. Has anybody found out where he's working?" I asked, looking in the direction of our waiter.

"Girl, Antonio moved to Atlanta and he's trying to open his own restaurant." Jewel finally leaned back in her chair.

"I knew you would know. Well, we're just gonna have to check out some other Houston restaurants. I heard Brennan's and the Magnolia Bar & Grill have a nice brunch. Jewel, Miss Fabulous Events, you can be in charge of that; it's part of your job anyway. And Capri, we got a little sidetracked, but are you giving the tickets up or what? You

THE SUNDAY BRUNCH DIARIES

know my *husband* loves the Houston Meteors and they may
be headed for the playoffs."

"Lexi, why are you saying *husband* as if we don't know
who your man is? I hate when women do that. And for the
record, I don't recall ever promising anybody season tickets. Anthony used to promise you when we were dating to
get on your good side. If one more person tries to get the
hookup, I'm gonna scream." Capri dabbed her mouth
with her napkin and reached for her water.

"Who's tryin' to get new on us now? But I guess being
a player's wife got you all high and mighty like that," Jewel
said.

Capri playfully smacked Jewel's hand. "You're trippin'.
I'm the same old Capri with just a little more bling." She
flexed her diamond tennis bracelet. Jewel, her eyes fixated on the flashing stones, looked like a deer in head-
lights.

"Anyway, *so . . .*" Jewel said as she snapped out of her
trance. She raised her eyebrows and looked at me. She
drummed her fingers on the white tablecloth, waiting for
me to respond.

"So what?" I asked as I tried to stay focused on the last
of my eggs Florentine.

"You know." Jewel raised her right eyebrow. "How
was it?"

"How was what?" The table was silent and all eyes were
on me. "Oh, oh *that!*"

"Yeah *that,*" they all chimed in.

"Well, it was, well, it was um . . ." My eyes focused upward.

"C'mon Lexi. You got to spill it." Jewel leaned in.

"W-e-l-l . . . *it was fabulous!*"

Jewel wiped her brow and leaned back on her chair. "Phew. *Thank God!* Just looking at Chris we weren't quite sure he could . . . well you know. He seems kinda dull."

I rolled my eyes at her. "Looks can be deceiving."

"Jewel is not speaking for all of us. Anyway, can we focus on something a little more suitable for Sunday afternoon conversation? I have an update or two," Angel interjected.

"What? You and Octavio are getting married?" Jewel said as she whipped out her BlackBerry.

"No, Jewel, we've had enough weddings for a while. You can put away the BlackBerry. No more 'Fabulous Jewels' soirees for a minute, please."

"Don't be mad because I'm using my gift for the glory of God," Jewel said, and sang, "Making people's dreams come true . . ."

"Did she say for the glory of God?" Jermane said, looking at me.

I just shrugged and shook my head.

"Anyway," Angel continued, "I'm officially a member of Lakewood Church and I think Octavio is going to join too. He really likes it."

Jewel began coughing. "What? Living Truth got us through law school! It's our home church. What's wrong with you? You know, there's way too many changes going on here." She raised her spoon for emphasis. "I mean, I know you needed a *whole* lot of deliverance, but I didn't think you were going to take it this far. First Bobby and Whitney break up, now this?"

"Are you serious? Kevin is rubbing off on you," I said. "No more reality TV for you."

"You know I'm joking, but still. Lakewood Church is *way* too big."

"Jewel, this is not something I decided. It's where the Spirit is leading me now. It's where God wants to plant me for the season I'm in now. People act like God can only be in one church."

"Who's saying all that? Anyway, all I'm saying is that you better not start recruiting folks to Lakewood. We're all happy where we are," Jewel said as she filled her glass with water.

"Angel, I understand. I'm glad you are being obedient. You don't know why God is calling you to Lakewood. You may turn out to be a ministry leader. Sometimes we can be so selfish." I glanced sideways at Jewel. "We can hinder another person's growth. Sometimes we can miss a blessing trying to please other folks!"

"Does that mean Octavio is giving up Catholicism?" Jermane asked.

"I'm not really sure. Lakewood's nondenominational. We talked about it a little, but for now we're just being Spirit led. Octavio's really getting a lot out of it. There are lots of other interracial couples there too."

"I knew it! You all have a little interracial ministry up in there?" Jewel pointed her butter knife toward Angel.

"Just when I want to think you have grown . . ." Capri interjected.

"I *have* grown. It's a valid question. *Never mind.* Angel, you go where the Spirit leads you." Jewel placed her knife on the table and patted Angel's hand.

"I'm glad I have your permission." Angel lifted her coffee cup toward her lips. "And for the record, I didn't need any more deliverance than you did, Miss Thang."

"Okay, I'm stuffed," I said after a few minutes. "I'd love to spend the rest of the afternoon bonding, but I got things to do." I pushed back from the table.

"I gotta get home too," said Jewel. "Aja will be back from visiting with her mama, Stacy, and you know I have to deprogram her. I swear, ever since Kevin and I got married, Stacy's been tripping. Can I help it if Kevin found me irresistible and was intrigued by my charm? Can I help it if his ex-wife gave up a good thing? Can I help it if she made some very bad life decisions? No . . . all I can do is receive the blessing and share all this love God has given me and breathe new life into the man and child she took for granted. I've been divinely appointed and anointed to—"

"Jewel, be for real," I said.

"Well, I just never thought I, Jewel Antoinette Whitacker-Eastland, would have to deal with baby mama drama. I'm *so* above that. It certainly was not on my 'ideal man list.' "

Capri turned toward me. "So, Lexi, you have time to meet this week to go over some paperwork?"

"Dang, I just got back from my honeymoon. But I guess it's back to reality."

"Lex, it's already early September. If we want this firm up, rolling and making money, we need to get refocused. We're behind schedule already."

"Yeah, hurry up so I can plan the opening reception,"

Jewel said as she dug in her purse for her lip gloss. She had already placed six tubes of MAC lipstick on the table.

"Who said anything about that?" Capri asked.

"Do we even need to discuss it? Who else would do the honors? Another Fabulous Jewels event that . . ."

"Sparkles like diamonds," we all chimed.

"You're just a bunch of haters, but I love you just the same," Jewel said as she applied her lip gloss.

CHAPTER FOUR

You've Been Served

"Come in," Rex said after he heard a light knock at his door. After a second or two the door opened. He was sure who it was and didn't bother looking up from his papers.

"I'm looking for Rex Richmond. I was told I could find him here?"

He raised his head slowly, squinting his eyes. He picked up his glasses and put them on. He was about to look back down at his papers, but froze as he studied the figure standing before him. She eased over to his desk and then walked around to his chair. He dropped his pen as she removed her silk head scarf and sunglasses.

She stood tall and confident, commanding his full attention with her body language. "I *said* I'm looking for Rex Richmond." She peered into his eyes.

He spun his large leather chair to completely face her,

but remained silent and seated. His hands had a mind of their own as they reached to loosen the belt of her coat and began to unbuckle it. Once it was open, he wrapped his hand around her waist and pulled her toward him. He then reached for her neck as she bent to kiss him. "Baby . . . umm, it's good to see you."

"You too," she said as her lips brushed his neck.

"Why am I so lucky?" he whispered as his eyes closed.

She laced her fingers through his. "Hmm, yes you are. What would your wife think about all this?" She leaned back to see his expression.

He opened his eyes, then grabbed her face with his hands. He looked directly into her eyes. He kissed her gently. "Let's not talk about that," he whispered, then reached down to slip off one of her red patent leather Gucci pumps.

"Baby, you've got to stop coming to the office like this. It's the middle of the week. I can't even think when you do this. I can't get any more work done." He wiped his forehead with his hand.

"Why do you think I do it?" Jermane said as she kissed her husband on the forehead. She stood behind him and massaged his temples. He reached for his glasses, then sat up in his chair. "If your father catches us in here one day, it would be a really embarrassing moment."

"Please, *my* daddy? With all the young women he dates?"

"Regardless, baby, I've got to get some work done. I have to say, this was a nice treat. I remember a day when you would have never thought to do something like this."

"I've been listening to Jewel. We've got to keep the marriage fresh." She rubbed his face with the back of her hand, then moistened his lips with a soft kiss.

"I know, but if you don't let me work, we won't have any money for that baby you say you want."

"Okay, but you have to promise . . . no more lawyers in the family. I want my baby to do something else. She can be a teacher, a writer . . . anything but a lawyer."

"I know what you mean. I think I'm feeling that burnout coming on. It's taking way too much to bring in clients these days. Can't rest on the firm name alone, but then again there's nothing wrong with lawyers. Besides, I always thought *this* lawyer was kinda hot," he said as he rubbed the cleft of his chin and raised his eyebrow.

"Yeah . . . I *guess* you can say that. But this lawyer's pretty hot herself." Jermane got up, put on her coat, and pulled the belt tight. She looked at him as she walked past his desk. "Smokin', as a matter of fact." She smiled and walked out the door.

Rex couldn't take his eyes off his wife until she finally was out of his sight. He had to admit her presence was a welcome relief from his otherwise overwhelming, taxing day. He was used to the workload, but recently some discoveries in the firm's archived files prompted him to wonder whether a partnership in his father-in-law's firm came with both fringe benefits and a tainted legacy. Rex reached into his desk drawer for some aspirin and grabbed the bottled water from his desk to wash down two tablets. He put his head on his desk to rest his thoughts. With his eyes closed, he replayed his afternoon tryst with his wife again and again until he finally relaxed.

CHAPTER FIVE

Lakewood Church

Angel stood in the pew, her arms encouraged upward by the lyrics flowing from the songstress. The lyrics were filled with words of adoration and worship. Soon Angel's strong hands were reaching toward heaven. The higher her hands stretched, the more liberated she felt.

She paused during the brief interlude, gazing at the huge sanctuary that felt more like a sports arena than a church. It seemed like every race and ethnicity of God's creation filled the seats—African American, Caucasian, Asian, and Hispanic, all worshipping the Lord together.

As she glanced at the smiling Hispanic woman to her left, whose infant lay on her shoulder, and the young Black woman to her right, casually clad in jeans and T-shirt, Angel knew she was truly in God's house. There was a sincere "come as you are" Spirit of God in the church. The love of the Lord consistently greeted her when she crossed the church threshold. She couldn't wait to arrive on Sundays to worship and hear the Word of God taught with such integrity.

Being at Lakewood even changed the way she looked at other races. Although she was in an interracial relationship, she wasn't sure she was entirely free from prejudice. Angel considered Octavio a man of color because of his Latino heritage, but her perception of white people was another story. Especially some who questioned her skills as a corporate lawyer.

The chorus of the song recaptured her attention. Angel fought back tears as the joy of the Lord arose in her spirit. Her week's fatigue and frustration dissolved in the living water of worship. She sang along with the congregation as lyrics appeared on the huge screen in front of the sanctuary.

In the middle of worship, Octavio's face flashed across her mind. She shut her eyes, once again, suppressing all thoughts that threatened her worship. *God, no other man has treated me better than Octavio. But help me to balance things out. Help me to prioritize my love for You over him. I need this time with You, Father. I need this cleansing and restoration. And Father, please usher him on this journey with me. Feed Octavio as You feed me.* Silently, she promised to ask Octavio to the Bible class she saw in the worship guide.

Angel finally silenced her mental disruptions as she looked upward. She spread her arms wide, allowing an anointed outpour to drench her soul. For in that sacred moment, her fellowship with God was all that mattered.

CHAPTER SIX

"Five-o"

"Good morning, Mr. Reynolds," I said as I watched
my husband standing there in his pants and bare
chest. *My baby's been working out.* Outside of his slightly
big ears, this man was close to perfection. *I said close. Give
me a break, we are newlyweds.*

"Good morning, sweetie." He walked over and planted
his full lips on my forehead. *He just really gets my day off to a great
start.*

"Uh, Mr. Reynolds, I know you're busy fighting Houston crime and all, but the next time I call you, don't take
all day to call me back. You know I worry. Don't let me
have to track you down again." I watched the definition in
his back as he leaned down in the closet to get his shoes. *My
baby is fine. Thank you, Jesus!*

"Lexi, did you have to call all over Houston looking

for me? That was *really* embarrassing. I've been involved
in something extremely serious. I'm taking care of business, baby, you know?" he said. "Oh, by the way, for the
millionth time, can you please tell Jewel I can't do anything about her speeding ticket. She's just gonna have to
break down and tell Kevin that this is her fourth ticket this
year. I'm not about to lose my job trying to get her a
hookup."

"Uh-huh, I'll take care of it." I sat up and rubbed my
eyes and opened my mouth wide to yawn.

"So how's the business planning going?" He sat down
on the bed to put his socks on, then grabbed his shoehorn
to slip on his shoes.

"It's going pretty well." I smiled.

He stopped and looked at me for a second or two.
"What is it?" he said, searching my face.

I paused a minute. *How does he know something's wrong?* I
shrugged my shoulders.

"See, I tried to warn you . . . friendship and business
don't mix."

"Chris, it's nothing really. I mean, Capri and I, we're
two mature women more than capable of running a law
firm. We've been through worse times in law school. I have
faith in our business *and* our friendship."

He stood, put his shirt on, and began to button it. I got
up to help him. "I'm nervous, but it's just because this is
a new venture."

"I'm just saying that, well you know, things happen.
Just make sure you get everything in writing and decide as
much as possible up front," he said.

"Hey, who's the lawyer here?" I kissed him on the lips and grabbed him by his belt hoops.

"Hey, who's the *law* here?" Chris said as he grabbed my bottom.

"I can't believe you." I playfully slapped his hands.

"Can't help it, babe." His eyes fell to my backside. "You look good in my T-shirt. Anyway, it just sounds like there's *something* you're hesitant to tell me."

"Okay, the only thing I'm a *little* concerned about is, well, Capri had that cushy situation at that big firm. I'm just not sure she has the hustle to build a practice."

"Don't underestimate Capri. She's a New Yorker; that East Coast attitude can definitely come out every now and then."

"It's just different for me, you know? This is our bread and butter. No offense, honey, but we need both our incomes. We just got this house. I'm taking cases now, just for the money, and I don't enjoy criminal law. Capri doesn't have that kind of pressure."

"Hmm, I see." He grabbed his brush from the dresser. "Baby, you just do what you do, and let me worry about the money. I can take care of us. I'm your provider." He placed two fingers under my chin and looked in my eyes and didn't release me until he saw my face soften.

I love this man. "O-k-a-y, Chris, just remember you said that. I've recorded this statement and I'll be sure to remind you if money gets tight." I smiled and grabbed his hand and placed it around my waist.

He took his other hand and lightly tapped my bottom. "Who's the man? Who's wearing this badge? Who has the

State of Texas entrusted with this gun? Who did you say makes you feel safe and protected? Who did you say was your provider?" He suddenly raised his arms to make his muscles pop from under the sleeves of his police uniform.

"G-O-D. You know, Jehovah Jireh—our provider; I believe *He's* the one who really does all that." I folded my arms, waiting for him to get it.

"Oh, yeah. Well, you know, underneath Him. You know what I mean!" He reached in for a kiss. "Ooh baby, morning breath."

I playfully punched him in the arm.

"Okay, I'm running a little late, babe, I gotta go." He pulled away and tucked his shirt in a little more.

"Not without praying you don't." Our eyes locked. He knew better than to argue because we prayed together every morning.

"Okay, but a quick one this morning. I love to hear you pray, but sometimes you get a little long-winded, sweetie. And when you start praying for your friends, it's on. I don't mean no harm, baby, but they can take care of themselves now, you gotta let them go."

"Baby, I know what you're saying, but I've always prayed for my friends. It's just a habit now. Anyway, God has a way of making up for lost time. Just be quiet and grab my hands." He placed his hands in mine and closed his eyes.

Father, we thank You for another day. We asked for Your provision and protection. Lord, send forth angels to surround us today. Father, I ask that You order our every footstep. God, as we go forth into the world, help us to be a light. Help us to honor You and all we do. We expect great things to happen today. Father, I ask You to cover us, our families, and friends in the blood of Jesus. Help us to walk in a spirit of agreement. In Jesus's name, Amen.

"Amen," Chris said as he lifted his head. "I'm gonna keep this law firm venture in prayer. You and Capri gotta stay tight; we can't mess up the chance for playoff tickets."

I reached out to tag him, but he dodged me and headed for the door. "Love you," he mouthed as he hurried down the steps.

CHAPTER SEVEN

Diamonds Are Forever

"Fabulous Jewels Events . . . where every event sparkles like diamonds! How may I be of service to you today?" Jewel sang her salutation like a commercial jingle.

"Jewel, knock it off. You have caller ID on your business phone. You know it's me," I said.

"This party no longer recognizes this number, since the party to which it belongs went and got married unbeknownst to this party, her best friend, to whom this phone belongs."

Jeez. "Jewel, knock it off. I'm sorry I chose to have the wedding of *my* choice. I apologize that I deprived you of planning another one of your sparkling whatever events."

"It's Fabulous Jewels Events . . . where every event sparkles like—"

"I get it! I get it! Do you have to quote that stupid phrase at every opportunity?"

"It's called branding, sweetie. Anyway, Lexi, you hurt my feelings and you know it. I'm one of your best friends. While you were lying out on the crystal blue beaches of the Cayman Islands, I was back here trying to negotiate with caterers and florists for *you.*"

"Jewel, it's been almost two months since I got married. I thought we squashed this already. And for the record, I didn't tell you to do any of that. Let me make up for some of it at least." *Why am I apologizing? Oh that's right, it's Jewel.*

"Okay, how do you plan on making this up to me?" Jewel said as she crossed her arms.

"Well, TSU's art gallery is hosting Grant Hill's art collection. They need someone to coordinate the reception. The who's who of Houston will be on the guest list. Come on, Jewel, you *know* you want this. I can just feel your mouth salivating through the phone."

Jewel sat up straight and took a deep swallow. Her heart started pounding. "Well, this doesn't completely make up for it, *but* I'll take it, I'll take it! So, how did you hook this up? Tell me, tell me, tell me!" Jewel said, barely able to contain herself.

"Girl, a sorority connection, that's all you need to know."

"Wow, this could be huge. This could be a serious Fabulous Jewels event that sparkles like . . . wait a minute, doesn't he play basketball? What the heck does he know about art? Oh, who cares? I smell other celebrity clients. And you're sure you can hook this up?"

"Just say the word."

"Okay. I'm in! I have to find something to wear. Like I was saying, come on Lexi, say it with me, this is going to be another Fabulous Jewels Event that . . ."

"Sparkles like diamonds," we said in unison.

I can't believe I just said that. Anything to get her to shut up about my wedding.

"Okay, glad that's done. Now, Jewel, the main reason I called was to tell you we're still having our housewarming on October 12, weekend after next. Nothing over the top, just a few people. Chris is gonna fire up the grill."

"Oh, okay. Do I have to bring a gift? I mean, y'all have been in the house for a minute and it's pretty much fully furnished, right?"

"Jewel, it's a housewarming. What do you think is appropriate? Never mind, do what your Spirit tells you and remind Kevin."

"Can we bring Aja?" Jewel put down her BlackBerry and pulled out her clear nail polish from her desk drawer.

"Yeah, you can bring her if you want. We're going to watch the game afterwards. Capri's coming. Anthony's in Dallas that night and they're playing the Mavericks."

"Whatever, I'll be there. Oh, that's the weekend Stacy has her, so it'll just be me and Kevin."

"So how's that going? Anymore 'baby mama drama'?"
I really hate using that phrase. I knew it was all over when Britney Spears had baby mama drama.

"I don't know. It's weird, before we got married, Stacy seemed so humble and accepting. But now she makes up any old excuse to call Kevin, like suddenly she needs his

constant attention. But it's got to stop; Kevin is *not* a
'rent-a-husband.' "

"Well, she *was* married to him and you do have custody
of her daughter. That has to be hard. Those feelings just
don't disappear. Especially after all they've been through."

"Whose side are you on? I don't think she has feelings
anymore. They *were* married, hence the past tense. She's
just lonely and homegirl ain't getting any younger. Let's
face it; all of us are not aging gracefully. I don't feel
threatened or anything. It's just aggravating."

"I'm sure eventually Stacy will get the point, but
Kevin's gonna have to check that situation before it gets
worse. I know you've talked to him about it."

"I have, but I think he just likes to keep the peace. But
I, Jewel Whitacker-Eastland, am definitely not into 'sharing is caring.' I'm gonna pray for her to get some business
of her own. Maybe in the back of her mind she still thinks
she and Kevin will get back together," Jewel said as she
began to slide some business cards in a few press kits as she
cradled the phone.

"Umm, I don't believe that. Then again, I've heard
stories about women who have set a permanent place at
the dinner table for their husband, truly believing he will
come back. Anyway, instead of praying Stacy gets a man,
why don't you pray that she's whole, or that God would
give her a Spirit of contentment?"

"What? Girl, *please.* Be for real. Is that how you were
praying before you met Chris?"

"Well, uh, sort of. Maybe not in the beginning, but I
eventually realized I needed to line my prayers up with

God's will." *Okay, I confess I was saying those "God, just send me some-body, anybody" prayers.*

"Yeah, as in God, 'will' you bring me a man? I'm just keeping it real. Old girl needs some testosterone in her life, just not my husband's."

"Okay, okay, I hear you, Jewel. I'll be praying for Stacy too, but I'm going to let Christ lead *my* prayer."

"Do what you need to do," Jewel said.

"Bye girl."

"Ciao."

CHAPTER EIGHT

The Brisket House

Our home was packed for the housewarming. Everyone seemed to be enjoying themselves. Some people were making themselves a bit too much at home.

"It's my prerogative," Kevin said as he danced around while waving his drumstick in the air. "Gettin' girls is how I live . . ."

I looked at Kevin and rolled my eyes. *The boy really ain't wrapped too tight.* Did he think he was the president of the Bobby Brown fan club or something? I couldn't even watch that show *Being Bobby Brown.* It was painful. I was embarrassed *for* him. But sadly, it looked like Kevin was a true Bobby Brown fan. *As long as he doesn't break into the Running Man, I'll be okay.*

"Y'all don't even need to sleep. Bobby Brown was the best performer at the *Essence*fest." He broke out into the

Running Man, moving his feet back and forth with all his might.

"That's it. He went there. I'm truly done," I said as I dropped my chicken wing on my plate.

"Kevin, up until now, I wasn't sure, but you have confirmed my thoughts. You're officially ghetto," Angel said. "Jewel, aren't you embarrassed? Look at your man." She nudged Jewel on her side and pointed toward Kevin.

"Y'all know Bobby Brown is the original King of R & B," Kevin said, trying to catch his breath. Isn't that right, baby?" He looked at Jewel.

Jewel just waved her hand at him and kept talking to Capri. "So girl, don't you miss Anthony? I mean, I don't know what I would do if I couldn't see my boo every day, coming home all sweaty and looking all cute in his little brown uniform. Now that he's about to move into management at the parcel company, he's looking cuter every day!"

Capri shrugged her shoulders. "I don't know. I'm kinda used to Anthony's schedule. I can travel with him anytime I want. I just like being home. It's too much of a hassle. I'd rather watch the games at our house in peace. When I go to the games and sit with the other players' wives, I've got to get my hair done, find an outfit, and get all glammed up. I'm just not up for the drama."

Jewel raised both her hands in astonishment. "Girl, I would *live* for that. Besides, the only person you have to talk to at home is Consuelo. Does she even speak English?" Jewel said.

"Yes, she speaks English. Jewel, this is why I'm his wife and you're not. I just don't get all caught up in the hype.

God knows I don't care about all that mess." Capri bit into her hot dog, then wiped the chili from the corner of her mouth.

"Well, you might want to travel with him every now and then," Kevin shouted over the music. "Because you don't want another Kobe situation." The music had ended and he was still shouting. Everyone had heard his last sentence.

Capri cut her eyes at Kevin, and Jewel mouthed "shut up" to her husband.

"What? I'm just keeping it real. I don't care how strong a man is. I don't care how 'rooted and grounded in the Word' he is, there's a *whole* lot of temptation out there in the world. Anthony better be prayed up."

"He had the same challenges before we got married, Kevin, and he wasn't out there. He's the same man," Capri retorted.

"Oh, so what you are saying, Kevin, sweetie pie, sugar dumpling . . ." Jewel interjected, "is that *you'd* have a hard time being faithful if you were in the same situation?"

"Uh, no baby, that's not what I'm trying to say at all." He looked at Jermane's husband, Rex, for support.

"Kevin, you're on your own with that one, my man," Rex said as he wrapped his arms around Jermane and kissed her cheek. "I got everything I need right here."

"Ah man, how you gonna play me like that? I should have known Republican wasn't gonna have my back. All I know is, I ain't in the NBA, and I've had my share of attention. Sometimes when I'm delivering packages, women are just all up on me." He started feeling his pecs. "When I'm on the road, women are just waving me down. Once they get a look at these bulging calves, it's over. Besides, I do recall when I dropped that package off to *you*, Jewel, the same thing happened. You were all up on me," Kevin said.

Jewel ignored his last comment, especially since she'd heard the story several times before.

"Kevin, man, you're always tripping. You've never heard me say I was a Repulican. And for the hundredth time, my name is Rex."

"Yeah, 'Rex the Republican,' you know you a lifetime member of the G. W. Bush fan club. You were talking all that noise a while back about Black Republicans. It's your fault the country is all messed up. Folks all irritable because they broke, we got a senseless war, and we might as well give Osama bin Laden his own reality show with all the videos he got coming out. And did I say the economy is jacked up?"

"Kevin, man, don't start this again. The man told you a hundred times he's not Republican," Chris said as he poured more sauce on the brisket. "Stop defaming the man's reputation."

"Now Clinton may have had his fidelity issues and I'm not excusing him for that. But we didn't have this kind of unemployment and at least Clinton could spell. If he were in office New Orleans would be rebuilt already. Dang, I miss my New Orleans grub: boudain and some hog cracklin'. Besides anybody who has Stevie Wonder at his inauguration is all right with me. *Very superstitious . . .*" He started to sing. "I don't know about Hillary, but Bill was the man!"

"Honey, why don't you just tell this man you are *not* a Republican," Jermane whispered in her husband's ear. Then kissed it.

"It's useless. You know Kevin's ignorant. We had one

conversation about the history of Republicans and ever since he swears I'm part of the party," Rex said.

Angel walked over to fix another plate. She rolled her eyes at Kevin. "Anyway, back to this fidelity thing. When Octavio and I were at church this past Sunday, Pastor Joel was talking about—"

"Here we go. Why do we always have to have the spiritual commentary from you, Angel? You act like none of us are saved. You are late on the spiritual scene. The rest of us have been going to church way before you got all saved and sanctified," Kevin said as he walked over and got a clean plate.

"I would have never thought it the way you behave sometimes," Angel added beans to her plate and went to sit by Octavio. She was about to go on, but Octavio lightly grabbed her hand. She cleared her throat, then smiled.

"Anyway, the game is getting ready to come on. Anthony's getting off the bench and finally starting again and I don't want to miss the beginning," Capri said as she picked up her paper plate and tossed it in the trash.

"Yeah, in a minute. I thought they were going to retire the old boy's number. And I don't mean that in a good way. It was looking shaky after that injury, but it looks like he's back on his game," Kevin said as they were leaving the patio to go into the house.

Chris looked at Capri and shook his head. "Just let it go."

"I know. Kevin's just special," Capri said.

When they got to the media room everyone got comfortable. Rex grabbed the remote to turn the volume up.

Brrrring. Before the game even started, Kevin's phone

went off. He pulled his phone out of his jean pocket and looked at the number reflected on the blue screen. He hesitated, then answered.

"Oh wow, okay. Yeah, I'll be there in a few minutes." He rubbed his bald head and started to get up.

Jewel's eyes pierced his face like daggers. "Where do you think you're going?" Despite their attempts to talk in low voices, I could not help but overhear.

"What?" she said with folded arms, awaiting an explanation.

"Baby, my ex got a flat. I'm just going to go run and fix it and be right back."

"Kevin, do I need to remind you that you aren't her husband anymore? Doesn't she have anybody else who can help her? What about her cousin Bootsy? You know she only does this because you'll jump up and do it. I put up with this before we got married . . . never mind, we've had this conversation before." She felt her nostrils flaring.

"I know, sweetie. *I know.* I just feel bad. She really doesn't have anybody. She's doing okay now, I don't want her to have a relapse. Baby, I'll be right back as soon as I'm finished. And you know Aja's with her; I've got to take care of my baby."

Jewel took a deep breath and let her arms drop. "Yeah, well, only because Aja is with her. But we need to talk about this, Kevin, we really need to set some boundaries here."

"Okay, I hear you." He gave her a peck. "I'll call you when I'm on the way back."

I quickly looked at Jewel, then refocused on the game.

CHAPTER NINE

The Ex Files

"Jewel, you know you were wrong! I explained what happened. But you wouldn't even let me in; I had to sleep on the porch. How you gonna lock me out of *my* own house?" he said as he weaved in and out of the traffic. They were late for church because she had finally let him in the house with just enough time to get ready for service.

Jewel didn't say anything, but kept staring out the window. She turned up the radio, but although they were playing one of her favorite Yolanda Adams songs, she didn't sing out as she normally would have.

"I told you. She had a bad spare, baby. We had to wait for the wrecker service and it took an extra long time. What else could I do? You're being just so, well, difficult," Kevin said as he focused on the traffic. "Where is this traffic coming from? Shoot, there's a highway shut down. If I had a chance to check the traffic this morning, I would've known to go the other way." He slammed on his brakes to keep from slamming into the back of the car in front of him.

"Kevin, I don't want to hear it. We're both so busy and it's rare that I get weekends off. You could have at least called me and let me know what was going on." She folded her arms and looked out the window.

"Jewel, you know I called you. As soon as I started to tell you what was happening, you started yelling, then hung up. Then you called back to yell some more, and I refused to deal with all that. You kept blowing the phone up and I knew whatever you had to say was going to be extra foul." His forehead crinkled and his hands formed a tighter grip around the steering wheel. "That's how you are, Jewel; you don't know how to deal with things calmly. Baby, this has come up before. You have anger and for-giveness issues."

Uh-oh. No he didn't. Jewel turned her face toward him. "I had a right to be angry. Oh, so now I can't express my feel-ings. I have a problem with forgiveness?"

"Yes. Jewel, do you realize I had to sleep on the porch of my own house last night, where I pay the mortgage? Granted it was a screened-in porch, but that's beside the point! That was just uncalled for."

"Well, you should have called me back."

His eyes focused on the traffic ahead. "Forget it, this is a no-win situation. Jewel, you may not be completely wrong, but your attitude is just messed up."

"I'm not hearing you," she said as she turned up the radio.

"Well, I'm glad to know that we've picked up a couple of demons on our way to church. You need to learn to be a little more understanding. You never know what people are dealing with," Kevin said, his eyes fixed on the road.

Understanding? Understanding? Please. Give me a break. "Understanding" will find my husband up in her bed. Jewel continued to stare out the window as they pulled into the church parking lot. She tried to ignore the couples holding hands. She remembered the teacher in the marriage ministry class said holding hands showed a couple's Spirit of agreement. When Kevin got out of the car Jewel hoped he wouldn't reach for her hand. He came to her side, opened the door, tried to grab her hand.

"C'mon girl, don't bring this mess up in God's house today. I'm not trying to block my blessing." He stood at the door and waited for her to get out.

"Oh, it's about your blessing? You really don't want to hold my hand? Why even bother?" she said. After hesitating a bit, she rolled her eyes, smacked her teeth, and placed her hand in his, but once they were inside the church she sat down and didn't look Kevin's way.

He smiled at a few familiar faces and nodded, and then thought, "She's really taking this too far." When the choir began to sing, Kevin totally focused on worship. Finally it was time for Pastor Graves to speak. "I want to tag this text, the power of forgiveness . . ." Kevin resisted all temptation to nudge his wife. He just sat quietly and attentively through the whole service. He knew a confirmation when he heard it. Jewel, on the other hand, tried to act as if none of the sermon applied to her. With her body slightly turned away from Kevin's, she couldn't keep from fidgeting. She knew that the Holy Spirit had climbed up in the seat with her and was all up in her business.

CHAPTER TEN

Computer Love

"Chris, why does it always take you forever to get ready?" *Jeez, I thought that was a woman thing.* While he was still in the bathroom I decided to put my multitasking skills to work. I eased into the home office to check and send a few e-mails.

I turned the computer on and started to log on to check my office e-mail. As soon as I typed in the first letters it immediately took me to something I'd never seen on my computer before. "This has got to be a mistake," I mumbled to myself. When I looked at several links it was clear that my eyes were not playing tricks on me. *Oh, Hell to the naw!* My first intuition was to shut it off, but I was intrigued by what I saw. "Ewww, that's disgusting!" "CHRIS!!!"

When he didn't answer I moved toward the bedroom. "CHRIS!!!"

He bolted out of the bedroom half dressed. "What in the world are you screaming about, Lexi!"

I looked directly into his eyes. "You have something you want to tell me?" I noticed his skin was still moist from the shower and he was looking way too sexy. Had I not been so angry, I would've been all over him trying to squeeze in a little lovin' before church.

"Lexi, we don't have time for this. If you have something you need to ask me, say it. We need to get ready to get up out of here in a minute so we can get a decent seat in church," he said as he started to finish sliding his belt through the hoops of his pants.

I held my hand up. "Uh-uh, brother. This can't wait. Now, I'm going to ask one more time." I placed my hand on my hip. "Do you have something you need to tell me? Am I not fulfilling my wifely duties? I tell you I'm tired one time and you resort to other kinds of relief? Porn, Chris?"

Chris's eyes grew narrow. He started scratching his head. "How in the world would you think that? Lexi, you know I've never been into any of that and I'm not going to start. That kind of stuff does nothing for me. Where are you getting that idea from?" he said, looking at her.

Well, you think you know somebody. "That mess just popped up on our computer," I said as I pointed to the screen. "Not one, but at least seven sites." I waited for an explanation.

He grabbed my shoulders. "Baby, I swear to you, and it's Sunday. I have never been to any porno sites."

"Chris, you better be telling the truth. I'm not going

to allow this spirit of pornography up in my house. It can turn into an addiction," I said as I pulled away from him.

He sat down in front of the computer. "Dang, this is some mess," he said, looking at the computer. "We're probably going to have to take it to get cleaned out. That's going to be embarrassing."

"Tell me about it. And Chris, you don't have to stare at it so long," I said.

"Okay, sorry, baby, but have you thought about the fact that we had a house full of people here last night? Somebody else could have used the computer, Lexi. I swear it wasn't me." He came from behind the desk and walked over to me.

He grabbed my face and kissed me softly. I took a deep breath. "Well, I suppose that could have happened. But I'm gonna go to God about this, and Chris, if you're not telling the truth you know God's gonna let me know." I stared at him one last time. "I'm gonna finish getting ready," I said before I walked off. I almost made it to the doorway and then turned around. "Whoa, so if it wasn't you, who in the world could it have been?"

"All I know was that it wasn't me, baby, but if it's one of my boys, I'm gonna find out. Their trifling behinds have me in trouble and I can't have that! I'll call my boy who works with computers to come and clean out our system. I'll just have to explain what happened. He knows me well enough not to believe this was my doing. At least I hope so!"

"God, I'm not sure what to do now. I mean, should we ask our friends about it? I don't want to accuse anyone.

This is not something you just blurt out. It's such an awkward situation," I said, then looked at Chris.

"I don't know babe, for now let's just pray on it and then we'll know what to do."

I looked over at Chris and watched as he repositioned his arm. Then he let out a grunting noise. As hard as I tried to fall asleep, I hadn't even dozed off yet. Still wound up from the weekend activities, I guess. I tried not to move, but decided I'd attempt to maneuver my way out of our nightly cuddle position. I slowly untangled myself from Chris's arms. I was a little chilly wearing his boxers and a tank top, so I threw on my robe. On the way out of the bedroom I grabbed one of my journals from my writing desk. I eased downstairs, and once I was in the kitchen I opened the fridge, searching for something to excite my taste buds. I settled for half a piece of carrot cake. I sat at the table devouring the cake as I started to write.

> *Dear Lord Jesus:*
>
> *First, I want to thank You for our beautiful housewarming. To have people in our lives who truly want to celebrate our blessings is special. Church service was wonderful today. It feels so natural to have Chris by my side at worship.*
>
> *Lord, on another note, I can't help but be concerned about the mess I found on my computer. Even during worship those images popped up in my mind. I don't sense in my Spirit that Chris was responsible for that filth. As You know he didn't even want to have a bachelor party. So, until You tell me otherwise, I'm just going to have to trust him. But Father, I ask that You*

expose the person and deliver them from this porn addiction immediately.

God, I know Chris and I may experience our own challenges. However, I'm going to resist the habit of trying to make everything perfect. Whatever trials may come, I have to trust that You'll equip us to handle it.

Father, it's a little scary. Marriages don't seem to have a fighting chance these days. I mean just today on a 20/20 news special they were spouting divorce statistics, and I heard it's even worse for Christians. Lord, what's really going on?

With a weak economy, crime rampant, infidelity and staggering unemployment, it's no wonder that people's marriages are strained. But then I think about the past, how marriages have survived slavery, the civil rights era, and poverty of the worst kind and much deeper tragedies that we've seen recently. I guess that's why I have an appreciation for my parents' marriage, now that I'm older. They had their disagreements, but they held it together until Mom passed on.

I guess it's just like anything else. We just have to trust You. But if Godly couples are supposed to come together to fulfill Your purpose it would seem that we would have extra protection, provision, and everything else. Lord I'm just going to look to You for guidance. Maybe it would help if Chris and I had mentors. If that is Your will for us, I pray that You would send an anointed Christian couple our way. I truly want to build a strong marital foundation, for You said in Your word, "a wise woman builds her home, but a foolish woman tears it down with her own hands." I'm going to need some help, Father!

One last thing God, You know how I allow fear to kick in every once in a while; fear that everything will fall apart, fear of failure, fear that something is going to happen to Chris . . . I pray You help me to rest in You whenever I sense fear creeping up in me.

When am I going to learn that everything I need is already on the inside of me and You have it all under control?

Anyway, I'm getting ready to turn in. I need to get up bright and early to "fight the good fight."

Forever Your daughter and servant,

Lexi

CHAPTER ELEVEN

Law Firm of Reynolds & Stanton

"Thank you, Ms. Wilson. I'll be sure to get back to you about the hearing," I said as we walked toward the front lobby of my law office.

"Okay, Mrs. Reynolds. I'll bring you the other half of the money. I promise. You've got to get my baby out of jail. He's not a thief and he's not evil. He's been set up. You know that place downtown was on the news for messing up everybody's evidence."

My eyes locked on hers, which begged for a sign that her grandson would be fine. My only assurance at the moment was an occasional nod as she spoke. She was feeble, her posture worsened by overwork, worry, and time.

"Yes ma'am, I know. We're going to do our best, but it *is* a process." I walked her out to the hallway and shook her hand. I held it long enough to feel her protruding veins, but also to calm her spirit. Our silent exchange was my unspoken bond that I'd do what I could. However, I knew it was going to be an uphill battle. Her grandson had been caught on tape. I felt for her. Instead of resting and enjoying her retirement, she was busy bailing him out. Our only hope at this point was a plea bargain, since he had an alleged accomplice. It's so discouraging to see some of our young men get in this situation. It's such a vicious cycle.

As we moved toward the elevator, it opened and Capri glided through its doors. Her hair, freshly permed, bounced in rhythm with her step. "Hello, ladies," she said, brushing by us with briefcase in tow as she strode toward our office.

When she passed by, the scent of Bond No. 9's Chelsea Flowers danced in the hallway. I became instantly irritated. Capri looked beautiful and polished as usual with her tailored suit, lightly layered cut, and natural makeup to complement her caramel skin. *What is this I'm feeling?* I looked down at my fingernails that were badly in need of a manicure. Without feeling my kitchen, I knew a touch-up was due. I tried to avoid checking my watch, but I couldn't help it. *1:13 p.m.* It's not that I wanted Capri to clock in or out, but I'd already worked a half day and she was sashaying in from her hairdresser's appointment, just starting her day in the afternoon.

When I made it back to my office I walked in and closed the door. Ms. Wilson had been draining and I just needed a moment. I sat and rubbed my temples. *Please Lord, don't let Capri come in here wanting to make small talk. Please God, fix my attitude, because I know it's bad.* I continued to rub my temples, take deep breaths, and tell myself I was just having a moment.

We'd only been in business a few months and I was feeling like this?

Brrrring. "Yes, Claudia."

"I have your husband on the line."

"Send him through." A smile danced across my lips and I sat up. *He must have sensed I needed him.* I leaned back in my chair and closed my eyes.

"How's the sexiest man in the city of Houston?" I said with the phone to my ear.

"What an ego boost. I'm glad I decided to call. I'm at lunch now. How's your day going?"

"Mmm, okay. Another grandmother who swears her baby's innocent."

"Umm, I remember when I was growing up, I wouldn't even *think* about doing some of the things these kids are doing. I grew up without a dad, so that single parent argument doesn't always work. Lexi, just do your best, baby, and try not to stress."

"I'll try not to stress; I think I'm just a little burned out. I was hoping I could have a date with my husband tonight." I leaned back in my chair awaiting his response.

"Uh, honey . . . That's why I called. I know Friday is our date night, but Nate's down here on business from Dallas."

"Wow, you guys haven't hung out in a while. I guess I have to take a rain check, but that's okay. I'll just rent a movie or something."

"Don't sound so pitiful, honey. You probably need the rest."

"Yeah, I am a bit drained," I said as I ran my finger

around the rim of the frame holding his picture. "So, y'all are just hanging out?"

"Yeah. Lexi, I know what you're thinking."

He was right. I loved his brother, but he was *very* single and always had some kind of investment or scheme he was trying to get folks to buy into. Didn't he know network marketing and pyramid schemes don't really work? Fortunately, Chris had resisted his brother's fast talk so far. "I'm just thinking that I trust my husband and I want him to have a wonderful time. Even though he'll be without me and this is usually our date night. But that's okay." I picked up his picture then set it back down.

"I know, I know, but how about I get us tickets to the John Legend concert to make it up to you?" he said.

"As long as you promise to hold my hand and whisper in my ear while we're there."

"You got it. I'll see you when I get home. Love you."

"Love you too." I hung up a bit deflated, but decided to make it a movie night for old times' sake.

CHAPTER TWELVE

Inquiring Minds Want to Know

Jermane decided to check in on her husband before she left to have tea. "Hey honey, how'd golf go this morning?" She cradled the phone in the crook of her neck as she finished applying her mascara. She slicked her hair back into a ponytail for a no fuss, but classy look.

"Good, honey. I need to run by the office for a little while," he said as he pulled out of the country club parking lot.

"I thought you weren't going in to the office today?"

"Uh, baby, your dad. He brought in a new client in this week . . ."

"I know, babe, I just don't want us to go backwards. I was getting used to our having more time together. You finally learned how to tell my dad no."

"Jermane, don't start. Didn't we go to Lexi's house-warming? And your dad no longer affects my schedule.

It's under control. Just don't stress me out by nagging me."

Jermane paused before adding another light layer of mascara. "Okay, Rex." She paused. "So when are you going to make it home?"

"It won't be too long. I need to go through some files. Jermane, I just think if maybe you started teaching like you promised you wouldn't be as fixated on my schedule. I know you could probably teach at the University of Houston or South Texas College of Law."

"Rex, I know I said that, but you also said there was no pressure. Are we in financial trouble? Do I need to work?"

"Jermane, don't get defensive. It was just a suggestion."

"Rex, why don't you just give me a call when you're finishing up."

He took a deep breath and said, "Alright, honey, I will." He knew if he went to the office now his father-in-law would be there. Maybe then Rex could work up the nerve to ask him some much needed questions. His future with the firm depended on it.

CHAPTER THIRTEEN

Delayed and Denied

There was no better sound to Capri than Anthony's SUV driving into the garage after a game. She heard the door shut and Anthony's size fourteen sneakers pounding the steps after several minutes. She ran in the bathroom and lit a few more candles, then met him at the top of the stairs wrapped in her silk kimono.

"I missed you," she said as he dropped his gym bag and wrapped his large, muscular arms around her. She felt secure enveloped in his large frame.

"I missed you too. Did you check out all my three pointers in the second half? I was on fire," he said like an excited kid.

"Yeah, I did. You hungry?" she said as he released her from his grip. She was happy for him but needed a break from basketball.

"Not too much. Just want to relax. I showered at the

gym and grabbed a quick bite with the fellas." He placed his full lips on hers. "Mmm, that's some good sugar."

Capri's insides got warm. "Well, I thought you'd want to take a nice little soak for your muscles." She felt his arm.

"Naw, I'm okay."

"Not even with me?" She looked into his eyes and raised her right eyebrow.

"Oh, you didn't say *that*. And don't do that, you know when you raise that eyebrow it turns me on," he said as he grabbed her from behind and kissed her behind the ear.

"Umm. Okay now, let's take it to the bathroom," she said, prying his hands away. "I ran the water and put in that soothing mineral salt you like. We can just relax. We haven't had much playtime since the season's started."

She grabbed his hand and they walked toward the large bathroom. They passed the huge vanity island in the middle of the room and the marble shower. The flat-screen television above the Jacuzzi remained off. The bubbles filled the tub and she let out a sigh at the gurgle of the water. The burning candles and caviar potpourri scented the room with a sensual Ebonywood fragrance. She'd made a special trip to the Bombay Company earlier that day to pick them up. The Bose sound system released the soothing sounds of David Benoit.

Capri watched as her husband peeled off his clothes. Her eyes scanned every indentation in his six-pack. She knew his body well, every muscle and curve, and the intricate designs of his crucifix tattoo. He got in the water first, as always. Capri liked the way her back fit in the cavity of his chest. She especially loved the way he kissed and played in her hair. That was one of the few times she didn't mind it getting a little wet. She looked forward to the way he'd bathe her arms with water and the feel of his large legs framing hers.

After they soaked for a few minutes, Capri realized her husband was practically asleep. She heard deep breathing and a little teeth grinding. *He never falls asleep in the tub, my big baby is tired.* He jumped when she kissed the inside of his arm.

"Oh, sorry, honey. I'm exhausted. You okay?" He grabbed her tight.

"Yeah, I'm fine."

"Tell me, how was your week?" he said quietly as he lightly stroked her hair, then wrapped his finger around one of her ringlets already softened by the steam.

"Umm, good. The firm's moving along. Lots of for-mer clients are sending business. I'm really excited. With Thanksgiving coming up, I'm hoping we can settle a few cases."

"You and Lexi doing okay?"

"Yeah, so far so good. I love being my own boss. I get to work at home or go in to the office whenever I want. I love working on the cases that I want to and no more being a slave to billable hours."

"That's great." He paused briefly and closed his eyes. "Baby?"

"Yeah?"

"How come you haven't come to the last few games? I like knowing you're there," he said as he buried his nose in her mane.

"I know. I just like watching from home. You should

see me. I can barely sit on the couch. I love being here in my comfy sweats jumping up and down, yelling at the top of my lungs. And, well, most of the other wives are so superficial. You know me. I'm just not into all that." She circled her finger on the inside of his palm.

"Baby, I don't care if you come in jeans and a T-shirt, as long as I know you're there. Do it just for me . . . I mean, you could at least come to the home games."

"Wow, you sound so pitiful. If it means that much, yeah, I can do that." She closed her eyes. "That's a small sacrifice for my handsome husband. And just for that I *will* wear jeans and a T-shirt, and put on a little makeup." She slid her fingers through his.

"Mmmm. Thanks sweetie."

"Now you can do something for me. I didn't go through all this tonight for nothing. I'm trying to get just a little lovin'," she said as she rubbed the thickness of his thigh.

ZZZZ

Uh-oh. No he didn't.

After a few minutes she woke him to get in bed. He managed to dry off and collapsed in the bed like a huge slab of concrete. She climbed in after him. The six-hundred-thread-count sheets did nothing to soothe her attitude. "Now, when *I'm* like this, it's a federal crime," she thought as she dozed off. "But there's always the morning, that may be even better," she said to herself as she rolled over with a smile.

apri hadn't realized how tired she'd been. She looked at the clock and noticed it was close to 9:45 a.m. She wanted to go to early service, but it was too late for that. She went to use the restroom and pulled on the door. It was locked. *What in the world? He never locks the door.* "Anthony, you in there? Why is the door locked?"

She could barely finish the question before the door flew open. "Sorry, sweetie. I don't know what I was thinking."

She paused momentarily, then walked past him toward the sink to wash her face. "Okay, um, are we going to late service today?"

"Yeah, yeah, whatever you want babe, whatever you want," he said as he rushed out of the bathroom.

CHAPTER FOURTEEN

The Future Has a Past

Angel waved her hand as she saw Octavio walk through the church lobby. She wanted to make sure they were going to be on time for their first night of the Bible lesson series.

She knew he'd be running late because of the weather. Houston didn't get much snow, but it had its share of the nasty mix of cold and rain, especially near the end of fall.

"Hey you," he said as he reached over to kiss her on the cheek. "It's a mess out there."

"I know. C'mon, we're only a few minutes late," she said as she grabbed his hand and led him to the escalator.

"Welcome to 'Living Victoriously!'" a young woman who looked to be in her early thirties said with enthusiasm. It was a very casual atmosphere since the series was being taught on Sunday evenings. She was dressed in jeans and a vibrant turquoise tunic. Her shiny brown hair was pulled back in a long ponytail, exposing her large hoop earrings.

"Hmm, she seems so spiritually mature for such a young age," Angel thought as she wrapped her hands around her Bible.

"My name is Amber. I'm a ministry leader here at Lakewood and I am so excited to lead this study. Part of becoming a victorious Christian is understanding how to apply biblical principles to your life. Jesus died so we could live life more abundantly and to the full! Our God is an awesome God. Amen?" she said as she raised her arms like a high school cheerleader.

"Amen!" chorused the thirty or so people attending.

She moved through the rest of her introduction, Octavio and Angel sat quietly and listened as she led the study.

"Let's start with the lesson 'Discovering Who We Are in Christ Jesus.' Sometimes the world has programmed us to see ourselves and each other a certain way. So, we have to do some deprogramming. It's not about what the world or your circumstances say about you, but what *God* says about you. You are not your circumstances! Say it with me: I am *not* my circumstances!"

"I am not my circumstances!" they all chimed in.

"So, before we begin to understand who *God* says we are, we're going to have an assignment. We need to discover who we are right now. We need to think about how our past and present circumstances have defined who we are. We want to clear away anything that may hinder us from hearing God clearly and keep us from embracing and owning who we are in Christ Jesus. We want to be the people that God originally created us to be. That's when we can truly tap into His power. Amen?"

"Amen," everyone echoed.

She passed out a one-page assignment. "I want you to really pray about this exercise, one of the most important exercises. It deals with your family. What impact did your mother, father, siblings, and anyone else who was a significant figure in your childhood have on you? There are specific questions in this exercise that will help you. Some of us may need to dig deep, but don't be afraid. Be bold and honest."

Angel noticed Octavio's body shift and watched as he quickly folded the paper and stuffed it in his Bible. She knew anything that dealt with his childhood seemed to cause instant agitation. He rarely spoke of it. In their friendship and relationship most of the focus was on her past issues. She was finally realizing that her man may have some healing needs too. *This class is gonna bless us both.* Peace settled in as Amber's voice led the closing prayer.

CHAPTER FIFTEEN

Brunch Unplugged

"We're going to be on *MTV Cribs* . . . this is really wild," Capri said as she adjusted her napkin. "I didn't think this was something I'd be into, but I'm kind of excited."

"Wow! I'd just love to do something like that! But who would come to our house? I mean, I've decorated it like a professional, but Kevin and I only have a little three-bedroom home. All of us can't live in Lake Olympia," Jewel said as she looked Capri up and down.

"Okay, there are people who would love to have a three-bedroom home," I said as I eyed my Creole cream cheese crepes. "Be thankful."

"Oh, don't get me wrong. I *am* grateful," Jewel said. She paused as she watched me about to savor a large fork-ful of food. "Lexi, dear, watch your carbs," she added as she tapped my hand.

I sighed deeply. "Jewel, slap my hand again and see what happens. I had a rough week. If I want to drown myself in food, that's my business." Just then I noticed I had dropped a bit of cream cheese on my new silk Nicole Miller dress. It was my one splurge in six months. *Shoot, can't have anything.*

"Goodness, you don't have to be so crabby about it. I'm just lookin' out for a sista—as long as it took for you to get Chris, you may want to work on keeping him. Just because you're married doesn't mean the work is done. See if I care if you walk around all bloated."

Gee, thanks for that reminder. Can we women get a break, God? It takes forever to get somebody, now we got to do stuff to keep 'em too? When will it ever end? I rolled my eyes at her and continued to chew.

"Anyway, Capri, I think that's fabulous. So when is it? I want to make sure I clear my schedule so I can be there!" Jewel said as she reached in her purse for her BlackBerry.

Capri threw her hand up in protest. "Uh-uh, Jewel. It's just gonna be me and Anthony," she said as she sliced her mushroom and onion omelet.

"Are you *serious?* That's so selfish. You know when they have all the rappers on *Cribs* they always do the cameo shot with their 'peeps.' You could do that," she said, waiting for Capri to agree.

"Jewel *please.* First of all, I'm a little too old to call anybody 'my peeps.' That's why the only person I was gonna tell was Lexi, so she wouldn't expect me at work that day," Capri said as she poured syrup on her pancakes.

I tried to give a half smile, but again, Capri seemed to be spending more time at home than at the office. *As long as the money comes in when it's supposed to.* I nodded my head and faked a smile.

"Okay, alright. Be that way. You know you're wrong for that. Isn't she wrong for that, y'all?" Jewel said as she waved her fork in the air.

"Jewel, no one else really cares," Angel barked, then grabbed a spoon to try her fresh berry parfait.

"Okay, I see how it's going down. I guess we'll just move on then. If you all don't care, then I don't care . . . Speaking of reality shows, did anyone see the last episode of *I Love New York,* the spinoff of *Flavor of Love?* I forgot to TiVo it this week."

"Are you *serious?* I *know* you don't watch that ridiculousness. It's so degrading. Not only is it time to 'take back the music,' it's time to take back the television, the videos, and the movies," I said as my head whipped in her direction.

"Please girl, talk about a stress relief, that show is *pure* entertainment. What can I say? It's my one guilty pleasure. Our life can't always be about CNN, MSNBC, or *60 Minutes.* We have enough real-life drama. Sometimes we just need to laugh," Jewel asserted.

"I can't believe Flava Flav and this New York character are making money off of that triflin' show. It's like they scraped the bottom of the barrel with that mess," I said.

"The *Flavor of Love?* Is that some type of new cooking show?" Jermane asked as she sliced her pecan-crusted catfish. "Does it come on the cooking channel?"

"Are you serious? No, this is the show with Flava Flav of the old rap group Public Enemy—uh, never mind." Jewel added more sugar to her coffee.

"Well, that's why Rex and I don't even watch much television. It's all garbage. I mean even regular TV is too risqué," Jermane said, unfazed by Jewel's frustration.

"Yeah, it's spilling over into books too. How come every person who lost custody of their kids, stripped, or did a porn movie needs to have a 'tell all' book? Every time I walk in a bookstore, all I see are covers with half-naked women holding a gun or some crap. I mean, that's definitely not *all* Black folks read," Capri said. "We just need something else to define our culture."

I cleared my throat. "Uhhh, speaking of porn . . ." Everyone looked at me with raised eyebrows. "Well, I wasn't going to say anything, but the morning after our housewarming, we noticed someone had been looking at porn on our computer." I waited for a response.

"How do you know it wasn't Chris?" Jewel asked. "I know that Kevin, as crazy as he is, wouldn't do that. But then again, that fool would probably tell me if had done it."

"Well, Chris swore it wasn't him. Besides, remember, he didn't even want to have a bachelor party."

"Lexi, you eloped girl. He didn't get a chance to," Jewel said.

"Don't start that again." My eyes locked with Jewel's.

"Don't look at me," Capri said, then folded her arms. "Lexi, I mean you've known Anthony from the jump and you know his character. That's definitely not his thing."

"Well, Rex is not lacking for anything at home, so I can't see him needing to do that. That's just disgusting," Jermane said.

"That's really trifling. Whoever it was definitely has an addiction if they have to use someone else's computer," Angel said. "There were a few other folks there, so it doesn't have to be one of our men."

"Hmm. Maybe sooner or later the truth will come out," Capri said.

Everyone was quiet for a moment. "I guess. Anyway, back to the state of our books and music. We have to take responsibility for our images. There are people out there who are supporting this crazy mess. It wasn't until Don Imus made his degrading comments about the Rutgers girls basketball team, that we even started dialoging about our images and the way we are viewed by the media," I said as I took another sip of coffee.

"It makes me wonder, do books and music that degrade Blacks sell well because that's what the public wants, or do they sell well because that's all there is to purchase?" Angel analyzed aloud. "I guess we just need to be more support-ive and proactive about what we want to see on the book-shelves and on television."

"Wait," I interjected, "I just thought of something. Maybe we should start our own book club?" I looked around the table for a response. "That would be one way to take action. We could talk about change or we could ef-fect change."

"Lexi, you know you are the infamous book club dropout," Angel taunted.

"Yeah, I know, but that's because you all weren't in them. C'mon. We need to try something different."

"Sounds good to me," Capri said.

"Okay, but we'll see how long it lasts," Angel said.

"Personally, I love the classics," Jermane said. "So you know what kind of books I'll be picking."

"Whatever," Jewel said. "I'll take any excuse to have a party. Oh, that reminds me, the planning for the art exhibit and reception is coming together splendidly. I have you all down as my guests. There's only been one glitch."

"What's that?" Jermane asked.

"Umm, it appears that Grant's bringing that Tamia woman," Jewel said with an attitude.

"You mean his *wife?*" I said. "I'm almost afraid to ask. Why is that a problem?"

"Well, I'd planned to be his official escort, of course. Besides, who knows what could happen? One can always 'trade up.' Then Capri and I can be in the 'players' wives' club together. I know somewhere in another lifetime I was rich. I'm destined to live the life of the rich and famous," Jewel said as she pulled out her compact to check her makeup.

"Okay, keep playing like that. God's gonna snatch away what you have if you don't appreciate it," Angel warned.

Jewel paused. "Girl, you know I'm playing. Kevin and I are *very* happy." She let out a quick laugh and slapped Angel on the wrist lightly.

"Yeah, okay. *Anyway,* I do give Grant Hill and his wife major credit for making it this long. So many people in the spotlight are tripping these days. Divorce, rehab, custody battles, jail . . . what in the world is going on?" Angel asked.

"I'll tell you what's happening," I said. "God is getting

tired. He's starting to sift through the world. He's allowed this mess to go on for too long."

"Yeah, I guess that's one way to look at it," Angel said.

"I mean really, money can't save you from everything. He's tired of the church tripping, fake ministries, and celebrities thinking they can buy their way out of anything. Look at Michael Vick, Britney Spears, and T.I. Some people want to say they're being made examples of, but at some point you have to be accountable." I realized I'd gotten on a roll.

"Dang, Lexi, calm down. I hear you, though. Just look at the NBA. Some people can't handle money and fame. God won't let foolery go on forever. He can't let the world think that people can do anything without any consequences. He's been patient long enough," Capri said. "That's why I thank God Anthony is responsible. He knows all he has is because of God."

"I'll tell you what other crisis is out of control. What's up with all the snow skiing? I mean, it's always been in the NBA, but dang, is the Black woman going out of style?" Angel demanded.

"Yeah, but I'm starting to see some sisters dating outside their race," I said. "Before I met Chris, I was thinking about it."

Everyone stopped eating and looked at me in disbelief.

"What? I got a little hyped up after seeing the movie *Something New*. Besides, true Christians do not discriminate," I explained as I finished off the last of my chocolate espresso cheesecake.

"*Personally*, I love me some chocolate," Jewel interjected.

"Let's face it. There are certain things that only a Black man understands. I don't want to have to explain why I tie my hair up at night with my jumbo silky scarf."

"Okay, Jewel, you had to take it to another level. On that note, I think it's time to go," Capri said.

I stood up and grabbed my purse. "Yeah, it's about that time."

"What? What did I say?" Jewel asked as she watched everyone head for the door. "And hey, wait a minute. We still have to pay the bill! My husband doesn't play in the NBA . . . you all, this isn't funny," she said as she grabbed the check and ran after them.

CHAPTER SIXTEEN

Dead Weight

"Add some more weight, man," Kevin said as he rested on the bench.

"You sure you can handle all this?" Anthony questioned as he bent down to reach for the weights. "I don't want to have to call Jewel to come get you."

"Man, just spot me." Kevin repositioned his legs on the floor alongside the bench. After Anthony added the weights, he attempted to lift them. His arms trembled. He raised the bars halfway, but then quickly dropped the weights back to the stand.

"Told you, man! You're gonna hurt yourself," Anthony said as he popped Kevin with his towel.

Kevin's chest heaved in and out. After a few seconds he spoke in between deep breaths. "So what's up for next weekend? I know all the women are getting together, so we need to plan something."

"Well, I got a ton of work to do," Rex yelled from the treadmill.

"Man, you always got work to do. I'm talking to the menfolk in this room that have a real life." Kevin sat up.

Rex frowned, then just shook his head. He grabbed his bottle of water and took a swig.

"Well, I gotta game Saturday, so you know what the deal is," Anthony said.

"We know, fool, we're gonna be there, remember? On Friday, my boy's having a bachelor party. It's been a long time since I've been to one of those," Kevin said as he wiped his clean-shaven head and forehead with a hand towel.

"You know Lexi would kill me if she knew I was even thinking about going to something like that," Chris said as his legs raised the weight on the leg press. "Naw man, I'll have to pass."

"Man, I can see now I'm gonna have to train you on the 'head of the household concept.' " Kevin shook his head. "Newlyweds . . . and this is your first marriage too? You'll learn. That 'honey-do' routine will get old," he said as he draped the towel around his neck.

"Man, that ain't it. I don't need to be up in that kinda atmosphere. Besides, that's never been my thing. Even *before* I got married. Besides, I've got to be careful with the line of work I'm in," Chris said, pausing between lifts.

"I'm only going for a minute. It's for one of my coworkers I'm tight with. Stuff like that's never interfered with my relationships. I don't get all caught up like that. It's those weak brothers who get all messed up over some body parts. Looking is one thing, but touching is another. I wouldn't go out like that, or hurt Jewel."

"Oh, okay. Then I'm sure you're going to tell her where you're going, right?" Octavio yelled as he paused between curl-ups. "This is coming from a man who just had to sleep on the porch."

"Okay, Marc Anthony, who told *you* about that?" asked Kevin. "Man, see women always running their mouths. But what Jewel doesn't know won't hurt her, and I better not hear about this from any of y'all," he said as he stood up from the bench.

"Anyway, Angel and I have plans Friday and Sunday, but I'll definitely be at the Toyota Center for the game," Octavio said.

"Yo, Mr. Conservative, I guess that leaves me and you. You know you're *way* too uptight for a brother. What's the craziest thing you've ever done? Run a red light?"

"Rex? He's the brother on a leash." Anthony started laughing as he ran over to Chris to slap his hand.

"Oh, so you all got jokes. Y'all underestimate me. Just for that, what time you want to meet after work?" Rex said as his treadmill slowed to a halt. "I've been looking for some stress relief anyway."

"Six-thirty. Let's grab a quick bite from the Fox Sports Grill at the Galleria first, then roll through the bachelor party after that," Kevin said.

"Alright, sounds like a plan."

CHAPTER SEVENTEEN

Let Sleeping Dogs Lie

"Angel, I may not make it to the Bible class this week," Octavio said as they walked toward Uptown Sushi.

"Why not? I thought you said you liked the class," Angel said while he opened the door to their favorite restaurant. Uptown Sushi had an industrial chic vibe with amber lighting and bar seating. It felt more like a loft space than a restaurant. It stayed packed thanks to its cool and sexy ambience. Angel looked around and noticed an eclectic mix of Houstonians; she and Octavio frequented the restaurant enough for her to recognize the regulars.

After they sat down at their table, the waitress walked up and greeted them, then handed them the menu. A few moments later she returned with two waters.

"I'll have the sake toro," Angel told the waitress after she closed the large menu. She noticed how the waitress's blood red lipstick contrasted with her flawless olive skin and silky black hair. Even in the dim lighting she noticed the explosion of makeup on the woman's face.

"Hirame for me," Octavio said.

The waitress, relieved that she didn't have to explain the menu, walked off quickly.

"So, what were you saying about the Bible study class?" Angel asked, continuing their conversation.

"I was just saying that I'm swamped. I'm up to my neck in work. I need that time to finish up a little research. You know we do the job of two or three people there over at the city attorney's office. So, you may have to go without me this week."

"Mmm-hmm," Angel said as she looked him in his eyes. She noticed how his baby-soft lips glistened as his words spilled out. Despite Octavio's habit of licking his slightly pink lips, they always appeared supple, smooth, and readily kissable. She watched as his hand slid over his buzz-cut hair. She liked his new look, but missed his dark thick waves. "Octavio," she paused. "What's going on with you? I've known you long enough, you're not being honest."

"Not sure what you're talking about." He looked away from her and toward the bar, where patrons swarmed.

"Every since we started this class, you've been acting a little weird, especially since we did those first lessons about family. Octavio, I know it brought up feelings about your childhood in Mexico and your father. But you have to move past the pain. Don't let it discourage your deliverance. Maybe the time's right for you to deal with this."

"Angel, I hear you, but I don't want to get into this now." He sipped on his water and noticed the couple next to them staring a bit. When he and Angel first started dating it seemed that people were always staring at them. Now it seemed a Black woman and a Hispanic man were no longer a novelty. However, every so often a look or stare reminded them of their unique relationship. "Can we just have a nice relaxing meal?"

Angel sighed and looked away. She refocused her attention on his eyes. "We don't have to, but you know I'm right. Octavio, if we can make it through all the mess I put you through, we can deal with this. If I had not faced my fears from my previous marriage, we wouldn't be together now." She watched his face for permission to continue.

He sighed and fumbled with his chopsticks. He finally placed them down on the table as a sign of surrender. "Angel, my mom called me a couple of weeks ago. My dad," he cleared his throat. "My father's in the hospital. He's pretty sick. I talked to him for a few minutes. That was the first time we spoke in years. I put him out of my mind a long time ago."

Her shoulders deflated and she sat back. "How come you didn't say anything before now?" She folded her arms, waiting for his response.

He shrugged his shoulders.

"So, what did he say? Where is he?"

"He's in El Paso. They say he may not have much longer to live. He's on dialysis. His voice was so, so . . . weak." Octavio dropped his eyes.

"Are you going to see him? El Paso isn't that far."

"I don't know, Angel. It's weird, he didn't sound like the man I used to know. I remember his voice as heavy with hate and anger." He looked around the room to avoid looking Angel in the eye. "Yeah, he was a hateful so-and-so. He treated Mom—well, all of us—really badly." He spoke slowly and his eyes were distant.

She could sense his pain. "We don't have to talk about this now," Angel offered.

Octavio's face softened. He swallowed and reached out for her hand. They locked fingers across the table in the busy restaurant. Octavio looked into her eyes and his mouth relaxed a bit.

"I'll be right back." He shot up from the table and headed toward the restroom.

Angel watched, resisting the urge to follow him. She prayed silently in her seat, while she waited for him to return.

After his date with Angel, Octavio headed home and called it a night. It took him a while to doze off as he thought about his father. He tossed and turned. He let out a groan and then a scream. He shot straight up. He grabbed his forehead. His chest and hair were both wringing wet. He rubbed his forehead, then reached down for the gold cross around his neck. As he ran his fingers over it, he tried to piece together his dream. All Octavio remembered was blood, some dirty boots, and a gun. He'd stopped having this particular dream when he was in his twenties. But once he'd spoken to his dad, the dream started again. Octavio's body was trembling. He looked at the clock; it was 4 a.m. He started to call Angel, but decided to get up and take a shower, thinking it'd be hard to fall back asleep. Before he went to the bathroom, he no-

ticed the slip of paper on his nightstand with the room
and phone number of the hospital where his father was.
Octavio picked it up and stared at it. Then he put it back
down. He got up and headed straight for the shower.
While he was in the shower, he tried his best to scrub away
his last image of his father. But it didn't work.

CHAPTER EIGHTEEN

Houston, We Have a Problem

"Anthony, wake up!" Capri shook her husband, who was passed out on the couch after finishing his workout. She finally slapped him lightly upside his head.

"Capri, what are you doing?" He turned to face her with his eyes half closed. He smacked his lips.

"You need to get up and go upstairs!"

"Okay, alright. It's not that serious—what's wrong with you?" he said as he sat up.

"What's wrong with me? What's wrong with me? I've been working hard all week and I was looking forward to some stress relief!"

"What? Why didn't you say something? I would have skipped my workout tonight. I can't read your mind."

"You know I understand basketball is a priority, but unless I make plans, you never seem to want to do anything. You seem all geeked up whenever we have to go to those players' association socials or when you want me to go to the players' wives functions. Or even those boring-behind fundraisers. Anthony, I just want to have some fun away from all of that. Just you and me." She pulled on his arm like a little girl.

"Couples time?" he said as he rubbed his head.

"Yes, Anthony," she said as she popped him upside the head again. "Couples time—Anthony, what's the deal? Can a sister get some lovin'?"

"Whoa, easy, sweetie. I've never seen you this determined before."

"That's because I've never *had* to be! What's up? You got a little something on the side?" Her New York attitude came out as she backed up and threw her hands open.

"Capri, I swear to God, that's not it," he said with his eyes now squarely focused on hers.

"Well, what is it?" she said as she looked him in the face with her arms folded. "I know it can't be me, because I look the same as when we got married, even better, I might add. Is this about me not coming to your games?" She placed her hands on her hips.

"Yes, I mean no. What I mean is yeah, you still got it going on and no, this isn't about you missing games," he said as he grabbed her and sat her on his lap.

She was already melting at his touch. "I know if Jermane and Rex can have a hot relationship, then we got to step up our game. Think about it, *Rex* . . . handling his business. You know how uptight they usually are. Anyway, you can't blame it on basketball, because we've never had these issues."

"Okay, okay." He started laughing. "I'm going to take a shower and by the time I get out, you better be ready and under those covers," he said as he ran his hand across her layered bangs.

"That's more like it," she purred. She jumped up and didn't bother to look behind to see if he was following her.

"Are you kidding me?" Capri sat up and rolled over on her back. "This *really* can't be happening." She placed her hand on her forehead.

"Babe, I don't know. You know this has *never* happened before." He stared at the ceiling. "Let's just wait a minute and try again," he said slowly.

"Anthony, all I can say is that nothing better be going on, or you're gonna see my East Coast coming out."

"Just cool out, Capri." His voice was a bit louder. "I guess I'm just a little tired."

"We've been trying this for the past forty-five minutes. Forget it, Anthony. You better make an appointment with the doctor first thing in the morning. You better come up with some reasonable explanation, or it's going to be *on*."

"Maybe it's the pressure from the games. This is the closest we've gotten to the playoffs and it's just a lot of pressure. Maybe that's it," he pleaded.

"Well, you better go do some yoga or something, because this is all out of order!" She got up, put on her robe, and headed downstairs for a pint of ice cream.

Anthony stayed in the bed and began to hit his forehead with his balled fist. "Ah man . . . This is messed up.

This is *so* messed up." While his wife escaped downstairs he slid to the floor and whispered a quick prayer:

God, I love my wife. She would never understand the real issue. If I'm being selfish forgive me. Lord, I can't be perfect all the time. Just don't let this be something that destroys us. Even in my weakest moments, Capri's never doubted my manhood. I'm going to trust that we'll be fine. Even though I may not be making all the right choices, Lord, I have to rely on Your grace and mercy. Thank You for loving me in spite of myself. In Jesus's name I pray. Amen.

CHAPTER NINETEEN

Legal Woes

Finally, I thought as I walked out of the opposing counsel's office. *Glad that deposition is over.* When I looked at the windshield my relief turned to anger. *Darn it! That's just great, a ticket.* I hadn't seen that sign when I parked earlier. I yanked the ticket off my windshield. *Boy am I glad this day is about to be over. I've had it.*

I got into the car, backed out, and headed into the start of rush hour traffic. *Okay, I have just enough time to get to the grocery store before the traffic really gets bad. Chris's aunt and uncle are coming in from Atlanta first thing in the morning and I need time to go home, clean up, and stock the fridge. Crap, I know Chris probably left the house a mess. He just doesn't think about that kind of stuff! It would really help me out if he did.* My anger subsided once I thought about the bottle of Riesling sitting in the back of the fridge from the housewarming. I was saving it for a special occasion, but it didn't get any more special than this. Add a slice of straw-berry cheesecake and it was going to be on.

I finally got on 610 North and figured I'd turn on the radio to ease the stress from my ride. "Hey . . . that's my jam . . . *I will love you anyway . . . Oooh, ooh, Sweet Thang . . .*" I started to snap one of my fingers. Then it happened. My cell phone starting ringing, interrupting my groove. I looked at the number. *Why would the office be calling now?*

"Hello?"

"Hey Lexi, this is Capri. How'd it go today?"

"It went fine. What's up?" I said as I jumped on the beltway.

"Well, did you know Ms. Wilson has been here waiting for you for about an hour?"

"No, I had no idea. Her appointment's next week. I checked right before I left the office."

"Well, she's here and has the nerve to be upset that you aren't here to meet with her."

"I really don't need this right now," I said as I pulled out onto the street.

"Well, she says it's urgent and that she has some new evidence."

"Jesus, Capri, are you kidding me? Can you *please* take care of this? I'm exhausted and I got a major headache. She'll be fine if you just meet with her and take down the information. She's the type of client that'll call the bar as-sociation on my behind and complain. It's partially my fault; I've been really holding her hand."

"I thought you were coming back to the office." Capri sighed loudly into the phone and sucked her teeth. "Lexi, you don't have to take *every* client. You need to screen these people a little better. I really don't have the time either because I have to go to a fundraiser tonight."

These people? "Capri, just talk with her for five minutes and see what she has to say. She just wants some attention. I would come back, but I'm on the other side of town. Besides, I have to get ready for Chris's aunt and uncle. You can spare five minutes, can't you?"

"Lexi, did you hear me? I have to be somewhere and I'm running behind as it is. Forget it, Lexi, I'll handle it . . . But you really need to start using more discretion when it comes to these clients. It's time to raise our standards a little."

Is she for real? As many times as I've covered for her behind? Where's the compassion? Part of our mission, I thought, was to help clients like Ms. Wilson. Is it just me or is this player's wife thing going to her head? I understand why she's upset, but we've always had each other's back.

"Capri, I appreciate it. Transfer me to the lobby and I'll let her know you're going to speak with her. I owe you one," I said calmly.

"Yeah, yeah. We'll talk this weekend," Capri said and hung up the phone.

After dismissing my exchange with Capri, I headed home. Once I made it through the garage, I walked in the house and did a quick assessment. It wasn't too bad, but Chris's aunt and uncle's home was immaculate. So I was determined to have a spotless house by tomorrow.

I was exhausted, but I knew if I sat down, I'd risk never getting up. I stopped in the kitchen and noticed a few dishes sitting on the counter from my husband's snack run. A few empty nacho bags and a big spoon with a trace of ice cream confirmed my suspicion. I let out a sigh and started putting the dishes into the dishwasher. Then I headed upstairs to the bedrooms.

I was in the middle of changing sheets when the phone rang. I looked at the caller ID. *Jermane.* "Hey girl, what's going on?" I said, a little out of breath.

"Nothing, got a minute?"

"Sure. But that's about all. I have family coming in town tomorrow, so I'm doing a little cleaning."

"Why didn't you hire someone? Oh, never mind," Jermane said, realizing she was talking to me. "I just wanted to have a little girl chat, Lexi."

"Jermane, the only time you call is if something is wrong. So what's going on?"

"It's probably nothing, but Rex has been a bit distant and a little more tense then usual. He brought up my not working and it's been a long time since he's said anything like that. And he's been keeping some odd hours."

"Well, you did tell Rex that now that you have your third degree you were going to teach, but that's another issue. I guess the only person in our circle of friends who has to work is me! Anyway, you're right, it's probably nothing. It seems as if the only time Rex gets stressed is if it has to do with a client. You should be used to that by now."

"He did mention some new clients. He claimed that was the reason for the odd hours," Jermane said.

"Well, just take what he says at face value and continue to pay attention to what he does. You know men are different from us. They don't talk a lot about their problems. On the other hand, we women like to talk about everything and get our emotions all wound up," I said, recalling the segment I saw on *Good Morning America* about the way men and women communicate differently.

"I suppose so, Lexi. I don't know, I still feel there's something different. Rex used to get all excited about his cases. I guess he's losing some of that fire. When my dad made him partner, it was one of the happiest days of Rex's life."

"Let me tell you, it's not hard to lose the passion. After you've been practicing a while, like anything else, it can become a love-hate relationship. You've heard me say that before," I added.

"Lexi, you know I tune you out sometimes. Just kidding, girl," Jermane added quickly. "Anyway, I just thought Rex loved the law as much as my dad does. Daddy never seems to lose his passion for the law. He's a tough old man. He's managed to build one of the most successful and well established law firms in Houston. And he started the business during a time when there were only a handful of Black attorneys in Houston, or anywhere for that matter. Rex should be proud to be a part of that."

"I'm sure he is, Jermane. I think you are worrying for nothing."

"Lex, you're right. I need to stop acting paranoid."

"Yeah, as long as you don't have the urge to hire the guy from that cheesy television show "Cheaters," you're alright. We all can get a little crazy. Perhaps it's just a little bit of your past creeping into your relationship," I said hesitantly.

"Huh?"

"Well, you know . . . the Naegel incident. I mean that did raise a little trust issue between you and Rex. So maybe you're a little suspicious of Rex now because you were the one who was creepin' a bit."

"Lexi, I thought we wouldn't go back there. It was a mistake, okay? One that was totally out of character for me, might I add."

"Okay, my bad. It's just that you would be the person I'd least likely suspect would hook up with a man like Naegel."

"A, we did not hook up and B, what do you mean with a man like Naegel? I'm a very desirable woman. I can be conservative *and* sexy. So I fell for the biceps, smooth talk, and sun-kissed dreadlocks. And before you start to judge me, Lexi, let me remind you, marriage is not easy. When real life kicks in, idealism and romance take a backseat. It can happen to anybody."

"Whoa, don't get so defensive, Jermane. I was just joking."

"Well, don't play like that. I just didn't think we'd ever revisit that time in my life. Anyway, Lexi, I just wanted to get your feedback, but now I need to jump off this phone. I have some fundraiser duties to work on. And just a few words of advice for you, a housekeeper *is* a worthy investment. If you ever need a referral, just give me a ring. It's not that expensive."

"Okay, girl, I'll keep that in mind. Well, I need to get back to cleaning up. But I will keep you and Rex in my prayers. Bye, Jermane."

As I pulled out the vacuum cleaner, I started having visions of a complimentary housekeeper mysteriously showing up on my doorstep. I also thought about Jermane's comments. I ran the vacuum back and forth, drowning out any thoughts of romance leaving my marriage. "That's simply not an option for the Reynolds household," I mumbled, then picked up a pair of Chris's underwear off the floor of the bedroom and tossed them in the hamper.

CHAPTER TWENTY

She Works Hard for the Money

"So I said, 'Capri, all I need you to do is meet with my client for five minutes.' Do you think I was wrong?" It was Saturday and I was headed on a rare shopping excursion. I also needed to de-stress from the company Chris and I had last weekend. My hands were on "ten and two" on the steering wheel, and I was trying to stay focused on the road.

"Well, *personally* . . ." Jewel started to say before Angel reached over and covered her mouth. "What are you doing?" Jewel protested once she freed Angel's hand from her lips.

"What Jewel was *about* to say was this is between you and Capri and she's not about to get involved." Angel cut her eyes at Jewel.

"It's not like I'm trying to get y'all to take sides." *Okay, maybe I am a little. That's the same thing Chris said. I'm not getting any support from anywhere!*

"Good, that's why we're not gonna talk about it," Angel snapped. She continued flipping through her issue of *Black Enterprise* magazine.

"*Fine.* Then everybody needs to get out." I turned up the radio to drown out my frustration. I started bobbing my head to the music and moving my bottom around in the seat. "Oh no they didn't!" I said when I recognized the song. I turned it up a little more. "Flashlight . . . neon light . . ."

Jermane leaned away from me and looked at me like I was crazy.

"This song makes no sense whatsoever, but it never goes out of style!" Jewel chimed in.

"Don't act like y'all don't remember this . . . *Ooh* . . . undergrad, Kappa party . . . summer orientation?"

I looked at Jermane. "Oh, sorry girl, you didn't go to a historically Black college. Aggie Pride! Go Aggies . . . Aggies in the front, let me hear you grunt . . . Aggies in the middle let me hear you wiggle . . ."

"Go Lexi, get busy, go Lexi, it's your birthday." Jewel clapped her hands and sang.

"They must be having the old school party mix. Ooh, wait, remember this one? En Vogue. 'Hold on to Your Love'—Woo' they are jammin'," I said as I fanned myself with one hand.

"Jewel, don't encourage her. Did you notice she almost ran that light back there? Lexi, girl, you need to focus on the road!"

"Angel, now come on, you know you used to throw down at those high school and college jams." I started to move my shoulders. "Oh, sorry, you may have to go back a little further than the rest of us—"

"Lexi, you're tripping." Angel paused and rolled her eyes. "Okay, yeah you're right; I *was* sort of throwing down at Howard too!" She and Jewel slapped hands.

"Y'all are *so* tired. See if Capri were here, she'd know what I was talking about! Capri is an undercover 'hip-hop head,' you know." *Dang, I miss my partner in crime.* "Those were the good old days because being a grown-up is for the birds!" I screamed.

"I know that's right." Jewel leaned forward slightly. "Bills to pay . . . work to do, ex-wives to curse . . . well you know what I mean," she said and leaned back.

"Now, Jewel, what would Jesus do?" I sang as I wagged my finger and glanced quickly in the rearview mirror.

"Well, Jesus wouldn't have baby mama drama in the first place." Jewel folded her arms and looked out the window.

I could always count on my sister-friends to raise my spirits and this shopping trip was definitely on time. I really needed to treat myself since I'd been working so hard. I know I'd have plenty of encouragement in the shopping area. Jermane had no concept of budget, but at least she could afford to go shopping. Jewel tried to have a budget, but often forgot about her debt diet. Angel had the most restraint, so she'd have to be my reality check.

Jermane's cell phone rang and she dug into her roomy Chloe bag. "Hey, honey," she said after finally retrieving it. "Uh-huh, okay, sure. See you later tonight." She slipped her phone back in her purse. She looked ultrachic in her large Dior shades, ruffled blouse, and skinny jeans. This was a relaxed look for Jermane.

"What's up with the Celine Dion ringtone?" Jewel looked over at her.

"That was Rex," Jermane said, ignoring Jewel as usual.

"How's he doing?" My eyes scanned the lot for a parking space as we approached the Rice Village shopping center. *Come on Lord, give me some favor, I need a parking space.* I hunched over the steering wheel as if that would help.

"He's doing well. He's taking some clients out tonight, so he'll be home a little late."

"Whoever it is must be a huge client for Rex to hang out," I said, wheeling the car around. "Yeah! Those people are pulling out! Thank you, Lord!"

"From what I understand, yes." Jermane peered out of the window.

"Rex has been out with Kevin a few times lately," Jewel added.

"Oh? He's never mentioned it. Well, I guess he could use a little male bonding," Jermane replied.

"Rex and *Kevin* hanging out?" I asked, keeping my eye on the car pulling out.

Jewel waved her hand. "Oh-uh-ah, I didn't like the way you just said my man's name. Kevin may act a little silly, but he knows where to draw the line. He doesn't even like clubs. Besides, he knows better than to stir up the wrath of Jewel," she said, pulling out her MAC lip gloss.

I had four large bags of clothes and knew it was time to call it a day. I went back and forth, debating whether to get that last suit at Ann Taylor. We were about to head over to Lot 8 when I realized that suit would take me way over budget. Casual wear was gonna have to wait. I still had part of the money from that case I settled before I got married. So I felt I had a little cushion. I hadn't touched it, so I figured it'd be okay to dip into it just a little for that suit. *It is a business investment.*

I walked up to the ATM and punched in my PIN number. When I went to savings to check the balance, my knees buckled. "What in the world?" I checked again and the same dollar amount stared me in the face. *There's several thousand dollars missing!* I immediately pulled out my cell phone to call Chris. I dialed frantically. *I KNOW this Negro did not go into our savings without telling me. I know he has better sense than that!* His phone kept ringing but there was no answer. *I'm not going to leave him a message. Some things are better left to do in person!*

"*Y*ou did what?" I heard what Chris said, but had to ask again.

"I—I took some of our savings to make an investment." His voice was trembling until the last word, as if he suddenly gained confidence in his decision.

I sat down on the couch and chose my words carefully. "Chris, why would you do something like this without even asking me? I worked hard for over half that money. This is crazy." I threw my hands up, then let them drop and slap my thighs. "What possessed you to do this? What about the conversation we had in our premarital counseling? What about the budget we made?"

"Well, Nate . . ."

I rolled my eyes and folded my arms. "Oh, you don't have to say another word. We've talked about your brother and all his 'investments.' Until now, you've managed to escape his schemes. This is the same brother who's tried out for *The Amazing Race, The Apprentice, Deal or No Deal,* and I don't know what else. He even auditioned for *The Real World,* knowing he was too old. I can't blame him for trying, but we can't afford to jump on his bandwagon of ideas now. Chris, why didn't you ask me first?"

"You mean why didn't I *talk* with you first? I don't have to ask your permission for anything." His eyebrows furrowed.

"What? You—" I took a deep breath. *Lexi, calm down.* I rubbed my forehead.

His face softened. "Alright, baby, I think we're getting just a little too excited," he said, realizing he'd probably crossed the line. "Just listen for a minute. Maybe I was wrong for not checking with you, but I wanted to do something for our future. I had to act quick." His eyes searched mine, begging for a little sympathy.

"So, it couldn't wait a day, or until we could discuss it? Be for real Chris, you didn't tell me because you thought I would say no." I got up and started pacing the floor.

"No, well, maybe," he said as he stood up. He grabbed my shoulders to halt my steps. "I know you've been working so hard, I just wanted to find some way to help. I was trying to do something to make things easier on you. Nate talked about all these other ways we could generate in-

come. I think this time he's finally found something legitimate." He continued to search my eyes for a connection.

"I mean, Chris, that's a nice thought. But it's the kind
of decision we should make together." I shook off his
touch and backed away. "So, can you tell me what you invested *our* money in?" I stood with my hands on my hips,
awaiting his answer.

"Uh, um . . . just a few stocks and . . . some property" were the words that crept out of his mouth. He
dropped back on the couch and his knee began to shake a
little.

In my mind I hit him. I pictured him lying on the floor
like a cartoon character, with stars above his head and bird
sounds. "Honey, it's a good idea, but just maybe not now.
It's not like we have all this disposable income. Capri and
I are still trying to get the firm off the ground and we just
bought this house!"

"Yeah, but the investment property was in the Third
Ward, and the value is gonna skyrocket."

"That's some expensive property already. A couple
thousand dollars couldn't have bought much." I was scared
to ask. "You didn't borrow any money, did you?"

He slowly shook his head up and down. "Yeah."

My mouth took off like a race car. "Okay, I guess you
forgot all about my law school loans. You know it's gonna
take a minute to get a return, don't you? I can't believe
you listened to your brother, who's been a financial planner all of two months? They did an exposé on *60 Minutes*
about that. Who does he think he is, Chris Gardner from
The Pursuit of Happyness?" I sucked my teeth and started walk-

THE SUNDAY BRUNCH DIARIES   97

ing toward the stairs. Chris stood up like he was about to
follow me.

I froze, then glared at the bookshelf. I reached over
and snatched our Bible. I had vowed I wouldn't be one of
those "preaching wives," but I couldn't help myself. "Maybe
if you won't listen to me, you'll listen to G-o-d," I said as
I started to toss him the Bible. "Proverbs 21:5."

Instead I opened it and read it myself. "The plans of
the diligent lead to profit as surely haste leads to poverty."
Then I tossed him the Bible.

After a few seconds, Chris muttered a pitiful, "I love
you, Cupcake." I turned and marched up the stairs.

CHAPTER TWENTY-ONE

Client Meeting

Rex felt like his head was spinning. Between the one drink he had had and the cigar smoke, he started to gag. The room was loud and musty. He couldn't wait to get to a shower and drop his Brooks Brothers suit at the cleaners as soon as possible. He grabbed a seat at the bar, his body awkwardly trying to adjust to the stool. The haze, boisterous patrons, and blaring music threatened his comfort zone and personal space. He dropped his head down toward the counter and rubbed his neck. When he looked up after a few seconds, everything seemed gray. A woman appeared, and his eyes tuned in to her presence like radar. For a few minutes, he was fixated . . . engaged in her presence. She was tall and voluptuous; her wavy auburn hair framed her porcelain face. The subtle sway in her hips was soothing. Their eyes locked and he tried to look away, but he couldn't.

"What's wrong with me? I must be tired," he said as his two fingers rubbed the bridge of his nose. He closed his eyes, temporarily shutting out the madness around him. His eyes sprang open and he noticed his clients engrossed in the atmosphere of the club. "It's definitely time to go home." He ran his hand from the front of his curly hair to the nape of his neck, and adjusted his rimless glasses.

As if reading his mind, his client, a rotund bald man, leaned over and said, "Rex, we're okay. We can find our way to the hotel if you want to go home."

He released a sigh of relief, shook a few hands, and sprinted for the door. On the way out, he couldn't help but try to take one last look at the scarlet-haired stranger. But as quickly as she'd entered, she'd disappeared. Despite a fight, her presence lingered with him to the car. As he focused on the road, visions of her fiery crown, cherry-stained lips, and blood-red stilettos bombarded his thoughts all the way home.

Once parked in his driveway, he grabbed the back of his head. "God, I'm not sure what's happening." He rubbed his tightening chest. "I'm just sick of entertaining these over-indulgent, self-absorbed clients," Rex thought. "And at what price? God, there's got to be a different way to make a living than this. Why do I feel so trapped?" He stared at the two-story mansion in front of him.

He leaned in, and took a deep breath. He turned on the light inside the car and examined his face in the visor mirror. He was looking for the man of integrity who had walked through the door of the firm on the first day of work. He noticed a few gray hairs had cropped up in his curly but close-cut hair. *There's got to be more to life than this.*

CHAPTER TWENTY-TWO

All of Us

"Come on in," Jewel said. She opened the door for Stacy, Kevin's ex-wife, and Aja. "Hey, sweetie, how did your ballet lesson go?"

"Fab-u-lous! We learned a new dance today." Aja tore off her little pink trench coat.

"What do you mean, 'fabulous?'" Jewel smiled, knowing exactly where she got that word from. She watched as Aja ran toward the cookies waiting for her. Before closing the door, she noticed Stacy had arrived in a new Honda Accord, instead of her old Corolla. "Hmm, nice car," she said as she turned and walked toward the kitchen.

"Yeah, it was time. I had problems with a cosigner, but it all worked out." Stacy paused and looked Jewel in the eyes, then put her hand on her hip. "And no, Kevin didn't cosign. I asked, but he said no," she quickly uttered as if reading Jewel's mind.

Oh, uh-uh! Jesus, see what I mean? Jewel paused to control her tone. She turned toward Aja. "Honey, why don't you finish eating your snack in the den? I need to talk to your mom."

Aja grabbed a few cookies and her glass of milk. "Don't leave without saying good-bye, Mommy." Her big brown eyes searched Stacy's for assurance.

"I won't, honey." Her mother smiled warmly. When she looked back at Jewel, her face maneuvered to a neutral expression.

"I guess now's a good time to talk about Aja's birthday party. I was thinking we could do a tea party," Jewel said, after Aja was out of sight.

"Umm, that's a cute idea, but I've already made arrangements at the Children's Museum." Stacy ran her hand through her cropped spiky hair.

For the old girl to be crying broke, her hair is always freshly laid. "Why didn't you let me know?" Jewel said as she picked up Aja's coat.

"Jewel, I *am* her mother. If I want to decide what kind of birthday party she's gonna have, I will," Stacy said as she frowned and rolled her neck.

Okay, Jesus, that's it. Please, give me a free pass to give her a beat down. P-l-e-a-s-e. "Stacy, I'm somewhat patient, but I draw the line when it comes to party planning." Jewel's right index finger wagged as she spoke. "I hope you didn't leave a deposit at the museum." Jewel took a deep breath and crossed her arms. "Never mind, we'll discuss it again later. There's something a bit more important I need to talk about." Jewel walked behind a chair, resting her hands on it. She failed to offer Stacy a seat.

"Oh? What would that be?" Stacy said with raised eyebrows.

"Um . . ." Jewel bit her lip. "I'll just say it. Stacy, I really think you've been taking advantage of Kevin's kindness. We need to set a few boundaries. Not to be rude, but Kevin's *my* husband now. You need to respect that." She watched Stacy's face for a response.

"Jewel, I'm not sure what you mean." Stacy pulled out her car keys from her purse, appearing distracted.

"I believe you know *exactly* what I'm talking about. There's no need to play games."

"I just think you're being a little insecure." Stacy turned and moved toward the door.

No she didn't—did she say insecure? Jewel walked after her. "Please, I don't possess an ounce of insecurity in my body. All I'm saying is you had Kevin and Aja, and *you* messed up. So deal with it."

Stacy stopped abruptly and turned to face Jewel.

Jewel took a step back. "Look, I don't have a problem with the time you spend with Aja. You're her mother, I understand that. But all this other stuff is *extra* and I'm not having it." She waved her hand in the air and it landed on her hip. Before Stacy spoke, Jewel walked toward the dishwasher. She opened the door to put away the dishes.

Stacy's face suddenly softened and her shoulders dropped. "Okay, Jewel, you're right. It's extremely hard to see my husband . . ."

Jewel snapped, "*Ex*-husband."

"Yeah, okay. It's extremely hard seeing my *ex*-husband with someone else. I know I hurt them; and yes, I admit,

I gave up too easily. It's hard, I mean seeing you with *my* life, in *my* house. You have no idea what that feels like. So excuse me if I want to make decisions related to *my* daughter who *I* gave birth to. I've paid for my mistakes. So if you want to deprive me of the few things that I want to do for Aja, go ahead and be my guest." She closed her eyes to control her emotions, forcing them shut to keep the tears from forming.

Jewel stood struggling for words, almost feeling sorry for Stacy. *Almost.* "Well, all I'm saying is we need to compromise a little more. I mean if Will, Jada, and his ex can do it, we can. For God's sakes, they created a whole sitcom about it, so evidently anything's possible. All I ask is a little more respect. For instance, when you call, you need to at least *speak* to me before you ask for Kevin. And some things, Stacy, you know you can handle yourself. You don't have to call Kevin all the time, acting like you need to be rescued."

Stacy looked down momentarily. When she looked up, her lips were tight, but her face quickly softened as she took a few steps toward Jewel. "I'll try . . . I mean to be more considerate. It's just that Kevin's always been there." Her eyes turned toward the floor as she studied the intricate pattern that replaced the old design. Slowly her eyes met Jewel's. "I—I've met some people at church, and things will, well, *are* changing. I have someone in my life now." She took a deep breath. "But Aja, she's still *my* daughter and that will never change. *I* gave birth to her. She knows I'm her real mother and you can't take that away, Jewel." Stacy's voice grew more confident as she gripped the keys in her hand tight. She felt a familiar pain shoot down the back of her head but resisted the urge to appear weak in front of Jewel.

Did she say she met someone? Thank you, Jesus, my prayers have been answered! Jewel still hadn't said anything aloud. Silence hung in the air, begging interruption. Soon Aja skipped into the kitchen, still dressed in her leotard and tights. *Thank God for Aja, this was becoming a Hallmark moment.*

"Here!" Aja handed them each a homemade card with a heart on it. "To both my Moms—God loved me so much He gave me two!" She grabbed their hands and held them.

Jewel and Stacy glanced at each other, their hearts softened by love's interruption. For the moment, they both surrendered to an unspoken truce.

CHAPTER TWENTY-THREE

The Backstreet Cafe

W e'd just settled in for our regular Sunday brunch fellowship. However, I was a bit distracted. After staring at Jewel for a moment, I finally asked what everyone else probably wanted to. "Jewel, girl, what's up with the hair?" I noticed it was about a foot longer since the last time I saw her, a week ago.

"Huh? Oh yeah. I made a trip to Weave Nation yesterday," she said as she flung one side of her newly lengthened mane to her back.

She doesn't seem fazed, so I guess we shouldn't be. "It really looks good. But I remember how you used to be such a 'weave snob.' " I have to admit she did look pretty glam. Her long layered mane pulled together her fashionable ensemble: a ruffled blouse, tulip skirt, and strappy sandals. Her healthy maple skin glowed with bronzer and cinnamon lip color.

"Hey, weaves are *totally* acceptable now. You can come with me the next time I go. My cousin Makeeba helped pick the perfect texture and color. She can look at you and tell instantly what you need. I went straight to the wall of weaves and found my exact match."

"Naw, I'll pass, maybe next time," I said as I rolled my eyes.

"Speaking of a new do, that's an interesting look you've been sporting lately Angel," Jewel said, glancing her way.

"Not that I have to explain anything to *you,* but I'm starting to lock my hair. I just need a change."

"Umm, it *is* a change. But you've always danced to a beat of a different drum," Jewel said inspecting Angel's hair with her eyes. "Are you having an India.Arie moment? I feel you. *I am not my hair*—I like that song, it's kind of mother earth."

"You totally misunderstand the message in the song. She's not pro-locks or anti-perm. She's really talking about defining ourselves by things other than our hair. Defining who we are by our Spirits."

"That's a nice thought, but Angel, c'mon, you know people judge by appearances first. Do you think Kevin was looking at my 'Spirit' that first day he met me?" Jewel brushed a strand of hair away from her eyes.

"Actually I do. He saw *something* in your crazy behind. Just think about it: 'pretty' walks up and down the street all day long; there has to be something that separates you from the next person."

"This is true, but my fitted jogging suit didn't hurt either. Men are visual," Jewel said as she waved her fork.

Angel dropped her shoulders. "Yeah, but when a man

is spiritually grounded, which I know Kevin is, that Spirit seeks out something besides the physical."

"Yeah, yeah. I guess that's why so many of us are breaking the bank spending money on hair, clothes, and anything else we can find," I said.

"I really don't see anything wrong with looking good," Jewel affirmed.

"No, I'm not saying that, but we need to work just as hard on the inside as the outside. I do have to admit, Houston *is* the land of big hair and Bibles." She scanned the room, noticing that half the women looked like they had the same hairdresser, shopped at the same store, and carried the same purses.

I was about to chime in, but I saw someone resembling Capri walk through the door. *Wait a minute; that is Capri.* She'd been missing in action from our girl get-togethers, tied up with Anthony and his social calendar. Recently, they'd been popping up in the Houston society papers—*Paper City, Onyx,* and *Gloss.* For someone shunning the limelight a minute ago, Capri seemed quite comfortable in some of the photos.

"Oh wait, there's Capri." Jewel stood, waving her hand as she strode toward us.

"Hey, ladies," she said when she finally reached our table. I barely recognized Capri. She looked like she'd just made a stop at a makeup counter. She dropped her quilted Louis Vuitton bag on the floor and slid her Armani shades above her flat-ironed, shellacked mane.

"Hey girl, I thought you were meeting Missy?" I said, still distracted by the layers of makeup.

"Oh, we rescheduled. I really wanted to spend some

time with you all. Besides, I don't need to tell you how exhausting she can be," Capri said as she slid her chair out.

Missy, another player's wife, wasn't exactly a friend, according to Capri; but they sure had been hanging a lot lately.

"Hey girl, I saw you on TV in the stands the other night. You were looking quite fab," Jewel said. "Sit down, sit down." She brushed off the chair before Capri sat in it. "Omigod!"

Capri jumped. "What's wrong?"

Are you wearing that Tracy Reese dress I saw on Kerry Washington in this month's *O* magazine? I adore her clothes."

"Jewel, I thought something was wrong. If you must know, yes, it is. Anyway, back to basketball. As you guys know, I'd rather watch the games at home, but I've gone to a couple of games recently because Anthony asked me to. They're having such an awesome season. Can you believe it?" She grabbed a menu but didn't look at it right away.

Who are they, Eva Longoria and Tony Parker? And why is Jewel all but drooling over Capri?

"I need another cup of coffee." Angel waved the waiter over.

"Hey, that's about your third cup. You never drink that much coffee," I said, slicing my brioche French toast. *Mmm, this is heaven.*

"Okay, the truth. Coffee is my only vice." She grabbed her cup with both hands, pretending to hug it. "It keeps me sane. Since Octavio and I are purging from sex, it's been my one outlet," she said, biting her nails.

I drummed my fingers on the table. "My, my, my how the tables have turned. I remember those days. Thank you Jesus, Hallelujah, Praise God . . ." I raised my hands like I was getting the Holy Ghost.

Angel looked over, clenching her teeth. "Don't let me have to hurt you," she said as she raised her butter knife.

"Well, I hate to break the news, but coffee's a stimulant. It might make things worse," Jermane warned as she picked over her eggs Benedict.

"I *know* that. Just leave me alone." Angel threw up her hands.

"Well, since we're on the subject," Jermane said slowly, "Rex and I have definitely gone to another level in *that* area."

"What do you mean?" Capri asked.

"Well, normally a lady doesn't divulge such information, but I have to talk to somebody. Rex hasn't been himself. I mean we've been spicing it up, but he's wanted to try all sorts of stuff. Is that normal?"

"Why are you looking at me?" Angel said. "I don't even want to talk about it."

"No offense, Angel, but despite your new Lakewood membership, you used to be, well . . . out there," Jewel said, then sliced her salmon crème brûlèe.

Angel ignored her comment. "Anyway, when I used to be married, my husband and I were never bored. Unfortunately, that seemed to be all we were good at."

"Girl, that was about a hundred years ago." Jewel waved her hand and laughed; she suddenly got quiet when she noticed no one else was joining her.

"Well, Anthony, future owner of an NBA champi- onship ring, hasn't lost his touch." Capri blew on her fin- gers and rubbed her fingertips on her shoulder.

The waiter approached Capri to take her order. "I'll have the shrimp cheesecake," she said.

While she ordered, I playfully stuck my finger down my throat. Soon everyone was looking at me to add my two cents. I cleared my throat. "Umm, no comment," I said, then lowered my head and started slicing my lump crab cakes.

"Uh-oh, sounds like the newlywed fire has fizzled al- ready," Jewel said. "Told you to stay away from those carbs."

"For your information, there's no problem in the Reynolds household. Besides, a true lady doesn't discuss such things."

Jermane cleared her throat. "I believe the conversa- tion was about Rex and me." She put her hand on her chest.

"Oh yeah, well, Jermane dear, all is well; you better be glad he's spicing it up with you and no one else," Jewel said, then sipped her fruit sangria.

"Yeah, I guess you're right," she said, then bit the side of her mouth slightly.

"Okay, enough about that. What's up for the holi- days?" Jewel looked around the table.

I knew Jewel's routine, she was sniffing around for party planning opportunities.

"My dad's coming down and also some of Chris's fam- ily. His mom is gonna do the cooking," I said.

"Well, you know Rex and I always have our annual din- ner," Jermane added.

"Yeah, the big soiree for the firm clients," Jewel teased. "Well, I'd like to invite everybody to our house for Christmas Eve, for a little party. Nothing fancy or over the top. Capri, can you and Anthony make it?"

"Ah, yeah, we should be able to." The waiter finally arrived with her food.

"You can spare a few minutes for your old friends, can't you? We'll let you off the hook for New Year's, but you gotta come hang for Christmas Eve." Jewel patted Capri's hand.

Capri smiled halfway and nodded her head. "We'll be there."

"Oh, I guess you don't care if Octavio and I make it." Angel folded her hands and leaned back in her chair.

"Girl, you know I want y'all to come. *Feliz Navidad, Feliz Navidad.*" She swayed in her chair and snapped her fingers as she sung.

Angel rolled her eyes and I let out a chuckle. "Jewel, that's *so* not funny. You are extra silly today."

Jewel raised her hands. "Okay, okay, before we leave, we have some other business. Remember we said we would start that book club? Let's start it in the New Year? Since we're all together now, let's talk about it."

A collective sigh escaped our mouths.

"C'mon, y'all said we needed some intellectual stimulation. January would be a great time to start. I mean honestly, in the spirit of our shero Oprah, we need to support our literary brothers and sisters."

Did she say "shero"?

"I'll plan the first meeting," Jewel offered. "C'mon, whataya say? I can make it fun, festive, we can do a whole book theme. I can get a cake shaped like a book, we can play games. We each should invite one guest. Capri, you should invite Missy," she said, working up her enthusiasm.

"Jewel, okay. We said we would do it," I said. *Anything to stop her whining.*

"Alrighty then! I'll send out the invites so you guys can put it on your calendar. In the meantime we have to find a name."

What she really means is she'll come up with the name and we'll all just agree. I'll give it sixty seconds.

"Yeah, yeah," Angel said as her eyes darted toward Jewel. "Just don't pick anything ridiculous for us to read."

"Ridiculous is relative, Angel. For example, I would venture to say that necklace you're wearing is *so* 'ridiculously' last year. However, maybe in your mind it's not. See? It's all in how you look at it." Jewel smiled.

Angel smiled back. "You know what? I'm just gonna place you on the throne of grace."

10-9-8 . . .

"Omigod! I got it!"

I knew it.

"The Shero Literary Sisters. That's it!" She looked around and waited for everyone to comment.

Oh brother.

"It's official then," she said after a few seconds. "Guys—guess what? Another 'Fabulous Jewels production!' Then *ooh*, maybe I can add author events to my services. Wow, another dimension in planning . . . think of the possibilities!" She gazed toward the ceiling.

She snapped out of her trance after a few seconds. "And everyone? I must remind you of book club protocol;

the host is free to indulge in his or her own literary pref-
erence. But keep your book selections clean. Wow, we can
even have a few meetings where the men come!" She
quickly took out her BlackBerry and began to make notes
to herself.

"What? The only way our men will come is if the TV's
locked on ESPN and we have some food," I warned.

"You never know. Anyway, this sounds like a great idea,
but keep in mind, many a friendship has broken up over
a book club," Angel added as she grabbed her clutch.

"Please, it's not that serious," Capri said, then dabbed
a cloth napkin in the corner of her mouth.

"Well, ladies, I need to get some work done before my
Bible study tonight." Angel eyed her watch, then waved to
the waiter.

"Okay, ladies, I'm excited. So in the spirit of Zora,
Langston, Richard Wright, Terry McMillan, Alice Walker—"

Before Jewel had a chance to finish, we all started
clearing the table and raced toward the door.

CHAPTER TWENTY-FOUR

Sunday Lovin'

ewel rushed home from brunch to spend time with Kevin. Brunch always put her in a great mood. Meeting her friends was a treat these days, since she was the only "mother" in the group. Factor in the time with her business, motherly and wifely duties, and it was a wonder she had any extra time at all.

Jewel drove up and was relieved to see Kevin's truck in the driveway. Lately his little excursions out of the house bothered her. She hated not being able to track his every move. Tonight Jewel had planned his favorite dinner to show him some attention and get them back on course. Stacy's number hadn't popped up on his cell lately, so Jewel had had a little more peace.

Kevin was reclining in his favorite chair with the remote when she walked in. Looking at him reminded Jewel of her father on Sunday evenings. Aja jumped from the floor where she was reading and ran toward her.

"Hey Mommy, how was brunch time? You bring me any dessert?" she asked as Jewel leaned down to give her a peck.

"Oh, it was great, sweetie, thank you for asking. No, I didn't bring you any more sugar. Has Daddy been behaving?" She watched for Kevin to stir, but his eyes were glued to the big-screen television.

"Yeah, he's been watching the game the whole time, yelling and screaming." Aja reached for Jewel's neck as she leaned down to hug her.

"Well, I'm getting ready to make some dinner. Wanna help?" Aja was still holding on.

"Yes, ma'am," she said as she smacked her gum and let go of Jewel's neck.

"Your dad give you that gum? Never mind, go and wash your hands. You tell your daddy he better not fuss when your dental bill comes." Jewel walked toward the living room and went up behind Kevin, rubbing his shoulders.

"Now, that's what I'm talking about. It's about time you remembered who's king. Now come on . . . give it up." Kevin grabbed her arm until she came around and sat on his lap. "Who's the king? Say it . . ."

"You are, Big Poppa." She kissed him on the neck.

"Uh-huh. You better recognize, before I go all Ike and Tina up in here."

"Kevin, don't even play like that." She wrapped her arms around his neck.

"Okay, baby," he said as their lips connected in a soft kiss.

"Ummm, don't start nothin' won't be nothin'," he whispered.

"Okay, Mom, I'm ready to start dinner," Aja said as she walked back into the room.

Jewel jumped up. "See you later, baby."

"Uh-huh. Later," he said, but he grabbed her arm and wouldn't let her go. She finally pried herself away. She bent down and kissed his bald head before heading to the kitchen.

*K*evin stretched his legs and rubbed his stomach as he and Jewel lay in their bed upstairs. "Dang baby, what's up? We had that good dinner, and you been all lovey-dovey. You aren't trying to kill me and cash in the insurance policy, are you?"

"You're being silly as usual. Can't I just be good to my man if I want to?" Jewel moved over and slid her head onto his chest.

"Yeah, but I'm kinda scared. I know you've still seemed a little irritated since the night I fixed Stacy's flat. That was over a month ago. You need to let stuff go, baby."

"I know. I'm sorry. I just don't like sharing . . . *anything.*"

"Baby, I know. But sometimes, you can get a little self-ish. Jewel, you know I'm not thinking about messing up. You have to understand, I had a life before you. You're just gonna have to trust me."

"I understand that, babe, it's just I still feel she can play on your sympathy sometimes. It's something about her I just don't trust."

He paused before he spoke. "I understand, but you have to put yourself in somebody else's shoes. Jewel, you've never been *really* lonely. You've always had great friends and a good family. You've had a stable life and you know your little butt is spoiled. Your mama and daddy spoiled you and I spoil you. I try not to, but I do."

"Well, should I be punished for having a decent family and friends? Besides, it may be hard for you to believe, but I *have* been lonely before."

"Jewel, please. People like Stacy haven't been so blessed. She's had it hard most of her life. I know you don't like me being close to her. I understand and I'm trying to be more considerate. I know she's a little too dependent. Before you and I got married, I was all she had, but she's stronger now."

"I'm glad you realize that. In the long run, it'll only hurt her and us. Codependency isn't healthy. They have classes for that, you know. I mean, I'm the one that's suffering."

"Okay, baby, I wouldn't say you're actually *suffering*. You have a nice home; Aja loves you just as much as her biological mom, and of course you have me! I do think Stacy's finally moving on, for real this time."

"She said she was seeing somebody," Jewel said waiting for confirmation.

"Oh, yeah . . . that." He took a deep breath.

"Kevin, I know you're not jealous. What was that tone in your voice?" Jewel felt her heart suddenly race.

"You know I'm not jealous. Umm, she's, well . . ." His voice trailed off.

"Kevin, be honest, what's going on? You holding back something?" She sat up and looked him in the face.

"Stacy's, well she's, she's sort of pregnant." He swallowed and waited for Jewel to speak.

"What?" Her eyes grew big. "Okay, Kevin, I swear to God, I will take you out right now. The baby is not yours, is it? I want the truth, I will hurt you." In one movement she straddled him, reaching for his throat.

He grabbed her wrists. "Baby, baby, chill out, chill out! Listen! I swear on my granddaddy Mojo's grave, Jesus Christ and all the disciples. The baby is *not* mine. It's some guy she knew a while back. She ran into him a few months ago. They seemed to be headed down the right path. I know she said they were going to church together. But—well she said it just happened."

Jewel sat back a little on his legs. "Kevin, I swear, I'll call Judge Hatchett. You better be telling me the truth." She paused and folded her arms. "This is crazy. You seem way too calm about this, like it's good news. I thought she was all saved and she's too old to go around having children out of wedlock."

"Jewel, she's still in her thirties; that's not old. Anyway, I'm not condoning it; she's got to answer to God for it. I didn't get into all that with her." He grabbed Jewel's shoulders.

"When did you two have all this time to talk about this? That's what I want to know."

He sighed. "I don't know, Jewel, just off and on. When she calls sometimes or drops Aja off. But nothing's going on, Jewel, I swear. I have a decent heart, baby, you know that." He stroked her face.

"Kevin, I know you have a good heart. That's one of the things that I love the most, but sometimes your heart gets you in trouble. I just don't know about this situation. Is this guy gonna be there for her? It's not that I'm *extra* concerned, I'm just not trying to have you running to the hospital in the middle of the night."

"She says he's in it for the long haul. I think they're planning to get married. You know, do the right thing."

"It's a little too late for that! Kevin, you can be so naive sometimes." Jewel's eyes started to tear; she was fed up with the entire issue. "This is just another one of Stacy's tricks, another ploy for sympathy." She got up, grabbed her robe, and headed downstairs.

"Jewel, everything isn't about you. This isn't even about us. Why are you so angry? You just don't know the whole—"

She slammed the door behind her and marched down to the living room. "I can't believe this. Pregnant . . . before I even get to have one child with my husband she goes and spits out another one? I thought she was all saved and sanctified. What kind of example is that for Aja? Well, I'm not going to allow Kevin to get sucked up in Stacy's drama. Men are so stupid . . . Ugh!" She mumbled something after each step. She started breathing heavily, feeling as though fire was shooting out of her nostrils.

Kevin knew his only option was to let his wife cool off. His safest move was to stay right in that bedroom. "I knew the night was going too perfectly," he said as he felt a headache coming on. "Lord, please, I love my wife, and

You know I'd never want to hurt her, but I swore to Stacy I wouldn't tell. What do I do, God? It's not my place to tell her business just to make Jewel secure. If Jewel knew how deep things were, she'd understand my behavior towards Stacy a little better. God, Jewel and Aja are my first priority, but soon something is going to have to give. I guess You're going to help me work all this out." He whispered as he rolled over on his side.

CHAPTER TWENTY-FIVE

Dear Mama

Jewel had been sitting in the living room for hours flipping channels and finally found old reruns of *A Different World*. It was one of her favorite episodes—the night before Whitley's marriage to the senator—but Jewel couldn't even enjoy it.

"God, you didn't teach me any of this in college. If I had known . . ." She sat with folded arms and refused to try to process the bomb Kevin just dropped. All she could do was mentally picture Kevin driving Stacy to the hospital after her water broke, while she rode in the backseat. "This is *so* not fair, God." Finally, Jewel stopped having her tantrum long enough to pick up the phone. "Who would I call this time of the night?" She checked the time on the television and it was 1 a.m. *Mama*.

She dialed frantically. After the fourth ring she heard her mother's voice and was comforted instantly.

"Hey, Mama."

"Baby, what's wrong, who died?" said her mother, trying to wake up.

"Mama, I'm sorry. I didn't mean to scare you. I know it's late . . ."

"Now chile, you know that never worked with me. I'm up. I'll go downstairs so I won't wake your daddy."

Jewel could hear him snoring in the background.

Her mother kept talking as she adjusted her scarf, wrapped her large frame in a terry-cloth robe, and headed downstairs to the kitchen.

"Okay, Jewel, what's the emergency that really isn't urgent?" She walked to the refrigerator to search for the Tupperware that held the leftover pot roast and side dishes from dinner that night.

"Mama, I've had it. I want a divorce."

"Please, Jewel, don't start your foolishness. I told you before you took those vows it wouldn't be a walk in the park. But *no*, you were all googly-eyed and in love with Mr. Brown Shorts. I know Kevin. He's a good man. I know you too, Jewel, and you're my baby, but you ain't perfect either. So what's going on?"

"Well, you know Kevin's ex? Mama, she just won't go away. I can't get her out of our lives. I mean, what am I supposed to do? When she calls, Kevin jumps. He's such a wimp. Whenever she's in trouble, off he goes to save her. She acts like he never got married."

"Um-hmm," her mother said as she spooned mashed potatoes onto her plate. She licked the extra potatoes that got on her finger and continued to listen. "So, whatchu gonna do about it?"

"Mama! Are you listening to me? This woman is trying to sabotage my life! She's like, like . . . a thorn in my flesh!"

"You just said it." She popped the top back on the Tupperware.

"What?"

"She's a thorn in the flesh. You remember in the Bible when Jesus said, 'Lord, if it be thy will take this cup from me?' "

"Mama, have you been drinking? Didn't you just hear me pour my heart out to you? I don't need some parable. Speak plain English."

"Okay, you better watch your mouth, baby. I can be there in record time with my belt if I need to."

"Mama, you've been watching too much Madea. Besides, I'm grown, remember?"

"Well, you know I like that Tyler Perry, but that's beside the point. I kept a supply of belts long before Madea showed up and you're still not too old for a butt whipping."

"Okay, Mama, can we get back to the point?"

"Like I said, 'Jesus asked, if it be thy will, take this cup from me' and what did the good Lord say?"

"Ma-ma . . ."

"What did He say, chile? I'm getting to something. Oh never mind, He said, 'My grace is sufficient.' "

Jewel let out a deep sigh. "Mama, what are you trying to say?"

"Well, sometimes God sends something or someone to wear down our flesh. No matter what we do, the thing or person won't go away, until God gets out of us what He wants. Sounds like He's trying to deal with some part of your flesh."

"Mama, that's not helping. I'm angry and I'm tired of dealing with this. I can't make Kevin see how she's interfering with our marriage. I know this baby mama drama is new to you. How much of this am I supposed to take?" She folded her arms and poked out her lip.

"First of all, you need to realize what you just said, baby; you can't 'make' a man do nothing. And as for the baby mama drama, you know I despise that phrase, honey, *please*. We had baby mama drama back in our day. We just didn't broadcast it. I never told you this, but one time some floozy from Dallas tried to claim your daddy had fathered a child out of wedlock. But we worked all that out behind closed doors. That's how we did. On the Q.T., the quiet tip. Turned out to be false, praise God. People had pride back then, nowadays, you pay people two hundred dollars to go airing all their business on Maury Povitch. Just no discretion. You know that man does entire shows on paternity testing? His wife is a respectable journalist. Connie Chung. You know her? Not sure how those two hooked up."

"Mama." *She can go on.*

"Okay, anyway, back to your daddy, you know it wasn't true. If it was, I'd be a widow because I would have killed him."

"Mama, you never told me about that."

"Like I said, we exercised discretion back then. But I have to admit. Women *are* much bolder now."

"See, you do know what I mean, Mama."

"Well, I'm not saying Kevin is right. He needs to step up and be a man. He needs to tell this woman he's married and you're his priority. Has he given you any reason to think he's cheating on you?"

"No, not really," Jewel said as she turned down the television a bit.

"Well then you really don't have a problem, just a *situation*. And you knew when you married him about the *situation* and its challenges. So what's changed?"

"Mama, she's pregnant and . . ."

"Oh, now you didn't say *that*. That's a *whole* other issue. Don't you worry, I'm going upstairs and get dressed. It'll take me two seconds to wake up Big Poppa, and we'll be on the road—"

"Mama, Mama . . . it's not Kevin's baby!" Jewel realized she was yelling and lowered her voice.

"Are you sure? We don't need no Anna Nicole situations. Whoa, chile, you have my blood sugar going up and whatnot. Who's the father?" she said as she placed one hand on her heart and scooped out some ice cream with the other.

"Some guy she's dating. I just tried to explain to Kevin that I wasn't going to be running to the hospital with her. She can barely take care of herself. At least that's the way she acts. She needs to cut the cord."

"Woo, I'm waiting for my heart to slow down. Don't scare me like that. Okay, let's relax. Let me wait and see what the Holy Spirit is telling me." She closed her eyes to have a quick talk with the Lord. "Jewel, honey, my Spirit is telling me that the woman is desperate. Despite her best efforts to move on, Satan has been holding her past over her. This baby means a chance for some kind of love in her life." She licked some ice cream off a spoon.

"But Mama, that's not my—"

"I know. It's not your problem. But you're not going to get any results if you yell and fuss at Kevin. He's going to have to get it for himself. I'm not saying for you to put up with some ridiculousness. But I hear God saying in the midst of this, he's working on your patience and empathy. Take your hands off the situation."

"Well, I just don't like this, Mama. Stacy puts on this big act, but I'm not buying it."

"Jewel, honey, I said be patient, I didn't say be a fool. You need to sleep with one eye open and one eye closed. The enemy can use anybody at anytime and he looks for the weakest link, especially in a marriage. That's why you need to stay in tune with the Lord. He'll let you know when you really need to be worried. I hear Him saying be cautious, but not worried. Be 'wise as a serpent, yet inno-cent as a dove.' Lord have mercy, I thought the child was saved and she done run out there and got pregnant. Well, I'm not gonna judge her and you shouldn't either. But Jewel, you need to stop your stubbornness with Kevin."

"Mama, what are you talking about?"

"Jewel, I know my child. It's okay to get angry, but you know you have a problem with forgiveness *and* you been punishing him by holding out with the lovin'."

"Mama! I'm not!"

"Hush, child. I'm telling you for your own good. That's the last thing you want to do."

"Mama, you're something else."

"Well, it's in the Bible and need I remind you, I'm still married to my high school sweetheart and I am a former homecoming queen, class of—"

"1966, I know Mama."

"And your daddy was . . ."

"Voted best looking, Black or white."

"And I'm still his queen and way beyond a size six and I ain't got no weave sewn in my head neither, but I did rock a wig back in the day, so I'm not gonna be a hypocrite."

Jeez. Jewel held the phone away from her ear, because she'd heard this part a million times.

"But anyway, you know I'm praying for you. If the Lord says anything else, I'll let you know. But for now, keep your friends close, but your enemies even closer. I got that from your daddy's favorite movie, *The Godfather*. And another thing, keep the home fires burning, if you know what I mean. You need to make a trip to Victoria's Secret."

"Mama, please! Anyway, why do I always feel better when I talk to you?"

"Because I know what I'm talkin' about. Now your father, love the man to death. But do you know how long it takes to train a man without letting him know he's being trained? That's an art form, sugar. It's a lost art. It's not all about looking cute all the time. That's a part of it, but it's about the way you make a man *feel.* We older ladies need to mentor you young women about that. It's not enough to get that degree, you need to know how to run a house and take care of a man."

"But what about Kevin, Mama? What is he supposed to be doing while I'm doing all this for him?"

"You work on your part and God will do the rest. That's why you stay focused on God. He'll let you know what to do. And another thing, if you panic and get all hysterical every time things look like they going wrong, baby, you won't last until your five-year anniversary. We have to know how to hold our tongue and control our emotions. It's not easy, honey, I know, but it's worth it. A man needs to feel like a man. Your Spirit isn't wrong about that Stacy; you need to work with God, instead of getting so worked up that you can't hear from Him."

"Yes, Mama."

"Trust me. God's never failed me yet."

"Okay. I feel better. I'll call you in a few days, Mama."

"Um-hmm. Now, it would be nice for you to call when you don't have some issue or a problem. Sometimes, you need to call just to say hello. Now you kiss that baby for me and how are the other girls . . . well, ladies. Lexi, Capri, Jermane, and Heaven . . ."

"Angel, Mama, not Heaven. Lexi's fine. She and Capri are practicing law together. Jermane and Rex are still doing fine and Angel is all into church now."

"You don't say? God truly is a miracle-working God. At least I know who's pregnant now. I've been dreaming about fish for weeks. Although I just don't feel like this is it."

"Mama, I know you want your own grandchild, but Kevin's ex is the *only* reason you've been dreaming about fish."

"Just wishful thinking. Oh well, I still have Aja. I guess I'll get some blood grandbabies one day before the good Lord calls me home."

"Mama, it's just not time for that. My hands are already full with Aja and my business. Anyway, it's late, I'll give you a call later in the week. Love you . . ."

"Oh, so now when *I* wanna talk about something, you don't have time. Ain't that nothin'? Well, I love you. I'll tell your father his baby's doing fine."

CHAPTER TWENTY-SIX

It's a Wonderful Life

How did December get here so fast? I remember I couldn't wait to spend my first Christmas with my husband, but I'm starting to feel overwhelmed. Between trying to decorate the house and shop for in-laws and thinking about the holiday meal, I'm about to break down. That's why I can't believe I allowed Capri to talk me into coming to the Galleria mall. I usually did all my shopping at outlet centers. I absolutely hated the mall during the holidays, especially this mall. You practically needed a makeover to walk the mall's "runway" show. It was 70 percent profiling and 30 percent shopping. But we came here for Anthony's favorite store, Sharper Image, and planned to go to TJ Maxx next.

Although other commitments had cut into our sister-friend time, nothing would break our Christmas tradi-

tion. We had one day when we did our "marathon shopping" with a contest to find the biggest bargains, although
this year, Capri didn't seem like she was really trying to
win. We'd add up the price tags and whoever got the most
discounts had to pay for lunch. We were about to take a
break at the Kona Grill when Missy came prancing around
the corner. *Darn it!*

"Capri!" Missy ran over and planted two air kisses close
to her face. "Why didn't you call me? I'm trying to find
some gifts for my in-laws, but so far all I've been able to
do is buy things for me." Her eyes shifted to the bags in
her hands.

Surprise, surprise.

She lifted her arms and all I saw was Dior, Gucci, Bar-
neys, and Betsy Johnson plastered on colorful totes weighing down her petite frame. She was definitely a Galleria
ghetto superstar. Her slicked-back ponytail exposed
diamond-studded hoops, while shimmering makeup
highlighted her self-tanned skin. Her megawatt veneers
popped against her tawny complexion while her mouth
rambled on a mile a minute. Skinny jeans, a printed top
cinched with a wide leather belt, and platform pumps
showed off her supertoned figure.

"You know my husband and I are making plans to fly to
Paris for New Year's. Why don't you and Anthony come?"
She looked at me as if for a moment she thought about
inviting me.

I played it off and gazed at the crowd passing by.

"Oh, um, I don't know. It sounds nice. I'll have to talk
to Anthony." She turned toward me. "You know Lexi, my
law partner, right?"

"Yes, Lena, how are you?" I saw her eyes go from my blouse down to my shoes in two seconds.

"It's *Lexi*. I'm doing . . ."

"What do you mean you have to talk to Anthony? Girl, we're gonna have to work on your 'wifey' skills." She nudged Capri.

My eyes moved from the crowd of shoppers to the Godiva station in the distance. I wanted to run over there and drown myself in chocolate. I'd doubt the two of them would even notice.

"So are you all getting something to eat? I'm *famished*." She looked at us both.

Capri, don't you dare break tradition. I held my breath.

"Uh, yeah. We're just taking a break."

Missy stood there smiling. I braced myself for the inevitable.

"Oh, I know you have to finish up your shopping," Capri said, looking down at Missy's bags.

"Yeah, but I could break for just a minute. I need to get my second wind . . . thanks!" She moved toward the Kona Grill restaurant hostess. "They have fabulous chicken satay here."

Capri looked at me and shrugged her shoulders as Missy marched ahead of us.

I rolled my eyes, and walked slowly behind them. *A lunch date with her couldn't be all that bad. Suck it up, Lex, you've got some things going for yourself too. You're a lawyer, you've got a great husband, you got your "cute" jeans on today that fit like a glove and your cropped jacket, so you can hang. Besides, you've been through worse. Your makeup looked good when you left this morning . . . Be open, be open.*

My self-talk helped for a minute, but soon it was all downhill. After lunch Missy dragged us to just about every store, most of which I couldn't even afford to breathe in. I thought Capri was going to cut this shopping excursion short, but soon she was whipping out her credit card at every turn. While they laughed and charged, I tried to find "a way of escape that I could bear." I finally drew the line when we reached Tiffany's. I quietly chanted "To the left, to the left" before I made my exit.

"Baby, how was shopping?" Chris asked me as I walked right by him. I realized I hadn't spoken to him since I entered the kitchen. "It was alright."

"Just alright?" He said as he flipped through the channels and continued, "Baby, what are we going to eat tonight?" He didn't take his eyes off the television.

"I ate at the mall. Can't you fix yourself something or order take out? I'm sorry babe, I just wanted to get finished with that holiday madness. I should have checked in with you."

"I'll let you slide, Lexi, if you come rub my back."

I rolled my eyes. I'm beginning to think Chris thinks I'm his personal servant. It's always about *his* wants and needs. "Chris, what about *my* back, or *my* feet? I'm tired," I said and my words were sharp.

"Okay, babe, I was just kidding." By this time he was standing at the doorway of the kitchen. "Hey, what's going on with you?" He walked over and grabbed me around the waist and pulled me into an embrace.

"Nothing, Chris, nothing." I let him hold me for min-ute. "I'm gonna head upstairs and stretch out on the bed."

"You want me to take your bags upstairs?" he said, eye-ing my packages.

"Just drop them in the den. I need to wrap some of the gifts. And stay out of my bags," I warned as he started grabbing the bags.

In seconds I'd changed out of my clothes and into my old sweats. I curled up on the bed. I tried to watch a movie, but I was restless. I reached over to scribble a few words in my journal.

> *Dear Jesus:*
>
> *So much is changing. I don't know, maybe I'm just jealous of Capri and her friendship with Missy. But I know that I need to resist the temptation to question Capri's loyalty. She'll always be a close friend. But God help me to understand what it is about Missy that bugs me. Is it her money? Her confidence? I guess it doesn't matter God. It's on me to keep a decent attitude. Help me, Lord, to search deep within myself, and then reveal to me any insecurities or sin I may be hiding in my heart.*
>
> *Also Lord, help me to continue to remain in You. I know You are the only One who can fill my Spirit. I love Chris, but there are moments when I know I rely a little too much on him to feel special. He is not responsible for my happiness, but I have to be honest, there are days when I want Chris to just spoil me and take care of me. Is that wrong, God? Does that make me a bad wife? I guess the first several months of our marriage I was so absorbed in him; I really didn't make much time for anything else. Now I'm craving alone time. I'm craving time with my girls*

*again. Gone are the days of chatting on the phone at all hours,
I'm barely keeping up with birthdays and other life events. I can't
imagine how life would be with children. But I guess if that day
comes, You will show me how to deal with it all.*

*God, I suppose I need to really focus on what this season of
my life is about. This is the tightest my budget has been for
holiday shopping, but you know what, God? I really don't care.
I'm not going to stress and overspend like I've done in the past.
Nope, this year, I'm going to focus on the true Spirit of the
holiday.*

*Oh, I almost forgot. Father, I lift up Rex and Jermane. I
don't know if there's anything for her to worry about, but she has
some concerns about Rex. Holy Spirit, You said if we lack
wisdom that we could obtain it from You freely. Father, I pray
that You would cause Jermane to seek You in all things regarding
her marriage. I pray that You would remind Rex and Jermane to
seek You first and then You will add other things to their lives.
Father, I pray that You would reveal to Jermane any issues
regarding her husband before they have the opportunity to hinder
her relationship with Rex or their marriage in any way.*

*God, I also ask that You continue to order my footsteps
daily. Father, I can only be the person You created me to be
through Your power. Lord, I pray that You keep Anthony and
Capri rooted and grounded in Your word. Continue to allow
Anthony to represent You as a servant and vessel while he is out
on that basketball court. I pray that we all continue to give You
the honor and praise in all things. Help us not to lay up our
treasures here on earth, but to store up our treasures in heaven.*

Until next time,
Lexi

I put the pen down and warmth filled my body. I began humming and soon I started to meditate on my blessings. As I dozed off for a nap, a Spirit of assurance washed over me. A few moments later my entire body was peacefully still. I slept for several hours. I awoke to Chris rubbing my cheek.

"Babe, you awake?" Soon he was kissing my neck, and I knew what that meant.

"I'm so not in the mood," I thought. I turned my back to him and wrapped his arm around me. *Spooning would have to do tonight.*

CHAPTER TWENTY-SEVEN

"Jewel-tide Greetings"

*B*efore Chris and I could reach the doorstep, I heard music blasting from Jewel's house. Cars were parked up and down the street. I was about to call Jewel on her cell phone when she finally answered the door. The bass bombarded my body, while a powerful haze threatened to choke me. I coughed as we walked through the door and my eyes started to water.

"Hey, girl!" Jewel said as she hugged me. "Sorry about the smoke—gumbo rue, my aunt's cooking up another pot." She was dressed in a red sweater trimmed with sequins, blue jeans, and red pumps. This time her hair weave was a curly, wavy texture. I was surprised she was so dressed down, knowing her propensity to overdo hostess attire. For a moment, I wanted to stay outside so I could breathe.

"Come on in. Besides gumbo, Kevin's uncle is on the

barbecue and there's some crawfish in the backyard. We have tons of cakes and pies and a whole tray of banana pudding just for you, Lex." She grabbed my hand and walked us through the living room. It was packed with people and it was obvious somebody had slipped something in the eggnog. *So much for the little get-together with friends.*

"I didn't know this many people could fit in here," I said. "Isn't this a fire hazard?"

Chris looked at me and shrugged his shoulders. We'd been to a few stuffy parties over the past couple of weeks, so at least this one was a little more relaxed. I heard Kevin's loud mouth coming from the kitchen.

"Man, you crazy! If I could win a date with anybody in the world it would be Halle Berry. Talking about some Gabrielle Union. She's fine too, but—What?" He stopped talking and looked toward the doorway after his friends began to signal him. "Oh, hey, hey baby." He walked over and tried to kiss Jewel.

"Boy, please," she said and waived him away. "Like you have a chance with either one."

"Chris, man, wassup?" Kevin said as he shook Chris's hand. "About time y'all got here. I have whipped *everybody,* I mean *everybody* in just about every game of spades. Finally, some real competition."

"You are always talking smack. I don't have any problems giving you a beat down in your own house. Baby, fix me a plate."

I took a deep breath, then smiled at Chris. "Okay, sure." The house was full of Kevin's family. It was obvious they were related because all of them were loud. According to Jewel, they could wear the heck out of a welcome.

"Jewel girl, how are you going to get these people out of your house?" I asked her as I looked around.

"Easy . . . no alcohol."

"That'll do it. But I think someone pulled a fast one on you with the eggnog. You might need to smell it."

We finally made our way over to the food table. There were Hefty paper plates on a paper tablecloth with plastic ware. The nicest things on the table were the punch bowls. This was nothing like Jewel's regular affairs.

"Girl, I know what you're thinking, but I'm not bringing all my good stuff out so Kevin's people can mess it up. Wait a minute, that's the doorbell."

"How could she tell?" I thought, as I watched her fight to get to the door. When she reached it, I heard a squeal.

Soon she was walking back with Capri in tow.

"Hey, Lexi," she said, giving me a hug. "Okay, you're not still mad at me for the lunch thing with Missy, are you?"

I waved my hand. "Girl, please. Where's Anthony?" I said as I looked past her.

"He's in the kitchen watching the card game. *Whoa,* it's hot up in here." She started fanning herself.

"I wouldn't leave him alone too long. You know how some of Kevin's relatives are. I wouldn't put my purse down either."

"Lexi, you know you're wrong!" We all started to laugh because we knew it was true. Capri grabbed her purse strap a little tighter.

"I'm gonna take a plate to Chris, but do y'all want to go to the sun porch? It's a little less crowded. This is a bit much."

"Yeah." Capri and Jewel walked off toward the porch.

I finally made my way over there and dropped in a chair. "Was that Kevin's ex I saw in the living room with a date?" I asked.

"She finally found somebody? Jewel, you know that's the only reason you invited her," Capri said.

"No, not really. I'm just trying to work with the situation." Jewel sat on a nearby lounge chair.

"Jewel please, you've come far, but not *that* far," I said as I sipped on some wassail.

"Anyway, Capri, have you made New Year's plans yet?" Jewel asked.

"Uh, yeah. We're going out of town." She smiled a little.

"Oh, okay, that's nice."

What? We always do Dick Clark on New Year's Eve. Another tradition broken . . .

"Anthony surprised me, we're going out of town. He already made the travel plans. Where's Angel?" Capri said, changing the subject.

Okay, I'm just gonna play crazy. I'm not even going to react to what she just said. We always spend New Year's Eve together. "She said she was coming, but I don't know. She's with Octavio; they went to church earlier."

"Dang, they're definitely becoming the 'un-fun' couple," Jewel said. "I mean Jesus *is* the reason for the season, but you gotta celebrate, shake your bon-bons, step in the name of love—" A big crash stopped Jewel's rambling.

Curious, we all looked off toward the noise.

"Okay, who broke my sorority plate!" Jewel said.

"We were out of plates and I . . ." Kevin's Uncle Pookie said.

"All you had to do was ask. Kevin, come clean this up!" Jewel yelled.

"Ah, it ain't a real party unless somebody breaks something," Uncle Pookie said, holding the drumstick he was able to save.

I wanted to laugh, but Jewel looked serious.

Jewel just shook her head. She was starting to fuss when someone put on "Step in the Name of Love" by R. Kelly. All of a sudden, there was a crowd of people swinging out in the living room.

"Aw, baby, it's just a plate," Kevin yelled. I watched as he grabbed her hand and hugged her.

Before Jewel could say another word, he swung her around and they started to two-step in the kitchen. I think Jewel may have realized it wasn't about the plate. We all took a moment to appreciate the festive atmosphere of family and friends.

CHAPTER TWENTY-EIGHT

"Angel" Tree

Octavio jumped on the marble island and watched Angel maneuver over the stove.

"I know you don't have your butt on my countertop," she said without turning around.

"Angel, how many times do I have to tell you? You don't put any fear in my heart." He pulled his phone out after it started to ring. He read the number and slid it back in his jeans.

"Somebody you don't want to talk to?" Angel said as she piled the chicken, drowned in marsala sauce and mushrooms, on a plate.

"My mother, she always calls on Christmas Eve. But the last time we spoke she was still nagging me about going to see my father."

"Well, she has a point." Angel turned toward him to look into his eyes.

"He barely understands what I'm saying anyway." He paused. "Hey, did I tell you you're looking mighty good playing chef? You need to do it more often." He walked over and pulled her away from the stove. He grabbed her and began to hug and tickle her.

"Okay, stop. I said stop!" She couldn't contain her laughter. She tried to break away, as he held her wrists.

He finally let her go, but not before he pecked her on the cheek. They moved over to settle on the couch and eat.

"This is good, babe," he said with his mouth half full.

"Thanks, Octavio, but can you finish chewing before you talk?" Angel said as she watched him continue cleaning his plate.

When they finished their dinner, Angel went back in the kitchen to check on her Christmas cookies.

Octavio walked across the hardwood floors and reached to touch one of the ornaments they had hung on her Christmas tree. He peered out the large windows that wrapped around the expanse of her high-rise loft. Octavio could see all of downtown including the city attorney's office building where he worked. In the distance he could even see the Aquarium's blue lights and Ferris wheel. "The view is a really peaceful sight from up here." He closed his eyes, allowing the image to remain in his mind.

"I'm sorry, baby, what'd you say?" Angel said as she removed the cookies from the oven. "Sure you don't want some?"

"I'll try one, but I'm craving that apple pie," he called and walked back over to recline on the couch.

When Angel returned, he admired how relaxed Angel

was in her yoga pants and tank top. She handed him a slice of pie and dropped down next to him. She sat back, focusing on the flat-screen television. "Church was nice today, wasn't it?" She sipped on a cup of fresh-brewed coffee.

"Yeah, it was. You know Jewel's never going to let us hear the end of it since we stood up her and her fabulous party," he said as the warm apple and ice cream melted in his mouth.

"She'll get over it. Besides, Lexi called and said there was plenty of food, but the party was too crowded, loud, and . . . ghetto." She grabbed the remote.

"I wasn't in the mood for all of that," he said as he rubbed her leg.

"Me neither. So, what will it be? We can have a holiday movie festival or we can watch something else." She started scrolling through the television menu.

"Doesn't matter to me," he said as he shoved another piece of pie in his mouth.

"You always eat too fast. C'mon . . . get in the spirit." She slapped his thigh. "We have *It's a Wonderful Life* or *The Grinch,* and you know Lifetime is having a holiday movie marathon. We can always watch an action flick."

He smiled and leaned over to kiss her. "I love you, you know that?"

"You still didn't answer my question," Angel said.

"Well, I'm really not in the mood to watch some cheesy holiday movie." He grabbed the remote from her hand. "You know I'm not big on holidays; not everybody had a Brady Bunch Christmas like you."

She stopped eating and turned to look at him. "Okay,

you don't have to be so touchy. I thought we were having a great day." She grabbed the remote from him.

"I'm sorry. Holidays bring back some unpleasant thoughts."

"Okay, let's just relax then. No more talking."

Without saying another word, he placed his head on her shoulder. She switched to the jazz music cable channel. Then she grabbed Octavio's hand to pull him off the couch. He pulled her into his arms and they started to sway.

After about twenty seconds, she pushed him away. "Okay, that's enough."

"What? I was just getting into it." He looked her in the eyes before she walked away. He followed her to the couch. He leaned his head back and brought his fist to his head. "Angel, I can't do this."

"Octavio, yes you can."

"Angel, I love church and I love you. But all the prayer in the world won't keep me from wanting you." He looked her in the eyes and locked his fingers with hers.

It didn't help, the way his steel gray cashmere sweater fit his broad, snugly frame. His cologne left a trace on her skin and she was hypnotized by the scent. *God, please help me.*

She walked toward the window and stared at the lights. He got up and stood behind her. He ran the back of his hand gently against her face. "Baby, I need you."

She closed her eyes. "I—I can't."

"Remember how it used to be." He kissed her on the neck and rocked her back and forth in his arms. She began to sway with him.

"Please, stop," she whispered quietly as she grabbed his

hand. He raised and kissed the back of her hand. "Octavio, Octavio . . . *stop!*"

ctavio sat up, thinking about the leftover food in the fridge. He was about to get a plate, but changed his mind. He let his body fall back on the cushions. *I can't believe I'm on the daggone couch. I really can't believe this.* After tossing, turning, and releasing a few sighs, he finally dozed off.

Later, in her room, Angel rolled over and felt the empty space next to her; all kinds of thoughts consumed her mind. She kicked the covers off. *I know I'm not having a daggone hot flash. I'm too young for that!* She knew what was up, she was battling her flesh. She finally started dozing when she heard Octavio screaming.

"No, no, no!!!"

She grabbed her robe and ran into the living room. She went over to shake him. His shirt was off and he was wringing wet. "Octavio, Octavio!"

He finally jumped up. "Huh? What? I didn't do it, I swear, I swear!" He started rocking back and forth as he grabbed his knees.

"Octavio?" Angel was kneeling next to the couch, trying to shake him into coherence.

"Angel? Angel? I didn't do it." He yanked her off the floor and grabbed her tight. He was shaking.

What in the world is going on? Angel didn't say anything, waiting for Octavio to speak first. He finally released her and walked to the bathroom without uttering a word.

He came back after several minutes. He took her hand

and walked to her bedroom. He pulled back the covers for her to get in, and he climbed in behind her. He placed her head on his chest. "Baby, I need to talk."

"You don't have to if you don't want to," Angel said quietly as she put her arm around his waist.

"I need to get this out. I have to . . . Angel, when I was a kid in Mexico—I guess I was about eleven—it was a few days before Christmas . . ." He swallowed hard.

Angel lay still.

"My father, he—he killed a man."

"Octavio, oh my God, no wonder—" She tried to sit up, but he grabbed her.

"No, wait, just let me finish. I need to say this. We were at the park for a holiday festival. My father and another man had gone out into the woods and started drinking. I followed them. Soon they got into a fight over some money. My dad stabbed him to death and I let out a scream. My father heard me. When he found me, he grabbed me and ordered me never to tell, holding that same knife to my throat. The authorities never found out who really did it. Angel, there was just blood everywhere . . ."

She reached up and kissed him gently on the lips, wrapping her arms around him tight, and spoke calmly. "So all this time, you've kept this to yourself?"

"Crazy, isn't it? . . . all these years." He gently brushed his hand over her cheek. "I guess during the Living Victoriously Bible study the Holy Spirit started dealing with me. It really started getting worse when that prayer partner laid hands on me."

"Octavio, God led you to that class. That incident and

your father have had a strong hold on you. None of it was your fault, so you need to let go of any shame," Angel said quietly as she rubbed his forearm.

"I know that now. I can't believe I kept this mess inside all this time. I'm not sure what I was more afraid of, my father or the guilt. I knew what happened. I was a witness and I never told."

Angel could sense his hurt. "That fear has no power over you now. You've been delivered."

"Baby." He started to kiss her hair, then her face.

She closed her eyes and wanted to totally release herself to the moment. "Octavio, I can't . . ."

He grabbed her chin. "Yes you can . . . just forget it." He rolled over with his back toward her. "Don't you understand? You're all I have. I need you right now. I need you to make it alright." He curled his body into a ball.

She pulled him back toward her.

He pulled her close to him and took a deep breath. "Angel, you're my family." She touched his face, then his lips, and felt his pain. "I can't let you push me away too."

A ngel pressed her face into her sheets. She rolled onto her back. *God, I'm sorry. I tried, I tried.* Her eyes began to tear up and she quickly began to wipe them before Octavio came back in the room. "I messed up," she said quietly.

Octavio was walking toward the bedroom with breakfast when he heard her prayers. His heart sank when he made out her words and the guilt began to taunt him. *God, what are we supposed to do?* He took a deep breath and walked in with the tray.

"Morning, babe," he said as he placed the tray across her lap.

"Hey," she said with a faint smile.

"Look," he stared into Angel's eyes. "I know we messed up and it's my fault. It's just that, well, I hadn't touched you like that in a while."

"Yeah, I know," she said, her eyes downcast.

"Angel." He grabbed her hands. "I'm proud of your relationship with God. I'm not quite there yet, but I promise not to pressure you again."

"It was my choice, it's not like you forced me," Angel said.

He looked down for a minute. "Why does life have to be so complicated?"

She sipped her juice, then spoke. "How 'bout for now we just say a little prayer. Then maybe we can talk about some boundaries," she said. "Maybe make a list of things we can and cannot do."

"Angel, a list? Is it *that* serious?" Octavio dropped his head for a moment and rubbed his neck.

She wasn't smiling. "Yeah, it is."

He didn't respond, just leaned over and kissed her. He pulled back and smiled. He brushed her lips with his two fingers, then grabbed her hands . . . for prayer.

Jermane was relieved their big holiday party was over. But she couldn't help but smile, thinking about the new faces, many of them socialites who'd showed up this year. A small part of her felt proud that her annual holiday part was always a "must attend" on the Houston social circuit. Even Shelby Hodge, the entertainment reporter for the *Houston Chronicle* had stopped by.

"Babe, wasn't this year's party the biggest and most well done yet?" Jermane asked, but he didn't answer her. "Rex, did you hear me?"

He finally looked up from his book. "To tell you the truth, Jermane, I'm kind of getting tired of doing this every year. I mean it's the same people. The same food, the same conversation."

"Rex, what's really your problem? I thought you always enjoyed this?"

He put the book down. "I don't know, babe, I'm sorry. Jermane, what if I just up and decided one day that I didn't want to practice law?"

She looked over at her husband. She studied his face, and finally spoke. "Rex, what's going on with you? You're one of the best lawyers in Houston. Is it my dad again? He hasn't really interfered in our marriage and he's given you freedom at the firm. He's not on you about your hours anymore."

"It's not that," Rex lied. He wanted to tell her the truth. He wanted to tell someone, but he just internalized it all. "I mean Jermane, these people that come to our house every year don't show up because they like us. They're just nosy. I know you grew up in Houston and maybe you're used to it, but there are times when I just can't stand it all."

"Rex, stop acting weird. You know, maybe you need to

make a little change. I mean try a different area of practice. Or maybe we just need to get away for a short vaca-
tion," she said, trying to probe her husband.

"Is it that simple, Jermane? There are days when I just
want out. There are days I just want to be free. I don't want
to have to worry about your father and the firm's reputation."

"Wow, where is all this coming from?" Jermane
grabbed his arm and her eyes commanded his attention.

He took a deep breath. "I don't know, Jermane. I
didn't come from money. This world can be overwhelming. I feel like I'm losing myself in all this. You don't understand. You think your father is God, but he's just a
human being," he barked.

"What! What are you saying? What does my father have
to do with all this?" Jermane's eyes begged for an answer.
"Why do you want to quit your job. Tell me now!"

He grabbed her hands. "Jermane, calm down. I'm
sorry for getting you upset." He grabbed her and drew her
to his chest. "I'm just thinking out loud, babe. There are
just times when I need a real break, that's all." He brushed
her hair back with one of his hands. He held her again and
rocked her lightly. "I've just been spending time with
Kevin and I see how carefree he is. I mean he works hard,
but he still has time to enjoy life. I feel like a robot, like I
have to be 'on' all the time. I have so much invested in this
firm," he said.

She pulled away from him. "Rex, I just think you're
going through a phase. You accomplished so much at such
an early age. I think you are the only one pressuring yourself to do more." She grabbed his hands and kissed them.

"Jermane . . . I think it's a little deeper than that, but I'm going to work it out." He stood up and started getting dressed. Before she knew it he was headed toward the steps.

"Where are you going?" She jumped up to follow him.

"Jermane, I just need to get out for a minute. It'll be okay. Don't worry, I'll be back soon."

She wanted to stop him, but she resisted. She looked out the window a few minutes later and saw her husband pull out the driveway.

Hours later she looked at the clock. It was midnight and he still had not made it home. She checked her phone and there was a simple text message. "I'm okay, will be home soon." He'd sent the message at 11:30 p.m.

"Rex rarely sends a text message," she thought. She picked up the phone and called, but he didn't answer. After about twenty minutes she heard him come in the door. After about forty-five minutes he came upstairs, but she'd given into sleep by then.

CHAPTER TWENTY-NINE

I've Been There

Any other night, I would have been missing Chris. He was working late at a second job, and I was looking forward to taking one of my nice long baths. I'd just finished reading a little of *Your Best Life Now*, by Joel Osteen, and went to the bathroom to run my bath water. As I looked around I thought about all the pink I used to have in my bathroom before I got married. Now it was a neutral mix of eggplant, cream, and gold.

Normally I rush to strip down and jump into the water. But I slowly peeled off my clothes and stood in the mirror. I began to count the things I loved about my body. "I love my hair." I ran my fingers through it. "I love my skin tone, my smile, my hips, and my curves." I turned to look at my backside. "Not bad, not bad."

I remembered seeing photos from a few years back.

Looking at them now, I realized how good I'd looked. But at that time, I couldn't see it. Why was it so hard for me to see myself as God did back then?

I loaded my CD player with a few discs: Joss Stone, Robin Thicke . . . *gotta have some old school* . . . Angela Bofill, *The Best of Anita Baker,* Sade . . . *darn, I wish she would make another CD.*

I shut off the water and added some Carol's Daughter Mango Melange bath salt and oil. The aroma gave my Spirit an instant lift. Just when I eased into the water, my phone rang. *Don't answer . . . don't answer.* I look at the caller ID . . . Jewel. Uh-uh. I decided not to answer and slid a little further down in the water. A few minutes later, the phone rang again. I was too nosy to ignore it, so I peeked at the caller ID again. *Jermane—nope,* not tonight. I dropped the phone back on the floor and slid down again, letting water cover my shoulders. I positioned my head against my bath pillow and started repeating my affirmations. I've memorized so many from Pastor Joel and Living Truth's Bible study.

"I'm getting better and better in every way. My best is yet to come. I have the favor of God. It's a New Year and a new season. This will be my best year yet . . ." I had barely uttered my fifth affirmation when the phone rang again. I reached down and looked at it. *Angel.* This time I answered.

"Hey girl, what's up?"

"Just in the tub. What's going on?" I closed my eyes.

"Oh, sorry to interrupt, I know how you are about your goddess 'me time.' I can call you back."

"No, that's okay. We can talk." I leaned back and let the warm water envelop my body.

"Just wanted to chitchat; it's been hard getting back into the swing once the holidays have wound up. Maybe I'm just getting a little tired of the corporate game. Sometimes I wish I could work for myself like you and Capri."

"Why can't you?"

"I don't know. At one time I never imagined giving up a regular paycheck, or this lifestyle for that matter. But recently, somehow all my shoes, outfits, and other stuff don't seem to matter as much."

"Hmm. If it's really your heart's desire, God will let you know. Just pray on it. You never know, the three of us in a law firm may be our destiny!"

"*Interesting.* Well, who knows? I never thought I'd be all up in church either. I'm just going to stay open to hear from Him. Enough about work, I have something else to talk about. It's about me and Octavio."

"What's going on?"

"Okay girl, what I want to know is how *you* survived. I mean the celibacy thing. I give it to you, girl; I had no idea what you were dealing with! The celibate lifestyle is not designed for a woman over thirty-five."

"First of all, Angel, let me say I wasn't perfect. I fell, got back up, fell, and then I really had to put my entire focus on God. Then I started to realize having sex outside of God's design can take away from the future. Maybe that's why so many people get bored after marriage. They experience everything beforehand and there's nothing left to do. I don't know. Angel, all I can tell you is it's a trip. It requires total commitment. There is no magic formula. Trust me, I know your struggle."

"Lexi, we got weak on Christmas Eve. I wish I could tell you I felt horrible, but it had been so long—"

"Say no more, sister. Angel, you're just gonna have to stay prayed up."

"Yeah, I know."

I took a deep breath. "Okay, seriously, is there a reason why you're putting off marrying Octavio?"

"I don't know, fear I guess. My first marriage ended *so* badly. I'm over it, but it's hard to take that step. That marriage started out great too. I guess I'm afraid. People change, Lexi."

"I know, but maybe your first husband wasn't your divine mate; Octavio could be. The bottom line is, nothing is promised. Nothing is guaranteed. But Octavio is a good man."

"I'm praying, Lexi. But please, I need your prayers too. I've got to get rid of this fear. I almost lost him a while back and I want to give him the love he deserves."

"I got your back. In the meantime, you have to believe that if God's in you, he's not going to let you fail. If it is His will for you to leave that job and if Octavio is your divine mate, nothing can hurt it or stop it. The past is behind you, old things are passed away, and all things are new."

"It's not that simple."

"I know. That's why I'm gonna stand with you. Sometimes another person's faith can make the difference in a breakthrough. Not everyone understands that celibacy struggle. Not everyone is real about it either. I've been there. Angel, I know the type of prayer required."

"That's why I love you, girl. You have such a gentle but determined Spirit. I'm praying for you too, girl. I cover your marriage in prayer on a regular basis. I'm really thankful I have friends that lift each other up."

"Yeah, but it hasn't been the same. I do miss some of the old days." I started to smile. "It seems like Capri and I used to be really tight. But we just don't share and talk like we used to." I sighed.

"Lex, now I'm going to speak the truth in love. You know you've never been good with change. Things can't be comfortable all the time. Is this about Missy?" Angel asked.

"No, not really, well a little. But it's bigger than that. Not only do I feel we aren't as tight as we used to be, we are having little issues with the practice."

"Lexi, first you have to trust the friendship you and Capri have. You know, she's exposed to an entirely different world now. You don't know why God brought Missy into Capri's life, you can't question it. Second, what kind of issues are you having with the practice?"

"Well, I guess you're right on the friendship note. I guess I'm just a little selfish when it comes to my friends. As far as the practice, I don't know, I feel like I'm taking things a little more serious than Capri. I mean I'm there all the time. I seem to turn over more cases than she does. I don't think she understands how critical it is for us to build this business."

"I think you two need to just talk it out. Going into business is like a marriage; you need to communicate. If you don't, things will just get worse. Instead of holding things in, like you always do, you need to put all the issues on the table. I'm sure you two can work it out."

"Yeah, I guess you're right." *I do tend to hold things in.*
"Angel, on another note, I want to let you know that I'm really proud of you."

"For what? I haven't done anything."

"Yes you have. You've been faithful at Lakewood and I can tell you are really trying to grow. God is about to use you in a great way. I just feel it."

"Well, I don't know about all that. Especially after my recent lost battle with my flesh. I really don't want to blow it with God." Angel took a deep breath.

"Angel, you have to repent and let it go. You've come a mighty long way, my sister. You may not be where you want to be, but you're definitely not the person you used to be."

"Thanks for seeing it, Lexi. Sometimes you need to hear from someone who's been down this road."

"Trust me, I understand. I don't ever want to excuse sin, but don't be so hard on yourself. If you repented, let it go. Well I love you, girl, but now that Chris is out, I'm trying to enjoy this peace and solitude."

"Okay, go ahead and get your relaxation on and enjoy your bath. Have a good night."

When we hung up, I realized what's kept our friendship circle strong is our commitment. We are committed to each other personally, spiritually, and sometimes even financially. I can count on my "divine divas" to speak in truth and love, and to have my back. After a few minutes of quiet meditation I began to pray.

Father, I know we are all changing and growing and I have to trust Your process. My friends have been my family for so long. We've all grown so much. God, change has never been easy for me. I tend to want to hold on to people and things. So I release my friends to You, have Your way, Lord, especially with Capri. We all need new experiences, and marriage is a different journey. Also, I pray Your will be done with Angel's job and her relationship with Octavio. Father, I ask that You wipe away any negative impressions her previous marriage has left. I thank You for keeping the door to her anointed future wide open. Be with her in mind, body, and Spirit. In Jesus's name, Amen.

Literary Divas

"Girl, did you read the book?" I whispered to Jermane as we gathered in Jewel's house for the first meeting of the Shero Literary Sisters book club.

"Please, I've been busy dealing with our landscaper, preparing a dinner for some of Rex's clients and trying to figure out what's been going on with my husband lately," Jermane said quickly before sipping her peach tea.

"One day I think I have him figured out, and then the next day he says something totally out of character. The other day he was talking about finding his purpose in life. I think he's been talking to Octavio too much lately. But his hanging with Kevin these days, has me more concerned than anything else," Jermane said as she picked up a shrimp brochette from a nearby tray.

"Well, I wouldn't worry about Kevin. I mean sometimes all it takes is a little male bonding. All Kevin does is watch a little sports and run his mouth. Besides, if Rex is having thoughts about a career change you have to find a way to be supportive," I said.

"Umm, I guess."

I can tell she wasn't at all accepting the advice I'd just offered. "I did read some of the book though." I tried to redirect the conversation. "I believe Capri's coming with Missy."

Angel had walked over. "I'm looking forward to the discussion. I read the entire book and I thought it really was a good selection," Angel said as she spooned some fruit salad onto her plate. "Lexi, you said Capri is coming with Missy?" She bit into a chocolate-covered cherry.

"Yes, but I'm not sure why she's bringing Missy. A book club meeting just doesn't seem like her type of thing."

"Lexi, behave," Angel said, then dabbed her mouth with a napkin.

"What? Well, I just don't see what a person who used to 'shake her money maker' in music videos would get out of something like this," I said.

"She used to dance in videos?" Jermane put her hand on her chest. "My goodness, I never met a real video girl."

"Lexi, I thought you said you would keep an open mind?" Angel said as she dabbed the corner of her mouth with a napkin.

"Okay, okay. I'm looking forward to her contribution to the discussion. That's all I'm going to say." I put a few more pieces of shrimp brochette on my plate and sat down.

"Okay ladies, ladies, may I have your attention please?"

Jewel stood in the front of the living room and clapped her hands. "Attention! Attention! It is my sincere honor and privilege to welcome you to our inaugural Shero Literary Sisters book club meeting."

I let out a little yawn and Jewel cut her eyes at me. "What? It wasn't on purpose," I mouthed. I'd been up half the night trying to read the book. I took another bite of one of the appetizers piled on my plate. *At least the food is good.*

There were about ten ladies present, including Angel and Jermane.

"Okay, how many of you read the book?" Jewel asked. A little over half the group raised their hand. "Okay, it's fabulous you all came, but how are we going to have a book discussion if you all don't read the book? Never mind." Before she spoke again, the doorbell rang.

"That must be Capri, I'll get it." I jumped up and walked toward the door. I looked outside, it was Capri and Missy. I immediately doused myself in Jesus joy.

"Hey ladies, come on in, we are just getting started." I smiled at Missy and she smiled back. *You're on my turf now, sister; you better recognize.* At least she was dressed down in jeans and a silk kimono top. She still worked her signature stilettos and Fendi bag.

"Ladies, come, come, have a sit," Jewel said as she pointed toward two empty chairs.

"Okay, as I was saying. We have to read the books to get the full benefit of the book club. With that said, I have a few other rules." Jewel picked up her clipboard from the coffee table and began to read the paper attached.

Angel stood up and politely grabbed the clipboard from Jewel's hands. "Jewel, this is meant to be a relaxed and fun activity."

"Well, I'm just trying to keep things professional, but if you insist. So I'll start. Does someone want to give us her overall impression of this splendid literary work?" she asked as she sat down in her specially decorated hostess seat.

Missy raised her hand and immediately began to speak. "Yes, I thought the main protagonist was a bit self-indulgent, but likable. I also thought the author meticulously developed her plot. However, her overuse of metaphors often got in the way of some of the novel's most pivotal scenes. Other than that, I thought the theme of redemption and restoration was eloquently crafted."

Everyone's mouth hung open. "Oh yes, I have a degree in African American literature." She raised one eyebrow and focused on Jewel.

"Well, um . . . um . . . that was, um, something. What an excellent comment to initiate our dialogue," Jewel said. "I'm so glad to know we have a *serious* reader in the house." She smiled at Missy and clapped her hands.

Angel looked at me from across the room and I just shrugged my shoulders. After Missy's comment, the book club came alive. At the end of the meeting everyone surrounded her like she was an award-winning critic. I saw Missy reach into her purse and pull out a mini–photo album. Lo and behold, she was showing pictures of herself and Capri in Paris. *That's the last straw.* Jermane and I stood at the table and helped ourselves to some cake.

"Is it just me, or is she just a bit irritating?" Jermane whispered.

"I'm so glad it's not just me," I said as I shoved a fork-ful of cake in my mouth.

"And really, who hasn't been to Paris?" Jermane asked.

Me.

CHAPTER THIRTY-ONE

This Is Not a Test

I decided to take the afternoon off. I had to wrap my head around what had just happened. I was like a zombie. When I walked in the house I bumped into the large couch. I dropped my purse to the floor. The earth tones in my living room did nothing to soothe me. I started to turn on the television, but sat in silence instead.

"This is a joke, right?" I said as I looked up at the ceiling. Each time I wanted to get excited, something in the pit of my stomach smothered the emotion. I walked to the refrigerator and pulled out an entire tray of banana pudding. I grabbed a big wooden spoon and started scooping out portions of my favorite dessert and stuffing them into my mouth. Then I placed the dish on the kitchen counter. "Why am I so upset about this?"

I paced back and forth. I paused and began laughing

hysterically. Then I finally said it aloud: "I'm pregnant and gonna be somebody's Mama?!?"

I sat on the kitchen bar stool. The tears trickled and soon soaked my brand-new blouse. I couldn't totally re-joice because the two people I wanted to tell, Chris and Capri, had me ticked off right about now. Regardless of what Capri claimed, she was changing. She acted like I was dipping into the bottom of the barrel to find my clients. When we first started law school she was so committed to the community. We talked for hours about making a dif-ference. All of a sudden she'd forgotten how to give back. *It's probably Mitzi's fault.* I had decided that if she couldn't re-member my name, I wouldn't remember hers.

And don't get me started on Chris. We had yet to see a major return on any of his investments. Just thinking about it made my neck tense and I could feel a big knot rise up in my neck. I massaged it with my hand and closed my eyes. Panic tore into my thoughts again. Who was gonna cover for me at work when I got sick or when I was home with the baby? If I couldn't count on Capri to have my back now, what was I gonna do then? *Dang, Chris and I didn't budget for a baby until* after *next year.* I took several deep breaths.

So, Lexi, now what? I had to tell somebody. My dad? But I couldn't tell him before Chris. I couldn't tell any of my girls, especially Jewel because she would just run her mouth. Maybe Angel, she was good about keeping things in confidence and she had some sense.

"Okay, Lexi, you're speaking to yourself in third per-son, and that is *never* good," I said as I raised my finger. I finally put my hand under my blouse and allowed my fingers to dance across my stomach. Instantly, I felt this over-whelming sense of peace, and a huge smile came across my face. *It's going to be alright, God. I just hope Capri comes to her senses before she is out one godchild!*

"Angel?"

"Hey girl, what's up?" Angel said as she picked up the phone.

"What are you doing—did I catch you at a bad time?"

"I was just doing some yoga; I can take a break. What's going on? You sound a little funny."

"Nothing . . . well, yeah, there's something. Umm . . . not sure where to start . . . Okay Angel, I need a little marriage advice."

"Sure you want it from me? Remember, I can tell you what *not* to do," she said as she sat on her mat, crossed her legs, and began to lean her head to the side to stretch her neck.

"Well, I still think you give good sound advice when I need it."

"Enough said."

"Well, I just have a couple of issues and I need to know if I really have a reason to trip the way I am." I took a deep breath. "Okay, you know I love Chris to death and he *is* a really good man."

"Lexi . . . do you always have to beat around the bush? That's one of your worst habits. Just get to the point."

"What do you mean *one* of my worst habits? Never mind, okay here it is. Chris lied to me. Well, not really.

What I mean is he made a major decision a few months ago without consulting me. And, well, due to some recent developments, it . . . well, it was just wrong."

"Okay, I need more details, Lexi."

"He spent part of our savings. Okay, a *huge* part of our savings for some investments. And now . . . and now . . ." I started to cry. I grabbed a tissue and blew my nose.

"Lexi, it's rude to call someone stupid. So let's just say . . . sometimes men do some 'not so smart' things. It won't be the first or the last time. Did you talk to him about it?" Angel said as she stopped the yoga DVD but continued to stretch.

"Yes, but he acted like it wasn't a big deal. So I said I would just trust him," I said as I picked up the tray of banana pudding and started shoving the spoon in my mouth again. *Uhh, I'm getting nauseous.*

"Did he at least acknowledge the fact that he was wrong?"

"Yeah he did," I said through what I hoped would be my last spoonful.

"Okay. I'm not saying take it lightly, but don't magnify this one thing and forget about all the good things that he's done," Angel said as she stretched out her legs.

"It's not just that. I've been working extra hard to build a law practice. I've made a lot of sacrifices. When he made that decision, I felt like he took for granted all the hard work that went into earning that money. Angel, I don't know how much longer I can work like this. And now, and now . . ." I put the tray to the side and grabbed another tissue.

"Lexi, tell me what's *really* going on."

"I don't know. It seems like *nobody* understands. Capri can't relate to my situation. She works because she wants to, not because she has too. She practices the kind of law she wants because she doesn't really need the money. I don't always get that choice. Don't get me wrong, I like to help people, but I don't want all the criminal cases. I mean, it's not like I'm jealous, but she's *always* had it easy. Besides, she's not my best friend anymore . . . Chris and his brother Nate . . . the stock market's down and . . . just how are we going to put the baby through college . . . ?" I tried to get the rest of the words out in between sobbing.

"Whoa, whoa, whoa . . . back it up. Lexi, I can't even understand you. Did you say 'baby'?" Angel stopped midstretch.

"Uh-huh," I said, nodding my head as if she could see me.

"Sweetie, are you pregnant?"

"Yes." My tears flowed down my face like the Dunn River Falls in Jamaica. "Lexi, Lexi, honey, calm down. This is wonderful! I'm so happy for you. I'm so happy for you!" Angel said.

"Yeah, it is pretty great, isn't it?" I managed to say in between tears and heavy breaths. I wiped my eyes with my sleeve because I was too spent to find a tissue.

"Yes, it's a major blessing and I'm so glad you shared it with me. This changes everything. Okay, you need to relax. It's obvious the hormones have kicked in, dear. Second, Capri hasn't always had it easy. Remember, she did lose both her parents as a child. You do need to be up front with her about your feelings, because 'business is business.' Girl, God will work all this out, leave it up to Him. Lexi, you always insist on putting extra pressure on yourself. Let Chris be a man and take up the slack. He's more than capable or God wouldn't have sent him to you."

"Woo, I feel better already. Angel, I can't believe it. I had to talk to somebody. I haven't even told Chris yet about the baby. He hasn't made it home because he's working late. Besides, I want to wait for the right time. So please don't tell anybody."

"I won't. Now, I want you to get some rest. And by the way, my sister, am I detecting a little spiritual drought? Have you been putting regular time in with the Lord lately, or are you running on empty? I'm not talking about a prayer here or there either, I'm mean real true time with God."

"Guilty as charged. I don't know what it is, Angel. I used to study the Word every morning, but over the past few months, it's been a challenge. And don't even mention midweek Bible study. I feel so undisciplined. When I was single, all I did was spend time with God."

"I'm gonna pray for you, Lexi, but you've got to do your part. Sometimes we can move away from God little by little and before you know it we are totally depleted. That's the worst feeling. Then we want to ask, 'God where are you? I haven't heard from You; You seem so far away . . .' "

"Okay, Angel, I got it. I'll take my spiritual butt kicking like a woman." I managed to leak a smile. *My, how the tables have turned. Angel ministering to me? But she is right.*

"So, tomorrow morning instead of rushing in to work,

why don't you spend the morning in praise and worship? You need to take a 'Spirit break.' The beauty of working for yourself is you're able to make your own hours. You've got a lot to be thankful for, so we can't have you all depressed. Lexi, you're going to have a baby, snap out of it, sister!"

"Okay, okay, you're right; I *do* have a lot to be grateful for. Angel, thank you. I know the Lord had me call you for a reason."

"No problem, you've done it for me . . . a million times. I do have one request, though," she said after a pause.

"Sure, what is it?"

"In your prayer time, please lift up Octavio. His father is in the hospital and he needs to make peace with him. I don't want to get into the details, but Octavio is obviously hurting and needs some closure. I'm afraid if he doesn't go see him soon, his father won't be here much longer. If Octavio's dad passes before he sees him, I don't think he will be able to live with himself."

"My pleasure, I got it covered."

"Thanks, Lexi. Men are special. The most logical thing would be for Octavio to go see his dad, but he won't even talk about it. I know God is going to move his heart soon."

"Okay, I'll definitely be lifting him up. This has been one crazy, emotional day. I was tripping big-time."

"Like I said, Lexi, your hormones are probably doing a few somersaults, so give yourself a break." She paused. "Oh no, I just thought about something."

"Yeah?"

"Baby shower—Jewel. For God's sake, we're going to have to keep this from her for as long as possible. It's inevitable. We're in for another Fabulous Jewel . . ."

"*Please*, don't say it. That will be enough to send me over the edge," I said.

"Get some rest . . . love you, girl."

"Love you, too!"

As soon as I hung up the phone with Angel, I realized I had not made anything for dinner. I just don't see how my mother used to do it. She "brought home the bacon, fried it up in a pan" and whatever else it took to keep my dad around *and* faithful.

It was too late to thaw out any meat so I was really in trouble. "Uh-huh, I got it! I'll order Chris's favorite . . . Chinese." I picked up the menu and ordered sweet and sour chicken, egg foo yong, and fried rice. A few minutes later he walked through the door.

"Hey honey, what's for dinner?" he said as he walked in and kissed me on the cheek.

"I had a long day, so I ordered Chinese. It should be here soon."

He picked up the mail from the counter and started thumbing through it. As he was doing this, I stared at the father of my child. *Wow, God, you don't waste any time. How did we get here? I mean, I know how, but you know what I mean.* I started smiling.

Chris looked at me. "What's up with you? Why do you have that weird look on your face?"

"Oh, nothing," I said.

"Something's up, but I'm too tired to even try to figure it out. Anyway, Lexi, you know this is the third time this week we've had takeout. I've been working extra jobs these past few weeks and it would be nice to have a home-cooked meal more than once a week." After looking at a few envelopes he dropped the stack on the counter.

My smile turned upside down. *Boy did he spoil the moment.* "Chris, you were fine with takeout when we were dating. Nothing's changed."

"Well, sometimes it's good to challenge ourselves. Besides, if you love somebody, then you try to do things that make them happy," he said as he looked in the refrigerator and pulled out some juice.

"If you love somebody, you don't go into the joint savings and spend money without their permission."

He slammed the fruit juice carton down on the counter and looked at me. "Lexi, it was a bad decision. Why are you rehashing old stuff? Have you ever made a mistake? No, of course not, because you're perfect. Anyway, you know I'm doing an extra security job here and there to make up for what I did and build our savings back up. You know what I'm doing, so stop nagging me!"

I held up my hand. "Um, did you just raise your voice? My father doesn't even talk to me like that. You attacked me first."

"You know what, Lexi? I'm gonna call it a night if you don't mind," he said as he unbuttoned his shirt and walked toward the stairs.

"Well, I don't know where you're gonna sleep because all your dirty uniforms are in a trail to and over the bed. You want homemade food? Then you might try cleaning up after yourself." *Darn, why do I always have to have the last word? Sorry, God, but I'm working on it.*

The doorbell rang as I was about to follow him upstairs, so I went to the door and got the food. I took out one plate and piled the food high. I sat at the table and stuffed my face, for the second time that day. I knew I'd pay for it in a few hours.

As I lay wide awake with my back toward Chris, I noticed the moonbeams slicing through the blinds. Chris slept away from me on the other side of the bed. Normally we'd be all wrapped up together, like a cub snuggled tightly under the mama bear. Boy was I missing and needing that right now.

I started thinking of special ways I could tell Chris about our baby. How could I make it memorable . . . the wording, the timing, all of that? Tears formed in my eyes again, before I knew it. I lay there whimpering.

After a few minutes Chris rolled over. "Lexi, baby . . . what's going on?" he said, still half asleep.

"I just have a few things on my mind," I said in between sniffles.

"Okay, then, get some sleep," he grumbled with his eyes still closed. He scratched his head then smacked his mouth together.

"Chris . . . can we talk?" I rolled over and pushed him until he opened his eyes.

"Lexi, I'm tired. C'mere." He pulled me closer and wrapped me up in his warmth. "Be quiet, we both have to get up in the morning."

"But Chris . . . I—"

Zzzzz.

"Great."

I shook him, then punched him softly. "Chris! Chris, I'm pregnant!"

"Uh-huh," he mumbled. A second or so later he jumped up. "Did you say you were pregnant?"

"Y-e-a-h."

He reached over and turned on the lamp near the bed. "Are you sure?" He looked me in the eye, then scratched his head. "Lexi, when did you find out? Why are you just telling me now? I mean, did you know all day? I can't believe you're just telling me now."

I sat up. "I found out earlier today. I was trying to come up with a creative way to tell you. You know . . . something you would remember. Then you ticked me off."

"Lexi . . ." He was finally coherent. "Wow!" He rubbed his eyes. "This is a blessing, aren't you happy? I mean, how do you feel?" He grabbed my shoulders, then kissed the top of my head. "You don't even seem excited."

"Of course I'm happy . . . and scared. I know this is what I've been wanting, I mean a family. But Chris, I feel like everything is happening so soon. This is so soon, Chris. I certainly wasn't expecting this. But I guess God has other plans."

"C'mere, sweetie." He pulled me toward him, gave me a big kiss, and brushed my hair from my face. He noticed my cheeks were still damp with tears. "Big baby," he said. "I love you. I don't want you to ever doubt that, okay?" He brushed my face with the back of his hand.

"I know you love me," I said as he pulled me so close I could feel his heart beating.

We spent the rest of the night too excited to sleep. We lay in the dark calling out just about every baby name we could think of until finally we dozed off at around four a.m.

CHAPTER THIRTY-TWO

Study and Show Yourself Approved

I made myself a cup of raspberry tea and pulled back the curtain to look out the kitchen window. I wasn't focused on the tangerine sun creeping up from the distance, instead, my eyes were fixed on my yard. *I actually have a lawn.* Everything had happened so quickly since we eloped. Moving into the house, organizing the firm, it had all been so overwhelming. I took a deep breath and really tried to be in the moment. I blocked out thoughts of the office and any other nagging feelings that had been getting the best of me.

While looking out the window, I thought about the lawn in front of the house where I grew up. It was a small, quiet neighborhood where you could leave your door open. I called it "the United Nations," as it was filled with Black, white, and Asian people. We played outside until the streetlights came on and even sometimes after. I re-

membered catching lightning bugs and picking clover. I
remembered my first skateboard, bicycle, and roller skates
and the cuts and scrapes that came with them. I remembered rolling down the hill of my backyard and sliding
down the huge hill in my neighbor's backyard on a sleigh
when it snowed. There were lots of smiles, warm hugs, and
laughter. I remember my dad's car driving up every day
around the same time. I helped him carry his briefcase in
the house, even though I know he carried most of the
weight.

I wanted that type of home and more for my baby. *God,
I'm so scared to bring a child into this world.* Things weren't the same
as when I was growing up. There was so much out there in
the world: a lot of anger, filth, pain, and danger. *How will
I ever protect my child?*

I decided I'd sit in the screened-in porch to study the
Word. I loved nature; it was God's sanctuary, pure and
peaceful, especially early in the morning. *Boy, it's been a while
since I got up to read the Bible.* I grabbed my pashmina shawl
from the living room chair and my Bible from the bookshelf and headed for the porch.

I sat and started searching random verses. It wasn't
coming easy. I moved from chapter to chapter, but nothing really spoke to me. So I paused for direction.

*Okay, Jesus, I apologize. I haven't really been studying, but I'm here
now. Help me to focus on You and what I'm supposed to accomplish during this time with You. Direct my eyes; give me an open heart and mind to
receive whatever Word You have for me. In Jesus's name. Amen.*

Once again, I opened the Bible. Nothing. I waited and
waited. Finally a Word.

"Worship."

"Lord, I'm not really in the mood for singing," I whispered.

"You don't have to sing. Meditate. Look at all I've done. Take in all I've created. Think about the manifestation of your many prayers."

I put the Bible down and looked out on to the backyard. The sky was so clear. I rubbed the softness of the shawl wrapped around my shoulders. I walked outside and released the air from my lungs. I moved toward the middle of the lawn and raised my arms. I heard music. A red bird danced from one tree to another. I noticed the pinecones on a nearby tree and the acorns that crunched beneath my shoes. I heard the neighbor's dog scratching the fence and looked down to find clovers, in my own backyard.

After a few minutes, I went back inside. I opened the Bible and turned to Psalm 113:3. "From the rising of the sun to the place where it sets, the name of the Lord is to be praised." I started humming quietly. Then a song was stirring in my Spirit and soon the words were fighting to come out . . . softly. "I lift up my hands, standing unashamed." My hands started to rise. "I worship You, Father, exalting Your name . . . I lift up my hands . . ." By the third verse, I was singing at the top of my lungs, my heart filling with each verse until it felt it would leap from my chest with joy.

I sang from a deep-rooted place. "Falling in love with J-e-s-u-s . . . is the best thing that I've ever done." I fell on my knees and put my head down. I felt God's hands wrapped around me.

"Thank You, God, for loving me. Thank You, Lord,

for answered prayer. Thank You for blessing me. I worship You for who You are."

I felt God's presence, His touch, His warmth. After a minute He raised me from the floor. I went to the Psalms again. My eyes scoured the pages until I reached Psalm 127:3. "Children [are] a reward from Him."

God . . . it is a reward! I know you'll give me everything I need to be a great mother. Lord, you know I'm frazzled at times. I can barely keep myself together, but I know you'll guide me every step of the way. That's it! I just have to take one step at a time . . .

I turned and read more, this time from Proverbs 22:6. I read aloud, "Train a child in the way he should go, and when he is old, he will not turn from it."

His words liberated me, released me from my fears, and I let out a sigh of relief. Just like that I'd fallen out of fellowship. But this morning, I reconnected with God. It felt good hearing that clearly from Him. *I really must rededicate my mornings to prayer.*

Suddenly, the Lord put Capri on my heart. I decided to buy a card and let her know I was thinking of her. We used to do little thoughtful things like that for each other, throughout our friendship. *I can't wait to share my news with her!*

Angel was right. I needed this praise break! I made sure I prayed for my friends and my business, and added a special prayer for Octavio and Angel. I covered all our marriages in the Blood of Jesus. Then I was off to work with a renewed Spirit.

I had a spring in my step as I walked to my office building. While on the elevator I smiled at the older white gentleman standing next to me. He smiled back and his eyes twinkled as if he knew I was blessed. Yes, my light was truly shining. Normally, my eyes are fixed forward and my mind is running wildly down my mental to-do list. But not today, I was at peace. I was prayed up and ready to face the world with confidence. In one hand I held my briefcase and in the other I clutched a card for Capri.

I walked off the elevator and into the office suite and heard voices.

"Girl, did you see that outfit she had on? You know that was wife number two. She used to be married to that R & B singer. I guess she didn't want to let that lifestyle go."

Capri's office door was open and I heard a familiar voice.

Missy. There was no way I could sneak by, but I thought I'd try.

"Lexi," Capri said as she caught me slinking past the door.

I froze, then faced her doorway.

"Hey, what's going on? Are you in a rush? Come in for a minute," she said.

I inched into her office. "Hey ladies, I would sit and chitchat, but I got lots of work to do."

"Hi, Lexi," Missy said and launched right back into her conversation.

She does know my name.

"Hey, Missy."

"How's every little thing? I haven't seen you since the book club meeting. Can't wait for the next one," she said as she waved her manicured left hand, with a rock so big it

was blinging up the whole office. She had her red carpet
look back on, with her hair pulled so tight I thought her
temples were going to burst. Her makeup, from eye
shadow to bronzer and lip gloss, was perfectly coordinated. She wore a fitted jacket, large Christian Dior belt,
and pencil skirt. The diamond stud earrings were the only
understated item adorning her body.

"So Lexi, you can't sit down for a minute? You work
way too hard, girl . . ." Missy said.

As soon as Missy looked my way, Capri rolled her eyes
and mouthed, "Please get her outta here."

"Oh, sorry ladies . . . as you can see, I'm getting a late
start today. Oh, here, this is for you." I handed Capri the
card.

Missy sat up taller. "Oh, Capri, girl is it your birthday? Why didn't you tell me? We have to go get something
to eat now. Right now! Wow, what kind of friend am I?"
she said as she playfully reached to slap Capri's hand. And,
quoting Ms. Beyoncé, "My mama taught me better than
that."

Just when I wanted to give Missy credit for coming up higher. She
couldn't quote Maya Angelou or Nikki Giovanni? It looked like her
well didn't go any deeper than an R & B track. Missy had
a high-octane personality like Jewel, but times seven. I
knew Capri could only take Jewel in small doses. So why
did she hang out with Missy so much? There had to be a
catch.

"It's not my birthday, Missy," Capri said as she reached
for the card. "Thanks, Lexi."

"Oh, anyway, like I was saying. She wasn't even invited
to the party and she showed up there hanging off his

arm . . . Check it out, it was on the E! Channel. She was a fashion 'trashy' in the 'trashy or flashy' segment to boot." Missy kept talking, giving me no further acknowledgment.

Her voice faded as I strode into my office. Once inside I closed the door and leaned against it, whispering to myself: "Lord Jesus, forgive me, but I cannot stand that girl. If she's going to be one of Capri's friends, please help me." My prayers must have been answered because about fifteen minutes later, Capri came down to my office alone.

"Hey, got a minute?" she said as she poked her head in the doorway.

"Yeah, sure," I said, as I looked up from my computer screen.

"Just wanted to say thank you for the card. That was really thoughtful."

"It was nothing. Just wanted you to know I was thinking about you."

"Lex, I know you're tired of seeing Missy. She shows up uninvited. It's okay every now and then, because, well, sometimes it's nice to have someone to relate to on the basketball thing. She's not that bad. It was fun at first because she was so intrigued by my being a lawyer. Anyway, all this NBA wife stuff is pretty new to me. I was just trying not to be so antisocial for Anthony's sake, you know? But I didn't know I was acquiring a shadow." Capri leaned against the side of the doorway and folded her hands.

"Capri, you don't have to justify your friendships to me. It's just that, like you said, she hangs around here as if she doesn't have anything else to do. We do have a practice to run and some of us *have* to work for a living."

Capri's right eyebrow instantly went up. "What do you mean *some* of us? Lexi, I do put in my time and if I want to have a visitor every now and then . . . well, I do pay for half the office space." She stood up straight.

I raised my hands. "Whoa, Capri, you don't have to get defensive. I didn't mean to offend you, but you just admitted that old girl shows up uninvited . . . often. I mean, we might as well hang out a shingle with her name on it." I clicked on my calendar to see what I had going on for the afternoon.

"But as long as I handle my business, it really shouldn't be that big of a deal," Capri said as she folded her arms.

I sighed. "Capri, it's not that big of an issue. As far as I'm concerned that's behind us." I took a deep breath and moved a pile of papers in front of me. I picked up a pen, but realized this was a good time to discuss some real business. "Since you're here, do we want to have a client meeting, maybe go over some cases right now?"

"Lexi, I know we need to do that, but I have to finish up a contract by five today."

"We've been putting off meeting for a while. We need to do some strategic planning and we have to meet with the accountant next week."

"Lexi, you pretty much know all my cases. I don't have as many clients, but they pay retainers. I may have a couple of settlements coming up. But you know how that is, sort of unpredictable."

"Yeah, I know, Capri, but you know we need to talk it over in detail. What's happened to you? You used to be so meticulous. And for the record, I have clients that pay too. Anyway, I just need to have a meeting to feel comfortable. I'm on a fixed budget."

"Why are you so stressed? Lexi, part of owning a business is to enjoy it. Why are you all of sudden so pressed for time? Our business is fine. Just don't pressure me, okay? You know if anything gets slow I got your back."

"I want to enjoy this as much as you, but this is a new business, Capri. We're not meeting some of our goals and I'm just a little nervous. I mean, yeah, you walked in the door with a few really good clients, but you know this is a hustle. I appreciate the fact that you would have my back, but I don't want you to have to carry me."

Capri took a deep breath. "Well, you know I got you. And besides, it wouldn't be the first time. Why are you tripping?"

My heart fell. I knew there was going to come a day when I would regret asking Capri for money when I was in solo practice. Did she realize she had just insulted me? She had watched me try to build this practice and knew how hard I've worked. Besides, I had a baby to think about now. *Boy, you think you know your friends, but I guess when your husband all of a sudden becomes an NBA player and starts making millions of dollars, anybody can change.*

"Okay, never mind. Yeah, it can wait. We can wait until we look up and all our books are screwed up. We can wait until we are in dire straights and have to answer to the IRS. Anyway, I'm gonna get some work done this afternoon and in between playing with Missy maybe you can do the same," I said with my eyes focused on my stack of papers.

"Okay, okay, Lexi, stop with the dramatics. We can

meet tomorrow morning. What's up with you? Why have you been so cranky these past few days?"

I looked up and relaxed my posture. My shoulders dropped. "I . . . well, Capri, I'm not sure," I lied. I was still a bit angry with her and didn't want to share my news. *At this particular moment, she doesn't deserve to share in my joy. I know, God, I know, I'm being ugly.*

"Well, Anthony has me a bit wound up too with the playoffs and some other issues, but things will work themselves out."

"What? Capri, I know you wouldn't tell the whole crew your business, but you and I, we used to be able to talk. What's going on?" My eyes focused on hers.

"Nothing, it's just *really* personal. It's about him and I just don't think it would be fair."

"Fine. Be that way." *Just for that, you may have lost your godmother privileges.* "Since you don't want to talk about it, I better get to work," I said as I opened a file.

Capri hesitated. "Well, fine." She went back to her office and I thought I heard her door slam shut.

Amelia, our legal intern, was the only other person in the office. After listening in as best she could, she picked her phone up and called her friend. She began speaking rapidly in Spanish. ". . . *Las chicas están locas.*"

"I heard that, Amelia," I yelled before I got up and shut my door.

CHAPTER THIRTY-THREE

Hoop Dreams

It had been raining off and on for weeks. So, the sight of sunshine glaring through the windows inspired Capri to embark on a cleaning marathon. She also wanted to work off the nervous energy surrounding Anthony's next game. They were one win away from the playoffs. She'd never seen him be so focused or work so hard. "Something might have come out of this sex drought," Capri thought as she sprayed and wiped the sliding glass door. She paused briefly to look out at her backyard. *Boy, I'm a long way from Brooklyn.* Her eyes focused on the infinity pool with the cascading waterfalls and outdoor kitchen. In the distance she could see Anthony's basketball court. *All this because somebody can dribble a ball.*

"I'd trade a chunk of this house if I could have my husband back," she thought aloud. *I miss those long nights. Not only am I deprived, but he's been cranky on top of it . . . but Missy says most of the players get irritable at a time like this.* Capri lifted her shoulders then sighed as she released them.

That Missy . . . she's definitely a character. After meeting her husband, Jason, Missy started to live and breathe the NBA. He seemed to worship the ground she walked on and didn't make a move without her. Now she was a self-proclaimed authority on this whole players' wives thing. Missy was the only one to really reach out to Capri. Although her conversation rarely went beyond fashion, *Star* magazine, *Vibe,* or E! Channel, the two of them somehow connected.

Capri refocused as she grabbed her bucket of sponges and cleaning products. She headed for the stairs, somewhat regretting the project she had started. Once in the game room she removed some of Anthony's trophies from the shelf. While dusting, she thought about Lexi. *The last thing I want is for this law firm to affect our friendship.* She stepped back, wiped her forehead. *The enemy will find any open door to cause division and strife. But I'm about to close the door on that sucker.*

Capri moved down the hall to the bedroom and immediately stripped the linen. *Hmm, time to shop for a new comforter set.* Although she admired the turquoise blue and brown décor, she was already bored with it. *Heck, maybe we'll redecorate the whole room. I could call that Naegel, Jermane's friend.* Capri put her hand on her hip and bit the side of her lip. *On second thought, I don't need any drama like Jermane had with her alleged decorator/stripper. I can't say I blame her; he was kinda fine. No, that is definitely not a good idea right now.* She closed her eyes, pictured his buffed reddish-brown body, sun-kissed dreads, and infectious smile. *Whoa.* She waved her hand toward her face, fanning herself, regaining her composure.

She stepped toward Anthony's closet with hesitation. In contrast to hers it was always in disarray, except for his sneakers, of course. Most of his massive collection of sneakers was neatly stored in a specially made wall display. A few pairs were still scattered on the floor amid sweatpants and lost socks, so she started there.

When she lifted the first shoe, she marveled at her husband's foot size. She picked up another and heard something rattle. She reached in the massive hole and pulled out a plastic bottle. *What's this?* Capri turned and read the label. She immediately went to her office and got on the computer. Her fingers typed with lightning speed until the information popped up. After she read it, she leaned back and took a deep breath. Her hands reached for the phone, she was about to dial his cell . . . then she slowly placed it back on the receiver. *It may kill me, but I can't talk to him until after the game tonight.*

"Man, Anthony could have hooked up better seats than this. We're two rows from the nosebleed section," Kevin said as he bit into a hot dog. "Look at Capri down there tryin' to look all cute. That's where we need to be."

"You better be lucky Anthony got us any seats. They're not that bad," Rex said as he scanned the Toyota Center. The music blared and an announcer's booming voice got his attention.

"Ladies and Gentlemen, we're proud to bring you the Hou-ston Met-eor-ettes!!!" A team of young women dressed in hot pants and cropped tops, shaking metallic pom-poms, flooded the floor, bouncing around various sections of the gym.

"Rex, man, focus . . . don't you see this is one of the highlights!" Kevin said as he started clapping. He stood up, mimicking the dancer's movements.

"Man, stop! You always got to act a fool." Chris yanked on his arm, trying to get him to sit down.

"Dang, I should have brought Angel," Octavio said as he tried not to stare down at the dancers and their skimpy outfits.

Rex, Chris, and Kevin all looked at him sideways. "Yo, that's your boy," Kevin said to Chris. "Man, you're trippin'. We love our wives and all, but you got to loosen up a bit," he said and started clapping again.

"I feel you though," said Chris. "Y'all know Lexi has radar. This would be the one time they'd flash me on the big screen. In a few minutes, I'd hear my cell phone. 'Baby, I saw you looking at those women' . . . then she'd throw a scripture on top of it."

"Yeah, you can look, but you better not let them see you do it. It's not like you become blind after you get married," Rex added.

"You know they have a ministry for that at Lakewood . . . for men struggling with temptation," Octavio chimed in.

"Man, we ain't in church . . . you are *really* killing the vibe," Kevin warned as he shook his finger toward Rex. "Besides, don't think our women don't look too. Rex, I know you know. That's why you all tight with Jermane now."

Octavio looked at Kevin, then shook his head. "Man, you know you wrong."

"What? I'm just keeping it real." He formed a mega-phone with his hands and yelled, still focused on the Me-teorettes. "These girls are talented." He clapped his hands along with the musical beat.

"Sit down, sit down!" a group of rowdy men behind him shouted. They threw a few pieces of popcorn at him.

Kevin looked around with an attitude and finally took his seat. "Look, I like to have a good time wherever I go. Shoot, we're about to make it to the playoffs."

"Not if your boy doesn't bring it. He's been a little shaky these last couple of games," Chris warned as his eyes focused on the floor.

"He's gonna be a'ight. He better . . . these ain't the best seats, but I still ain't trying to give 'em up," Kevin added.

The lights dimmed and the announcer's deep voice in-cited the fans to a noisy roar. The four men began to high-five one another and prepared to watch their boy play the game of the season.

CHAPTER THIRTY-FOUR

Girls' Night

apri was actually at the game and the rest of us had gathered at my place. It had been a close one and we were in the fourth period.

"I can't take it anymore," Angel wailed as she sat at the edge of my couch.

"I don't get it. What's the big deal? It's just a game," Jermane interjected as she buffed her nails. "Jewel, you're right, this diamond buffer is great."

"Lexi, hurry up and come back, they're going into overtime," Angel called as she jumped up and down.

"Okay, okay. I just wanted to grab some snacks during the commercial." I walked in with more nachos and salsa.

"You think Lexi's putting on a little weight? I tried to tell her to cut back . . . just look at her stuff those nachos down her throat."

"I hadn't noticed. But now that you mention it, her

face does look a little full," Jermane confirmed as she looked up from examining her nails.

"I heard that!" I said, and rolled my eyes.

"Anyway, so tell me what you found at Saks," Jewel begged as she grabbed Jermane's arms.

"Oh yeah, the annual sale. I missed it last year. But I was all in those racks. I saw four-thousand-dollar dresses marked down to a thousand. I picked up this darling Zac Posen cocktail dress."

"Oh," Jewel uttered after a swallow.

"I don't believe them," I said to myself, catching the rest of Jewel and Jermane's conversation. "They aren't the least bit into this game. Never mind, the game's back on. Oh please, hurry up and get those funky Meteorettes off the court! What is their purpose?"

"You know the deal," Angel said. "That's for the testosterone-saturated arena."

"Well, I know *my* Boo wouldn't even think about look-ing at those anorexic, plastic Barbie dolls," Jewel asserted.

"Shhh, they're starting again." I ignored Jewel, because we all knew she was fooling herself with that remark.

Angel cupped her hands around her mouth like a megaphone. "The clock's running down. Anthony, come on, brother!" she yelled. "Darn, he looks like he's slowing down."

"Yeah, but brother's been playing his heart out." I watched as the players ran up and down the court. "This game has been *too* good. Any more time-outs left?" I dipped my nacho in cheese sauce and stuffed it in my mouth.

"No, none. They're gonna have to play smart," Angel

said as she watched the Meteors' point guard dribble the ball up the court. "Oh no, he walked!"

"I can't believe it! I just can't believe it. You don't walk in the NBA!" I moved to the edge of her seat and grabbed the top of my head.

"Take it easy, girl," Jewel said as she patted my arm. She finally decided to focus on the television screen to see what all the commotion was about. "Look at Missy, she looks a hot mess. Normally she looks good, but she's a 'fashion don't' tonight. Where's she going in that beret? Is that Diddy? What's he doing in town?"

"Two minutes. Come on, we can do this, we can do this. It's tied. Okay, let's keep it together!" I said as I leaned forward.

"No foul, no foul. Omigod, Anthony stole the ball." Angel watched the crowd going wild and everyone was on their feet. "He passed it to number thirty-two, umm, look at that chocolate Vernon Styles. Girl, he's *definitely* bringing sexy back!"

"Take the shot, take the shot!" I watched as they reached the other end of the court. Dang! He missed. "Get up, Anthony, get the rebound. Yes, he's got it!" I raised my hands.

"Why would someone want to put all those tattoos on their body? That has to hurt. And is all that ink sanitary?" Jermane watched curiously as Number 32 reached his long tattooed arm toward the hoop for a layup.

I raised my hands. "It's good!"

"Shhh! Aw man, the Suns scored a three-point jumper!" Angel and I screamed seconds later. The Meteors ran the ball to their end of the court.

"Anthony has it!" He fired the ball to his teammate, Troy Woodson, a rookie drafted straight out of high school. Woodson's eyes looked wildly around for someone to pass the ball to. "Dang, he looks confused . . . a minute and ten seconds left. They're down by one point, take it!" We watched as Troy tried to get the ball back up. He stood still and his hands started moving. "What is he doing?" Then a whistle blew.

"Oh, nooo!!!" Angel and I both cried.

"What—what happened?" Jewel said. Amid the excitement, I didn't even realize Jermane had left to watch television in another room.

"He called time out. There aren't any freakin' time-outs left!!!" I shouted, without looking at her. She grabbed the top of her head.

"So?" Jewel said.

"*So,* that's an automatic technical foul. Dang!!! I don't believe it," I said as I folded my hands and leaned back in my chair.

Before they knew it, the Houston hoop dream was just that . . . a dream. After the next two shots, the Suns beat the Meteors by only three points.

CHAPTER THIRTY-FIVE

A Dream Deferred

All Capri could do was stand there in the press area and watch the reporters bombard her husband. The reporters yelled as lights flashed from all angles. She was still very proud of him, and wanted to show her support. Anthony always kept his games in perspective, but this loss hit him extra hard. He could barely get the words out as questions were fired left and right. They analyzed every play and questioned his decision to pass the ball to the team's youngest player.

"Well, we gave it all we had and I have all the confidence in the world in my teammates," he said after a long pause.

Capri watched in silence, as the strong man she knew was suddenly fighting back tears. His voice was lower than usual and soon his head dropped in between his brief responses.

"Do you think this is the end of your quest to get to an NBA championship?" one reporter yelled.

After a moment, Anthony looked up and said, "All I can do is my best and give God the rest." On that note, he got up and walked out. Capri went out the back door and met him outside.

"Anthony, wait." She quickened her footsteps to catch up. Once he recognized his wife, he wrapped his long arms around her.

"I fought *so* hard—I worked for this, baby" was all he could say as he held her tight and stroked her hair.

"I know you did," she whispered after a long pause. In the car, Capri reached for Anthony's hand to hold it. They rode in silence as he did mental replays of the game. It took all she had not to ask about what she'd found in his closet earlier. Instead, she gazed out the window while they rode home in a safe but uncomfortable silence.

Capri watched the butter bubbling under the pancake in the frying pan. She gently tucked the spatula underneath to flip it over. The ringing of the phone snapped her out of a daze. She picked up without even looking to see who was calling.

"Hey girl, just wanted to check in. How's Anthony doing?"

"Hey Lex, he's okay. He's not saying much; I'm just giving him space. We slept in this morning—didn't make it to church."

"You know we were watching and cheering for him, girl. It's just a tough break."

"I know. I appreciate you calling. Anthony's strong, he'll be fine," Capri said as she cradled the phone between her neck and ear.

"Chris enjoyed the game and said the crowd's energy was crazy."

"It was. I just wish they could have pulled it off. I saw *The Chronicle*. They didn't beat up on Anthony too bad, but they showed little mercy for that young player. I feel so badly for him. People can be really cruel," Capri said as she reached in the refrigerator for the juice carton. "Oh, girl, I'm gonna have to go, I think Anthony's up. I'll call you back later. Thanks again for checking in. If I don't call you back, we'll talk tomorrow."

"Capri, wait, I have something to tell—"

Click.

"Hey, are you doing alright?"

"Yeah, I'm fine," Anthony mumbled as he plopped in the chair at the kitchen table.

"Are you sure?" Capri asked as she slid another pancake on the stack. She could still smell the soap from his freshly showered body.

"Capri, I'm fine. You don't have to tiptoe around me. It's over. Where's the paper?"

"You sure you want to read about it?" she said as she slid a plate in front of him.

"Capri . . . just give me the paper!" His eyes glared at her and a small vein protruded near his temple.

She jumped a little. He'd never raised his voice to her before. "Anthony, you don't have to yell. I just thought—"

"Well don't think for me. I said I was fine . . . never mind. I'm gonna put some clothes on. Maybe play a round of golf."

Capri didn't speak. She was still stunned at the tone he used with her. She couldn't move to the side fast enough before he brushed by her on his way out of the room. After a few seconds, she walked over to turn off the burner. For the first time in a long time, she fought back tears. *God, I'm doing all I know to do. I need Your help on this. How do I make him feel better?* She paused briefly. *What would Lexi do in this situation?* She was so used to just dialing up Lexi for prayer. *I guess I'm gonna have to figure this one out for myself, God.*

Several minutes later, Anthony walked past the kitchen in his golf shirt and khakis without uttering a word.

Before she could walk out of the kitchen he'd closed the door behind him. *He always hugs or kisses me on the way out,* Capri thought as she started to put away the food. Although she knew Anthony would be back to normal soon, his coldness made her numb. *This foul Spirit is not gonna come up in my house,* she thought, vowing to pray once Anthony was gone.

*A*nthony and Chris had spent all day out on the golf course and afterward they headed to Houston's for a bite to eat. "Can you seat us in the back?" Anthony asked.

The hostess nodded her head and led them to a seat in the back corner.

"Man, I just don't feel like talking to anybody right now."

"I know I'm not the best golfer, but it seems like you

got a lot out of your system on the course today," Chris joked, once they made it to their seats.

"Yeah, I did sort of whip up on you. Sorry about that, son." Anthony grabbed a menu, then placed it down. He noticed a man staring in his direction. He locked eyes with him and frowned. The man looked the other way.

"Hey, I'm just happy to get out of the house. Lexi was about to have me hanging up some drapes and mowing the lawn or some other crazy mess. She's been that way since—since, um, the weather broke."

Anthony nodded his head. It was quiet until the waitress came to take their order.

"Man, we had it! Why did I pass that ball?" Anthony hit his fist lightly on the table.

"Man, you got to let it go. It is what it is. There's nothing you can do, man."

"I just feel like I let so many people down. I'm so tired of 'almost' . . . tired of failing." He looked down at the table.

"Okay man, don't go to the extreme. It's just, just . . . a test."

Anthony rolled his eyes and shook his head. "Chris, no disrespect, but I don't need a sermon right now. The bottom line is I wanted this. Is that so wrong? It's not like basketball's everything, but it'd be nice to get a championship for once. We just blew it." His fist hit the table with a thud.

The waitress finally walked up, breaking the tension. They placed their orders after she returned with their beverages.

Chris looked around the restaurant to avoid the uncomfortable silence. He was still searching for words of encouragement. "Man, you got at least five years before you have to give up," he finally offered.

"Man, I'm starving. I hope they hurry up with the food." Anthony looked down, drumming his fingers on the table. "Man, I appreciate what you're tryin' to do. Just give me a few days, I'll be cool." He shook his head, "Just like that, it's over. All the hype . . ."

"That's just it; you can't get caught up in all that. People will love you one day and hate you the next, no matter how hard you try. But, if it's any consolation, Lexi thinks you're more than good enough," Chris uttered slowly.

"Huh?" Anthony snapped back from his thoughts.

"Man, you and Capri, if you want to that is, are gonna be godparents."

Anthony sat up taller, then leaned forward. "Are you serious, man? As of when?"

"She's a little over six weeks." Chris grinned and let his mouth spread wide into a smile.

"Dang, man, you are cheesin' *real* hard. Why haven't y'all told anybody?"

"It's not me. I wanted to tell everybody right away, but Lexi didn't. She just wanted to keep it to herself for a while. I don't really see the point, but she's my baby and I gotta make her happy. So you know you got to keep this under wraps. I just thought some good news would break up this basketball funk."

"Wow, man, you're gonna be a father. That's deep. It's cool, I'll keep it under wraps."

"Yeah, Lexi would kill me. I think she's gonna tell everybody soon. She won't have a choice in a minute."

"Well, it doesn't make up for the game, but at least we got something to celebrate. Congrats, man," Anthony said as he reached over to shake Chris's hand.

Capri kicked off the sheets after tossing and turning half the night. Although she was in bed by nine, she had only gotten about two hours of sleep. Several hours later, she finally heard Anthony come in. After a few minutes she heard his footsteps in the room, causing the floor to vibrate slightly. She smelled cigar smoke as he pulled off his shirt. *Anthony doesn't smoke cigars. What's up with that? Is that alcohol I smell? He doesn't even drink!* She didn't stir because she didn't want him to know she was awake, but she was steaming.

After a quick shower, he climbed in bed, assuming she was asleep. Her Spirit was telling her to just wait until the morning, but she couldn't help it. "Where have you been?" Her cold voice sliced through the dark, still air.

"Nowhere really, I played golf and got a bite to eat with Chris. You can call Lexi and ask her," he said with his back turned away from her.

"Oh, so now I have to call Lexi to find out where my husband's been? What's wrong with you? You've never ignored my calls."

"Capri, I'm tired and definitely not in the mood for this. You can ask me whatever you want in the morning, okay?" He pulled the covers tighter around him.

"No, it's not okay." She leaned over and turned on the light.

"Capri, I said I don't want to talk right now." He pulled the sheet over his bald head.

"Well *I* do." She wasn't backing down. "Anthony, you've been so rude and disrespectful. I haven't done a thing to you."

"Look, baby, this isn't even about you, alright?" He pulled the sheet back and faced her.

"Oh, it *is* about me. I've watched you work hard this season. I've been very supportive. I knew this was a sacrifice, but it's not the end of the world. This is not like you, Anthony, what's going on?"

"Capri, you're trippin'." He rolled away from her and closed his eyes.

"Anthony, look at me. Don't you care that I'm upset? You leave the house; I don't know where you're going . . . You come home smelling like cigars and alcohol. Where have you been, Anthony? What have you been doing?" She pulled on his firm shoulder.

He finally sat up. "Okay, Capri, I asked *nicely* if this could wait until the morning. I just want to get a good night's rest. Look, it's not always about you, okay?" He took a deep breath, rubbing his head. He finally looked in her eyes. "Maybe I don't feel like explaining myself. And yes, you've been supportive, but it's not like you had to sacrifice a whole lot to do it. Capri, I've *always* catered to you . . . since the day I met you. So your support should be a given. It's the least you can do. But if it's too much to ask, trust me, any woman would trade places with you in a minute."

"Are you *serious*? So what are you trying to say? I was

perfectly fine with my law career. You know I don't care about all this crap . . ." Her forehead wrinkled as she watched his face.

"*Please.* Maybe in the beginning you didn't. But once you got around Missy, you seemed to fall right in line."

"Anthony, what in the world are you talking about?" She grabbed the blanket and pulled it to her chest like a shield.

"I'm just saying, you seemed to adjust to this lifestyle pretty well. The last time I checked there was Gucci and Prada all up in your closet. Y'all live in the Galleria and have spa day every other weekend . . ."

"You were the one begging me to meet the other wives. You know that's where that stuff came from. I'm still the same old Capri. Anyway, we're talking about you."

"Yeah, you're right. It *is* about me. You are absolutely right. Capri, can you for once take care of me?"

"What are you talking about?"

He sat up. "You should understand what your man needs without me having to tell you. I'm the one always hugging and kissing on you. I'm always there for you, Capri. Maybe you're not aware, but sometimes you can be a little into self."

"Did you just call me selfish? You gotta be kidding me. Besides, you know I've never been a touchy feely person." She was wide awake now.

"Except . . ."

"What?"

"Except when you want to make love."

"I can't believe I'm even having this conversation.

Okay, so if we're being honest—and we are being honest aren't we?—"

He raised his eyebrows slightly but didn't speak.

"Well, why are you hiding that stuff in your shoe? Your back's been fine for over a year now."

He rubbed his eyes, then the bridge of his nose. "What? Capri you're trippin'. What makes you think I'm taking something now?"

"Well, are you?" She crossed her arms.

"Capri, I'm not gonna try to explain anything tonight. Besides, if you'd paid attention you'd know."

"Anthony, I'm your wife and I asked a question." He still didn't answer her. "You know what? Fine. I'm only asking 'cause I care. But whatever; I don't need this." She threw off the covers and was headed for the door.

"Wait, alright." He sat up on the edge of the bed. "Capri, you know, if you'd look up from that computer long enough, you'd realize other things are going on outside your world. Did you even know your best friend's pregnant? And tonight I had a drink just to celebrate with Chris."

The words electrocuted her, causing her to stop at the edge of the doorway. She couldn't believe what she'd heard. *Where was all this coming from?* She turned around abruptly. "Lexi? She—she's having a baby?"

"Yeah, that's right. She's pregnant. I thought as a woman you'd pick up on something like that."

Capri couldn't form any words with her mouth. She walked out of their bedroom to seek solace in the guest room. She felt as though someone had punched her in the stomach. Her insides churned. *Why didn't Lexi tell me? And why is my husband acting so crazy?*

After Capri left, Anthony slammed his body back on the bed. "Aw man, Chris is gonna kill me." He knew he'd messed up, in more ways than one.

CHAPTER THIRTY-SIX

Coming Clean

"Thank God it's Friday" could not begin to express Capri's emotions. It had taken everything she had not to ask Lexi if she was pregnant the entire week. When she walked into her house that afternoon, she immediately noticed a note on the entryway table. Anthony had gone to play pool at his teammate's house. She was a little relieved, since tension still lingered between them.

She dropped her briefcase on the floor. *I will not pick it back up until Monday,* she vowed. The house seemed so much larger when Anthony was gone. She walked upstairs and threw on her sweatpants and law school T-shirt. She came back down, grabbed some leftover pizza, and went into the living room. After devouring half the pie, she leaned back on the sofa.

As she lay there, she started thinking back to law school. *Boy, I thought once I'd made it through that, life would be smooth sailing. I never pictured myself married, much less to someone like Anthony. How could he forget how much it took for me to give my heart away? He knows none of this material crap matters to me.* Her eyes watered, but she kept any tears from flowing. She wrapped her arms around her body, hugging herself.

She wanted to get past her pride and call Lexi. She tried to quiet her thoughts, but Anthony's stinging comments invaded her mind. *He's taking things out on me, the person who cares about him the most. I'm the one who has his back. Have I really changed? What's wrong with treating myself every now and then? Am I selfish? I've worked hard most of my life and never given myself permission to enjoy anything.*

After dozing off Capri woke up two hours later. Anthony still hadn't made it back. She stood and walked over to a shelf and looked at all the pictures. There was one of Capri and all the girls on her wedding day. Next to it was another of Capri and Lexi at their law school graduation. She picked it up and smiled. After setting the frame down, she walked toward the phone. She grabbed it and dialed quickly. *I really need to talk to my best friend.*

CHAPTER THIRTY-SEVEN

B.F.F.

"Capri?"

"Hey girl, what are you doing?"

"Um, watching a movie with Chris." I pulled away from him and sat on the side of the bed. "Where are you going?" Chris whispered as he grabbed my arm.

I waved at him and walked out to the guest bedroom and future nursery.

"You don't sound like yourself. What's going on?" I said as I sat in the rocking chair.

Capri took a deep breath. "Lex, you're my girl and we've been through a lot. I know there's a good reason . . ."

"What are you talking about?"

"Why didn't you tell me you're pregnant?"

I took a deep swallow. *Chris.* "Umm, where'd you hear that?"

"Anthony. We were arguing. He accused me of being selfish. That's when he said I didn't even know my own best friend was pregnant and he's right." I heard her voice tremble and then a few sniffles.

"Capri, Capri, it had nothing to do with you. Capri!"

"I'm sorry, girl; I'm just a little upset. Anthony's been acting like a fool since that game. I'm sorry, Lexi, if I haven't been there for you as much. You have to believe nothing would destroy our friendship," she said as she wiped the tear that managed to escape from her eye.

"Girl, it's not you. I guess I'm still trying to believe all this is happening to me. I was so used to things not working out; when God started answering my prayers, I guess fear got the best of me. I'm embarrassed to say, I just didn't want to jinx anything. Some kinda faith I have, huh?"

"Lexi, you've been through a lot, I'm a witness. I sort of know what you are feeling. It took me forever to open up to Anthony. It had been so long since I even thought about a relationship. But you talked me into giving him a chance. Lexi, he's a good man. He's always treated me like a queen. And now that he's going through his own trial, well, I'm not sure I'm doing all that I can to be there for him."

"Capri, don't believe that crap. Just give him some time. He'll shake all this off. Men like to put the guilt trip on you every now and then. He's a big baby . . . they all are."

"Umm, you may be right. Well, I know one thing; Mr. Stanton better get himself together. It took everything I had not to go off on him."

I started laughing and Capri joined in. Then I said, "Girl, I'm trying to imagine Anthony towering over you while you're fussing at him."

"You know I fuss at him too. I'm from the East Coast; don't let the business suit fool you."

"Yeah, yeah, yeah. Girl, I remember when you used to threaten folks in law school, trying to be all serious."

"I must be getting soft. Anyway, back to you. Lexi, I can't believe you're pregnant! I mean, this is so amazing! How do you feel? I'm mean, what does it feel like inside?"

"Girl, I can't begin to describe it. I'm still in a daze. It was *so* not planned! And I'm terrified. I haven't told anyone but Chris and my dad." *Okay, so I lied just a little. But if she knew I told Angel before her . . . but so what? Dang, this is ridiculous.*

"So, I know I don't even have to ask who the god-mother's gonna be?"

"Missy," I said and started laughing.

"Funny."

"Well, you did sell our friendship out for her," I said as I got up from the rocker.

"Girl, please. There's no comparison. I just didn't know any of the wives; she sort of schooled me on all this NBA crap. Out of all of them, she's been the coolest," Capri said.

"She's alright. Anyway girl, you know we're going to have to wait as long as possible before we tell Jewel, right?"

"That goes without saying. Lexi, I can't believe I'm gonna be a godmother."

"You'll make a good one too. So, where's Anthony now?"

"He's out."

"Hmm. Well, you know what? I think we need to say a little prayer before we go. We gotta keep these men on the altar."

"I hear you. I knew I could count on you to break off some prayer."

"Oh *no*, sister, you'll be praying too. If you plan on making it through your marriage you're gonna have to learn to cover it in prayer more often. It's time for you to grow up in the Spirit, girl. Prayer is one of the greatest weapons in marriage. Without it, you won't have a fighting chance."

"I hear you. Yeah, it is time for me to step it up. I'm ready when you are." I started to speak.

Father, I thank You and praise You for all You are. You are Lord over everything. Lord, I thank You for the gift of friendship and I thank You for the gift of love. God, I ask that You would bless these marriages. I pray that You would give us wisdom, guidance, and understanding. I pray that You would continue to anoint these men to be head of the household. Where they are weak, make them strong. Father, we ask that You would help us to love them according to 1 Corinthians 13. God, I pray that we always have a Spirit of agreement with our husbands. Show us our role at every season of this marriage. Give us discernment and help us to prepare homes where angels love to dwell. Lord God, I pray that You would cover our marriages in the Blood of Jesus. Lord, I pray especially for Anthony, that You would not allow a spirit of negativity, disappointment, or failure to overtake him. Let him find peace and encouragement in Your Word. Let him know what Your will is for his life. Lord, let us always seek Your will in all things. We will be careful to give You the honor and praise at all times. In Jesus's name we pray, Amen.

"CHRIS!!!" I yelled as I walked back toward our bedroom.

"Yeah, baby," he said, still focused on the television.

"*Swee-tie,* that was Capri," I said as I sat on the bed.

"Um-hmm."

I leaned over and snuggled up to his ear. "Did you tell Anthony I was pregnant?"

"Uh-huh, yeah I kinda did." He turned to look at me with those puppy dog eyes.

I punched him in the arm. "I can't believe you. I mean, I specifically asked you not to do that. Now Capri's not speaking to me. She's extremely angry. Because of you our friendship is pretty much over."

"What? That's ridiculous."

"It's all your fault." I fell on my face and started to cry.

"Baby, baby, I'm sorry." He shook my shoulders.

I jumped on him and started softly punching him. "Just kidding! But you know you were wrong to do that."

"Baby, I'm sorry. It's just that I was trying to get Anthony in a good mood. He was down last weekend. He's excited about being a godparent. I'm excited too. I'm tired of holding it in."

"Well, I know you meant well . . ."

"Yeah, yeah," he said as he started kissing my neck.

"Don't even think about that," I said as I slid out from under him and leaned back on the headboard.

"Ah, I can't get just a little lovin'? Man, I hope this isn't a sign of things to come."

"Maybe, maybe not. But because of your big mouth, you gets none tonight."

CHAPTER THIRTY-EIGHT

Birthday Sweeps

I don't know how I get talked into these things, I thought as Angel, Jewel, Jermane, and I headed down the escalator of Crate & Barrel. I never come to shop at Highland Village. All my kitchen stuff comes from Wal-Mart or Target, and I think it's just as cute. But I do have to say, it was a nice change of pace, and they did have some nice things in there.

"Okay, I just want to peek in Anthropologie," Jewel said. Angel and I rolled our eyes behind her back.

"I just don't get that store," Jermane said as we walked out. "I guess it's vintage chic, but it does nothing for me." She looked completely uninterested from the time we walked in. I was really focused on a cute multicolored Tracy Reese frock, until I peeked at the price. Angel and I looked at each other and shouted "eBay" at the same time.

Jewel turned around and gave us that "I can't take you anywhere" look.

"So where we gonna eat?" I asked, hoping this little excursion was coming to a close.

"I don't know. RA Sushi is close. We can go there."

"No, I need *real* food," I said. *My stomach is getting nauseous even at the mention of sushi.* "How about Grand Lux?"

"Yeah, we can do that," Angel said.

"Doesn't matter to me, I'm ready to go," Jermane chimed in.

Once we got to Grand Lux and the food was ordered, we immediately launched into birthday plans. "So Angel, yours is coming up next. What do you wanna do?" I asked, eyeing the cheesecake being served to the couple at the next table.

"I don't know. I'm sort of through with over-the-top birthday events," she said as she sipped on her water.

"Girl, that's because your behind is getting old!" Jewel started laughing and patting the table with the palm of her hand. "Now me, I live for birthdays. It's like the world is saying 'Jewel we're so glad you're here.' "

"Don't make me hurt you," Angel said. "I guess right now, I'm trying to simplify my life. The other day I walked by my closet and noticed there was barely any room for another piece of clothing. I just started pulling out clothes to give away. I feel like I'm just hoarding stuff. I mean, how many Chloe bags and Manolos does a girl need to have?" She pursed her lips to blow a little air on her coffee.

Jewel turned her head slightly and focused on Angel.

She grabbed the table. "Girl, don't you give away a thing until I get to sort through it."

"Down, girl, down," I said as I patted Jewel's hand. "Hey, why don't you have one of those clothes-swapping parties for your birthday?"

"Yes, what a fabulous idea," Jewel exclaimed, almost jumping out of her seat.

"I was talking to Angel."

"That's not a bad idea . . . a party with a purpose. Whatever is left, I'll donate to Dress for Success and some other charities," Angel said as she buttered a slice of bread.

"And please, we *have* to invite Missy, you know she's got some good stuff to give away."

Angel rolled her eyes and shook her head. "Anyway, Jewel, feel free to plan the birthday festivities."

"Gotcha. We can do it the end of May. A week after your birthday." In less than two seconds her BlackBerry was in hand and she was typing away.

"Okay, I'll supply the guest list and the place."

"Angel, again, please remember to invite people that have good stuff," Jewel said, waving her spoon.

"Jewel . . . it's *my* party."

"Yeah, yeah," she said, scrolling through e-mails and typing.

"Well, I have plenty of clothes to donate to charity," Jermane said.

"Okay again, let's make this clear, *nothing* will leave the room, until I've gone through every item." Jewel looked around the table into each person's eyes.

"Okay, Jewel we got it," I said.

"With that settled, on to more pressing matters," Jewel said as she sipped her raspberry tea. "I have an issue that's been weighing on me, but I need to get the advice of my trusty sister circle." She grabbed Angel's and Jermane's hands. "It's Kevin's ex."

"So what else is new?" I said as I munched on a bread-stick.

"Well, this is serious, I mean, she's taken it to the next level. Homegirl is over two months pregnant."

I almost choked on my bread.

"Lexi, you okay?" Jermane patted me on my back. "Yeah, fine," I said, though I still felt a piece of bread in my throat. "It's not . . ."

"No, it's not Kevin's. He'd be dead by now."

"Wow, that's deep," Angel said.

"Yeah, it's freaking me out. I've already threatened Kevin. He better not even act like he needs to be there for her. She's got a man."

"Not trying to judge, but wasn't she all up in the church, singing in the choir and whatnot?"

"Yes Lexi, you are judging," Angel chided.

"Yeah, that's what I said," Jewel added.

"Hmm, I'm gonna have to think on this one." *Whoa, the drama never ends. God, we need a life manual. Oh that's right, You gave us one—the Bible.*

"Well, all I can say is you really need to put your foot down with Kevin and establish some boundaries." Angel stirred some Equal into her coffee.

"Thank God, I have never had to deal with baby mother's drama," Jermane interjected.

"Anyway," Jewel broke in, "I had a long talk with Kevin

and he knows how I feel. I just need you all to lift up this situation in prayer. She said the father is going to be there for her." She watched their expressions.

"Um-hmm." Angel was unconvinced.

"Oh no, I see trouble written all over this one," Jermane added. "I'm glad Rex knows how to act. Thank God I've never had to deal with anything like this."

"Jewel, I'm sure God's got it all under control." I noticed our waitress coming with our food and got a bit distracted.

"Is that all you can say? That's your answer for everything."

I shrugged my shoulders and kept on eating my bread.

"Well, I just can't take her anymore. I had to lay her out one day when she came over. I told her she needed to respect me and to stop manipulating Kevin. I don't know. I just don't trust her." Jewel's voice went from a strong, confident tone to a low softer voice.

"It's gonna be alright, girl. God's got it. What's done is done now. But it doesn't have to affect what you and Kevin have. The boy loves you to death. On that note, I'll be right back, gotta make a bathroom run!"

"Yeah, I don't know why that boy puts up with you. Then again Kevin's special, so y'all are made for each other," Angel said and laughed.

"Well, it's time to go. I got a party to plan," Jewel said as she removed her napkin from her lap and stood up.

CHAPTER THIRTY-NINE

What Happens in Vegas . . .

*K*evin quickly looked around the billiard hall before he refocused on the pool table. "So, fellas, check this out. Jewel's been really tripping lately. I mean she knows I'm faithful but she still can nag a brother to death," he said as he tried to line up his shot.

"Man, don't they all? After a while, I just tune Lexi out," Chris said. "Kevin, take the shot."

"Don't rush me." He leaned over the pool table, then stood up several times trying to assess his next move. "Why you been so quiet?" Octavio nodded toward Anthony reclining on the nearby lounge chair.

"I don't know, I was just thinking Capri's been tripping too."

"You know how it is when they start talking to each other. It's like they have a meeting and decide all together what the issue of the week is going to be."

"That's the one thing I can say about Jermane, she doesn't really get other people involved in our problems," Rex called out from his chair.

"That's what you think." Kevin lifted his pool cue from the table and placed it on the floor.

"Anyway, I heard they were going to have a party for Angel's birthday at the end of May, so you know they'll be stirred up then.

"Next month?" Anthony asked as he sprang up.

"Yeah, man, the last weekend. I'm taking Angel out the week before and she mentioned what the ladies were going to do.

"Aw, that's perfect. Fellas, my boy Kelvin Jeffries is having his annual White Party in Las Vegas that weekend," Anthony said.

"Ole boy from the Bulls? Man, you know it's going to be a gold digger function fo sho'. You tryin' to get us killed," Kevin said.

"Y'all know me. I can't remember the last time I went to a real party. It's just a little getaway. A weekend away with the fellas. It's not like we don't know how to act. Besides, it ain't like you got no money, what you worried about?" Anthony watched for their reaction.

"Hey, you don't know what I got in my bank account. Why do you think Jewel married me?" Kevin puffed his chest out.

"I don't know, man. You know I'm definitely not down with any clubs or parties." Chris shook his head slowly.

"C'mon man, Anthony said it's just going to be a getaway. My man needs some relief. I'm definitely down," Kevin said.

"You know you can't go anywhere unless you ask Jewel's permission." Chris started laughing and slapped Anthony's hand.

"Aw, man, forgetchu." Kevin waved his hand. "It's not like Lexi doesn't have you on a leash."

"Hey, I don't have a problem checking in, 'cause I'm not doing anything wrong." Chris folded his arms.

"Wait a few more years, dude," Kevin said. "G. Bush, what's up, you down or what?" Kevin lifted his head and looked at Rex.

"I don't know. It's just not something I would normally do. But lately, I have been needing to de-stress. I mean, cases are starting to run together and I'm not feeling the law right now. I do need a break. I don't gamble, but I'm sure I can find something to do."

Kevin leaned over Anthony. "Pssst. I knew that Negro wasn't gonna go."

"There's got to be a nice golf course in the area. Yeah, yes, I'm in." Rex's words built momentum as he racked the pool balls.

"Man, you don't go to Vegas to golf." Kevin frowned.

"Well, I guess there's nothing wrong with a little male bonding," Chris suggested.

"Yeah, we can take a limo to the airport and ride on my boy's jet," Anthony said. "This'll be good," he added as he smacked fists with Rex and Kevin. "I could use a break."

"I feel you, I feel you. And they can't make no excuses, because they got plans!" Kevin ran over and tried to bump chests with Anthony, but almost fell down.

Octavio started laughing, "Yo, dude almost fell!" He was pointing at Kevin as he regained his balance.

"Yeah, yeah, let's see you get away from Angel. She got you on lock, dude. Every five minutes we got to hear some scripture, dude. When we go to Vegas, man, leave some of that at home," Kevin warned.

"Man, you trippin'." Octavio got up to grab a pool cue.

"So look, we need to make a final decision tonight. Everybody's in, right? The women are doing their thang. The menfolk are just getting away. Nice innocent fun. So I got a yes from Kevin, I knew that fool would be in. Got my man Rex on board. Alright, alright. Chris? You know if you come the women will really know it's legit." Anthony stuck his fist out and Chris hit the bottom of his fist on top of Anthony's.

"Octavio, you in? Do it for me . . . for the championship I *could* have had."

"Man, I guess so." Octavio's mouth was saying yes, but his Spirit was saying something different.

"That's it. It's on. No backing out either. But remember, what happens in Vegas . . . stays in Vegas."

CHAPTER FORTY

Can I Go to Vegas?

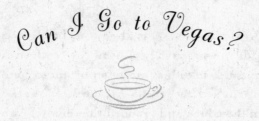

Take One

"No, Chris."

"But, Lexi, all my boys are going and you ladies will be celebrating Angel's birthday that weekend anyway. I never go away with the fellas." He followed her to the living room like a little kid.

She stopped in her tracks and he almost ran into her. "Boy, are you crazy? I'm with child. I could go into labor, anything could happen while you're trouncing around Las Vegas doing God knows what!"

"Lexi, do you have to be so dramatic? It's way too soon for you to go into labor. You'll have at least six months to go." He closed his eyes and opened them, waiting for me to respond.

"I'm not. How could you want to go to Vegas at a time like this? You should want to be with me to experience every second of the pregnancy." She grabbed his arms and her eyes began to tear up.

Dang, she's laying it on thick. I guess this is when the hormones start to kick in.

"Well, all I have to say is when your baby grows up and asks about the pregnancy, I'll be sure to let your child know his daddy felt it was more important to go to Vegas— aka 'Sin City'—than be with his mother." Lexi dropped down on the couch and grabbed the remote.

Chris plopped down beside her and placed his head on her shoulder. "Lexi, it's *one weekend.*"

"Um-hmm, whatever."

Take Two

"Boy, have you lost your mind? What could you possibly want to do in Vegas that you can't do right here in Houston? I know. You want to run around with some women. I knew it; you're tired of me already," Jewel said as she crossed her arms and turned her head away from Kevin.

Oh brother. He grabbed her chin with his fingers so he could look in her eyes. "Babe, it's just a simple little trip. Anthony's teammate has this event every year. It's just a little male bonding. Baby, I'm with you all the time. Whoa, wait, I didn't mean it like that."

"Oh, so now it's punishment to be with me?" She watched his face, but he didn't speak right away.

"Baby, you know it's not like that." He sighed deeply and then rubbed his forehead. "You know what? I don't have to ask your permission. I'm going and that's it!"

Several seconds of silence passed. "Okay."

"Okay what?" he said with a frown.

"I said okay, but Kevin Eastland, I will hop on a plane and show up wherever you are if I even think you are acting a fool. You better keep your cell phone on and answer when I call!"

Take Three

"Jermane, honey, there's a golf tournament and conference in Las Vegas I want to go to," Rex said.

"Okay, honey, that's nice," Jermane said on her way to Tootsies.

Take Four

"Octavio, I already heard it through the grapevine. But I promise you, you won't have a good time. You certainly don't need my permission . . ." Angel said as she continued to stretch her legs.

Octavio bent over and stretched out his arms. *Wow, that was easy.* "Well, baby, don't forget we'll celebrate your birthday the week before."

"Sounds fine with me," she said as they started their daily jog. Despite her apparent dismissal of the issue, Angel still barely said anything during their two-mile run.

Take Five

"What did you say was going on in Las Vegas?" Capri eyed Anthony as he was on the bedroom floor doing his daily push-ups. She was a bit distracted by his bulging biceps. She pulled her terry-cloth robe tighter, then began to sweep her hair into a ponytail.

"You know my boy Jeffries. He's throwing his annual all-white party on Saturday and a golf tournament that Sunday. Just fun, babe." He jumped up after finishing his push-ups, breathing a little hard.

"Uh-huh," she said as she walked toward the bath-room. "And why all of a sudden do you want to go this year?"

"I don't know. I just need to blow off some steam." Anthony walked into the bathroom and grabbed her waist from behind and kissed her. She looked at the reflection in the mirror of the two of them, then turned around to face him as she grabbed his hands.

"Anthony, what's really going on? You don't party. That's one of the things you said when I first met you. I felt so comfortable with you for that reason. I don't want to have to wonder what you're doing in a city like Las Vegas."

"Babe, you have to trust me to do the right thing. I would never do anything to hurt or embarrass you. But I need to get away." He kissed her on the forehead.

She looked down, and then up into his eyes. He took his hand and slid it through her ponytail, then pulled her toward him for a kiss. "Hmmm, it's been a while since I've had those lips," he said as he rocked her a bit in his arms.

He kissed her again. She left the conversation in the bathroom and decided to take full advantage of the moment. Regardless of his crazy Vegas notion, it was the first time in a while that she felt like she was kissing the real Anthony Stanton, with all of his passion and sincerity. Capri didn't want the moment to end because of some silly trip that might not even happen.

One Woman's Trash . . .

I looked around at the festive décor and wondered how Jewel came up with clothing-shaped cookies.

Her clothes-swapping birthday soiree seemed like a good idea after all. She'd managed to transform Angel's condo for another one of her "Fabulous Jewels events." Even though I was looking forward to the festivities, I was missing Chris. He let me know they had landed safely and settled into the hotel in Vegas. I refocused on my punch bowl duties.

"So, Lexi, I wonder what those men are up to. I hated to give in, but I finally told him just to go ahead and go," Jewel said as she finished arranging the skewers on the tray.

"What? You mean *you* didn't fuss at all?" I asked as I added a little more ice to the punch bowl.

"Girl, no. I'm just going to trust that he knows how to act."

"Um-hum. Well, all I can say is I talked to Chris for about an hour before he left. I made him rub my belly to remind him what he has back at home. I can't say that I have a good feeling about this. But he seemed determined to go."

Jewel paused to brush one of her ringlets away from her face. This week she had her curly weave in. "Girl, I can't wait to see what Missy's going to bring."

"Girl, is anything else on your mind besides clothes? Do you even like the girl?" I paused before I brushed a piece of my own hair away from my face.

"Yeah, I mean she was fun at the book club. You're the only one that seems to find something negative to say about her." Jewel dipped a piece of strawberry in the chocolate fondue for a taste.

"What? Please, I haven't given her a second thought."

"Umm-hmm," Jewel said as she arranged her T-shirt-shaped cookies on a serving tray. "Angel's gonna love these."

"Yeah, they are cute. Oh, there's the doorbell." I walked to open the door of Angel's high-rise and in came Capri, Missy, and two of Angel's coworkers, Reyna and Tara.

"Hey, ladies. Let me help you with those." Jewel rushed over and grabbed their shopping bags. She couldn't help snooping in them before she set them down. "Okay, I hope there are tags on everything."

"Where's the guest of honor?" Capri asked, then sat

on the couch and crossed her legs. She looked extra cool in her floor-length patterned sundress.

"Oh, I gave Angel a gift certificate for Isle Pedi-Spa. She should be back soon," I said.

"Ooh, I love that place, my favorite is the chocolate-covered strawberry pedicure," Tara said.

Missy put her hand to her chest. "No, darling, the vanilla latte with the vanilla paraffin dip is heaven."

Jewel was pulling things out of shopping bags to hang them on the rolling racks set up in the living room. "Are we talking about pedicures or food?"

Just then she heard keys opening the door.

"Hey, birthday lady!" Capri ran over and gave Angel a hug. "Girl, you are looking all refreshed."

"I know. I had the most fabulous pedicure, thanks to Lexi. I also had a facial around the corner at Beautique," she said as she patted her face.

"Well, you don't look a day over—"

Angel threw up her hand. "Don't even go there, Jewel. Wow, the place looks so festive." She looked around and saw the beautiful cake and pastel colors. The little miniature shoes and feather boas and other decorative items added to the fashion theme.

Once Angel got settled, she grabbed a plate and joined the other ladies. "So after we eat, we can have a little fun playing dress-up!"

"Not before we give you your gifts," Jewel said.

"That can wait, really. I just want us to relax and have a little girl time." Angel kicked back and started to eat. "Ummm, this is good."

"So what do you think they're doing?" Jewel asked after it got a little quiet.

"Who?" Angel replied.

"You know, the men."

"Girl, I don't know, and I don't care. It's my birthday celebration; I don't have time to worry about what Octavio is doing. We had a nice time last weekend."

Missy reached for some dip. "Well, if it were my husband, I would be right there."

"Dang, girl, you don't let that man breathe," I said.

"That's just me. It's a rough world out there. Girl, I know how good I got it. I'm not trying to give up my lifestyle. Besides I think my husband likes it. I don't hear him complaining."

"Well, Rex said all he wanted to do was play golf," Jermane said as she sipped her tea.

Missy let out a laugh. "Girl, is that what he told you? Yeah, okay."

"Please don't have Jermane getting all freaked out. Rex is old faithful. He doesn't have an ounce of dog in him," Capri said.

"Well, I wouldn't be so sure. No disrespect to you, but Jermane, your man is fine and he *is* a man."

Jermane's eyes got wide. "I know my husband. Trust me, he's faithful."

"Umm-hmm," Missy said. "That's what I said before . . . well, never mind."

"Anyway, this party was a great idea," Reyna said as she cleared her throat and changed the subject. "I came to find something new to add to my wardrobe, we don't have time to gab about some men." She walked over to the racks and started looking through the clothes.

Jermane began to fidget in her chair. She was two minutes from calling Rex to check up on him, but she was going to wait until she could escape to the bathroom later.

"Jewel, I got this first," I said as I picked up a lemon-colored cashmere sweater.

"No, I had it first, besides you can't fit this, it looks a little too small for you."

Oh no she didn't. "Jewel, you are one of my best friends, but I *will* fight you for this sweater."

"Fine, Lexi, I see something else I want anyway." She walked over to the other rack and picked out a Rachel Roy gold satin trench coat. "Omigod! I love this!"

"Yeah, I never wore it. I saw it on *Oprah* and thought I had to have it. I don't have any more room in my closet," Missy said.

"Jermane, where's your stuff?"

Jermane was just sitting there, still looking preoccupied.

"I said, girl, where's your stuff?" Jewel poked her in the side.

"Oh, it's mixed in there. Everything I brought was brand-new. All my stuff still has the tags on it."

"Girl, look at this Luca Luca dress." Angel pulled out the colorful dress and held it to her.

"That's cute, girl," Capri said.

"What do you think about this?" I looked at Capri after I'd donned a fedora and cocked it to the side.

"Mmm, no, just don't think it's you," Capri said, tilting her head.

"I do, I'm gonna keep it. I'm gonna try on this Calvin Klein pencil skirt."

Jewel caught me struggling to zip it. "Girl, that skirt is too tight on you."

"Jewel, be quiet. You don't have to hurt my feelings." I had to play it off.

"Well, she oughta be bigger than that," Capri said. As soon as she let the words fly out of her mouth, she realized she'd said a little too much.

Jewel paused for a minute and looked back at me, but appeared unfazed.

I cut my eyes at Capri. I took off the skirt and ran to the bathroom for the fourth time since I'd been there. On my way back I heard Jermane on the phone with Rex.

"So why haven't you called me? I know you talked to me earlier this morning, but you said you were going golfing. Well, you better call me before you go to this White Party tonight."

Dang, is that how I sound? Jermane is tripping.

After everyone had gotten their share of items and dessert had been served, Missy, Reyna, and Tara left. Then the five of us kicked back like old times.

Angel sat on the floor barefoot. "So I wonder what they're doing? I haven't heard from Octavio."

"I don't know, but something tells me they aren't sitting around thinking about us. We need to put on some music and have some fun!" I said.

"Girl, you're right. We need to do like we used to back in the day."

The next thing I know Jewel had put on the *Emancipation of Mimi* CD.

"Dang, Mariah Carey put her foot in that CD. It's one of the only CDs I lost and went and bought again," Capri said as she got up and started dancing.

"I know that's right!" Jewel said. "You gotta shake it off . . ."

"Go ahead, Jewel!" After a while we completely forgot about Vegas and had our own little party.

CHAPTER FORTY-TWO

VIPs

"Man, I thought you would never stop eating at that buffet," Anthony said as he trimmed up his beard with his razor. "Smooth as a baby's bottom," he said as he felt his face.

"That was some good food. No wonder Las Vegas has some of the fattest people in the world," Kevin said as he slapped a little aftershave on his face.

"It was embarrassing after a while. Doesn't Jewel feed you?" Octavio yelled from the bedroom.

"Man, why are y'all acting like women up in there? I've been ready," Chris yelled from the living room. Chris was still in awe of the spacious suite. He hadn't thought anything could top the ride over on Kelvin Jeffries's private jet.

"Perfection takes some time," Anthony said as he came out of the bathroom. "Where the heck is Rex?"

"Man, I haven't seen him since lunch. That fool's been gone all day. Anybody try to call him?" Kevin said as he dropped on the couch and grabbed the remote.

"Yeah, he called. He's on the way. He said he went to the mall to pick up something to wear."

"Dude had the most luggage . . . never mind," Anthony said. There was a knock on the door.

"I bet that's him now," Kevin said as he opened the door.

"What?" Rex said as he walked in and met their stares. "I told you I needed to go to the mall. Man, they have some nice shops out here."

"I can't believe he came to Vegas to shop, like we don't have a thousand malls in Houston," Chris said. "Oh, I gotta call my baby to see if she's feeling okay."

They all rolled their eyes. "Man, you gonna kill the vibe," Kevin said.

"Go 'head Chris. That's what you need to be doing. Don't listen to Kevin. That Negro stays in the doghouse," Anthony said.

"Well, he needs to do it on the way out, because we are about to head to the Palms," Kevin added as if he was in control of the agenda.

As soon as they reached the top floor their mouths dropped.

"Ah man, I knew it. None of these women have clothes on," Octavio said.

"I know, I know," Chris said, trying to keep his eyes

front and center. Part of him felt ashamed but the other half of him couldn't help but enjoy the scenery.

"Fellas, it's gonna be alright," Anthony reminded them.

"Look at ole girl over there in the white bikini," Kevin said. "Is there a pool up in here or what? Why you so quiet?" He looked at Octavio who was standing still.

"Nothin', nothing man. There's just a lot going on in here." He tried hard not to stare at the tall Latin beauty who had just walked by and winked. "God, please help me. I can't handle this right now." He repeated to himself, "I'm in love with Angel, I love Angel."

Once they got to the VIP area, bottles of Moët and Cristal started flowing.

"We need to make a toast," Anthony said. Although none of them normally drank, they each had a glass raised. "To my brothers . . . work hard and play hard."

After he took a sip, Anthony noticed a woman with shapely long legs appear in the VIP area. He stared for a moment. "Michaela?" he uttered.

"Anthony?" As she walked over to him, his mouth was still open a bit. He stood up, kissed her on the cheek, and grabbed her hand.

"What are you doing here?" he said, still holding her hand. He tried not to stare, but she hadn't changed at all from their college days, even though it'd been years since they'd seen each other. Her layered hair fell below her shoulders. Her skin was creamy and her voluptuous lips were moist with gloss. She wore a white kimono-style minidress with stiletto sandals. She was dripping with diamond hoop earrings and bracelets and wearing a huge diamond ring.

"Oh, I'm here on business. I do marketing for an apparel company and we're trying to promote some of our items. We have a contract with Kelvin and some of his teammates. I've been coming to this event for the past three years and I've never seen you here." She smiled and batted her extra-long eyelashes at him.

"I, um. We just decided to come." *Boy did that sound stupid.* "Umm, you want to join us?"

She looked around the cushioned booth and noticed all the men staring at her.

"Oh, I'm sorry. These are my friends from Houston, Chris, Kevin, Octavio, and that's Rex." They each reached out to shake her hand. She nodded and smiled.

"Michaela and I went to undergrad together." He tried to put his hand over his wedding band, but he remembered it too late. He knew she'd already seen it.

"Well, I gotta see a few people I know, but I would love to catch up. Gotta schmooze a bit, you know? You gonna be around for a while?" She smiled again and touched his arm lightly as she awaited his response.

She always got me with that smile. "Oh, yeah. Not going anywhere." He felt his phone vibrate. It scared him, causing him to spill his drink a little. "Oh, sorry about that, almost got it on you," he said as he quickly composed himself.

"No, don't worry about it. We'll catch up. It was good seeing you." She kissed him on the cheek. "Really good." She finally let go of his hand.

As soon as she walked away his friends rushed him. "Man, who was that? She had it going on," Kevin said.

"Man, we used to mess around back in undergrad. She's cool. She was the one that got away, I guess. I messed up," Anthony said. "Okay, fellas, show's over," he said as he snapped back into reality.

"Okay man, you're supposed to be the strong one, talking about this as just a night of innocent fun," Chris reminded him.

"Yeah, an innocent night of fun," Anthony said. He still could smell a trail of her perfume. "Yeah, yeah Chris," he said, fully aware now. "It's about the fellas tonight. Don't even trip, it's under control," he said as he refocused his attention on his boys.

Octavio was shaking his head. Rex just shrugged, then looked around, and Kevin started whistling. The music started pumping up. "Upgrade ya . . ." Once they heard the beat, they decided to leave the VIP area to mingle.

CHAPTER FORTY-THREE

Revelation

"Okay y'all I feel old," Angel said. All the ladies were in her bedroom. "I can't believe I have several gray hairs coming in."

"Girl, please, my mother was prematurely gray. It's not a big deal. Just get some hair dye," Jermane said. She got up and looked in the mirror. She turned around slightly to inspect her hips and thighs.

"Jermane please, you don't have an ounce of fat. You really make me sick," I said.

"Yeah, and she doesn't even have to work out," Capri added, as she rolled over on her side.

"That's not true," Jermane said as she sat back on the bed. "My energy level isn't the same."

"Ladies, this is a part of the process. We have to work a little harder, to be this beautiful," Jewel said.

"Yeah, this is true," I agreed. "It's just not fair, though.

I don't know why God designed some of the things the way he did."

"I'm thinking about doing that diet that Janet Jackson did. I can't believe she lost all that weight," Jewel said as she pinched the side of her stomach.

"Jewel, please, you would evaporate," Angel said.

"Well, I just have this paranoia about weight. Want to do it with me, Lexi? No offense, but you have picked up some weight."

"For the love of God, Jewel, I'm pregnant!"

She jumped on the bed. "Omigod! I knew it, I knew it."

Jermane ran over and yanked me up from where I was sitting. "Lexi, is it true? Oh sweetie, that's wonderful."

For the next twenty minutes I was bombarded with all kinds of questions *and* showered with all kinds of sister-love. I was glad I finally let the cat out of the bag to everyone. I felt like I might need four godmothers.

CHAPTER FORTY-FOUR

High Rollers

It was close to 1 a.m. Chris and Octavio had spent most of the night sitting in the VIP area. Rex had disappeared again. Kevin was busy eating and taking in the scenery, and Anthony and Michaela were talking again. They'd found a couch and sitting area outside on the balcony and gotten comfortable.

"So how'd you end up getting into this business?" he asked as he leaned back to get comfortable.

"Well," she crossed her legs. Anthony could not help but glance at them. "This is my husband's company. You remember I majored in fashion merchandising, but marketing sort of comes natural for me." She shook the loose wave away from her face.

"Um. So where's this husband now?" Anthony asked. *Darn, that sounds so predictable.*

"Working in New York. He stays busy. Typical Type A personality."

"So he lets you run around the streets of Vegas alone."

"He trusts me. Besides I'm a big girl," she said as she licked her lips. "What about you? Where's wifey?" She raised her eyebrows.

"Home. Other than games, I don't get away much. This was one of my first trips with my boys since I've been married."

"Yeah, I can tell. You all looked so stiff. Well at least I helped ward off some of the gold diggers."

"Yeah. You sure did, at least for a little while." He winked his eye.

"I've done my deed for the night. Your wife's a lucky lady. Well, Anthony Stanton, I'm getting ready to call it a night."

Before he knew it he'd jumped up to grab her hand. "You're gonna be okay, right? Do you need me to get you a cab or anything?" No, that was not the right thing to say. He was surprised at himself.

"No, no. I have a few friends still here. But perhaps we can stay in touch. Maybe we can do some business together." She reached in her purse for a business card. Right before she walked off, she grabbed a pen and wrote something on the back. When she placed it in his hand, he stood there speechless.

He realized she'd given him a room key and her room information on the back of her card. He shoved the items in his pants pocket. He rubbed the back of his neck, then his face. "Wow, this is wild." He reached in his pocket again and felt his cellphone. He pulled it out and noticed four missed calls from Capri. "It's all good, I haven't done anything," he thought. But he wondered why he was feeling guilty.

CHAPTER FORTY-FIVE

Lay Your Head on My Pillow

nthony cleared his throat and felt his chest. He rolled over and felt the other side of the bed. His throat was extremely dry. He didn't sit up right away. He just stayed there with his eyes closed. He noticed the clock on the stand. 4:30 a.m. He noticed it was still dark outside. As soon as he moved a little more he heard a sigh. It was coming to him. He wasn't in Houston and Capri was not the woman next to him. He quickly rolled over on his back and his eyes sprang open. He wanted to jump up, turn on the light, and run. *Oh crap.*

Anthony was paralyzed, unsure of what to do. Then he felt Michaela snuggle under him.

"Umm," she purred.

I'm stuck. Darn. In the midst of his panic, he noticed how warm and comfortable her body felt. She had on a large T-shirt, so he didn't feel all her skin, but it was her legs that did it for him. He wrapped his hands around her waist and allowed his hand to touch her leg slightly. *How'd I get here?* Then he remembered the bottle of champagne that was left in the living room of her suite. "Two old friends." That's how it all started.

She moved and grabbed his hand. She wrapped it tightly around her. He had to admit, it felt so right. But then he thought, "I'm kidding myself, since when does sin ever feel bad?"

She locked her fingers in his hand and brought his hand to her leg.

Oh no. Despite his thoughts he followed her lead. She rolled over and it was clear she was fully awake. She took her hand and traced his lips and finally reached up to kiss him.

Anthony didn't do anything. He didn't kiss her back, he didn't move her hands. All he could see was Capri's face. Then all of a sudden he grabbed her and kissed her back.

"*D*ude, where is he? Capri has called me twice. I can't be lying to her," Kevin said. "Soon I'm gonna get in trouble."

"Man, calm down. I don't know what he could have been thinking about," Chris said as he paced the living room floor. "I told you this was a bad idea. We couldn't just hang out in Houston. We had to come to the mecca of sin."

"Okay, let's not overreact. You have to admit, we had a pretty good time and most of us have been acting like we got some sense," Kevin said.

Rex poured himself some coffee. "What the heck are

we gonna do? It's still early, so maybe Capri will think he's still asleep.

A few seconds later, the door to the suite opened and Anthony walked in wearing his clothes from the night before. "Don't ask me jack." He walked past them and slammed the door.

"You go in there," Rex said to Chris.

"Naw man, I'm gonna wait a little while." Chris went and sat on the bar stool. "The man said he doesn't want to talk."

"I think we should give him his space," Octavio said. "Boy, I'm glad I didn't drink anything last night."

"Well, I'm headed to the buffet. A man can't deal with all this on an empty stomach," Kevin said as he walked out the door.

When Anthony walked out of his room after about two hours, he thought he was alone in the suite. He'd finally called Capri and told her he forgot to charge his phone. That was the first time he remembered lying to his wife. He went to the bathroom and when he came out, he noticed Chris was out on the balcony. "Darn, I thought I was alone," he said. He walked over to the glass doors and went outside. He sat down on the chaise lounge next to Chris.

"What's up, man?" Chris said, not trying to bring anything up. "This is a nice view."

Anthony was quiet. He was starting to feel the hunger pangs kick in. "So, I know you want to know what's going on with me."

"I'm not gonna say a word. You want to talk, we can talk. If you don't, that's on you, bro." Chris was still looking at the clear sky.

Anthony took a deep breath. "Chris, I don't know what happened. I saw her, all these old things started coming up from the past. All I knew is I wanted to spend some time with her. When we were together in undergrad, I left on a really bad note. I needed some closure."

"But Anthony, dude, y'all aren't back in college. You have a wife."

"Chris, man, don't you think I know that? I would never, ever hurt Capri."

"I don't think anybody ever intends to cheat on their spouse." Chris paused. "I take that back, some people out there have no respect for the institution of marriage. They let all kinds of foul Spirits come up in their relationship. Anthony, man, you got to keep things tight. You can't even play around. You know Satan is always looking for an open door. He'll dress it up right and the next thing you know, he will have a stranglehold on you."

"Chris, man, I know you're right. You know I have a strong relationship with God, but there is so much temptation. I've been slacking. I know how much you and Lexi pray together; maybe Capri and I need to do a little more of that."

"Anthony, all I can say is you have to be the spiritual leader of the home. You can't afford to slack off. You know how much the enemy fights a marriage between two Christian people? Do you know how powerful you all could be? It's extra work, but you gotta keep things covered. God entrusted you with this relationship."

"Chris, I know everything you are telling me is true. I can't put myself in a position like this again. Just one drink and the next thing you know we had knocked off a bottle of champagne. You know my system couldn't take all that."

"So?"

"What?" Anthony said.

"Did you?" Chris looked Anthony straight in the eye.

"Naw man, honestly I didn't. It got heated though. I had no business in her room," Anthony said as he put his head down.

"Man, I'm not gonna lecture you. But you gotta deal with it," Chris said.

"Chris, I just need a favor."

"Yeah man, whatever."

"Can you pray with me? I can't even go to God right now for myself."

"Now that I can do." Chris put his hand on Anthony's shoulder and began to pray.

Father God, we humbly come to You right now. First, thank You for allowing us to see another day. Thank You for not punishing us according to our inequities. Father, as I stand with my brother, we ask that You would cleanse and restore us. Father, we know without You we can't be good husbands or fathers. Lord Jesus, keep us from harm. If we opened the door to sin, we ask that You shut it immediately. God, help us to stay connected to You. Help us to walk in victory as we continue to seek and do Your will. Now as we end this prayer, we thank You that You do not condemn us, but You hold us responsible for repentance. And in order to repent we must change our ways. We thank You that You are a loving and forgiving God. In Jesus's name, Amen.

"Thank you, brother," Anthony said. When he lifted his head, he felt lighter.

"No problem, man. We all have tests." He looked at Anthony and noticed his eyes were a bit teary. "C'mon. I don't know about you, but I need to get some grub. I'm not sure anything is left, if Kevin has anything to do with it!" He hit Anthony on the back.

"Yeah, you right." Anthony managed to let out a chuckle. "I'll be ready in a minute. I need to call my wife before we go."

"Gotcha. I'll meet you in a few," Chris said as he opened the glass door to the suite.

CHAPTER FORTY-SIX

Confessions

Dear Father: I'm just learning how to talk to You. Chris told me all I have to do is say what is on my heart and I don't have to worry about exactly how to say it. I have a few things I need to do and I need Your strength.

Rex was on his knees and his hands were shaking a bit but he continued to pray in his mind.

I have some things to tell my wife. I love her so much, God, and I don't want to fail her. I want to be the man she needs me to be. The only example she has had is her father and he seems to have done no wrong in her sight. But I know differently. I just really need guidance. You already know what I've been holding in. It has caused me to look at her father differently. On the one hand, I knew he did what he had to do. On the other, I've lost so much respect for him I can barely look at him. I feel like everyday I'm wearing a mask.

She would probably hate me if I told her. God, why did I have to find those files? Why me? I would rather have not known. Now the responsi-

bility is weighing me down. If I don't say anything, I could put my own ca-reer in jeopardy.

Lord, I wish You would tell me what to do. To relieve the mounting stress I've been doing things that I know I shouldn't. My life's out of con-trol. I want to come clean with my wife. She's so beautiful, God, I don't de-serve her.

He started to weep. The words stopped coming. He felt his wife's presence as she knelt down beside him.

"Honey, what's wrong?" she whispered quietly.

He grabbed and rocked her.

"Baby, what is it?"

Rex finally faced her and grabbed her hand. He placed the palm of his other hand on her face.

"I'm sorry."

"For what?"

"I know I haven't been myself for a while. It's just, honey, I have something to tell you and I didn't really have the strength. Honestly, I have several things to tell you. I've been dealing with something and it's been causing me to make one bad decision after another."

She stood up and sat on the bed and he did the same.

"I'm scared, baby, just say it," she demanded.

"Well, I guess I'm struggling with staying at the firm. I was reviewing some old files I know I wasn't supposed to see. Baby, I saw the evidence myself. Your dad's practice has a shady history. Honey, he's paid off a lot of people. He's paid off ambulance people, police officers, and even a judge or two. I can't be a part of it. I could lose my li-cense."

She took a deep breath and hung her head down. After

a long pause, words slowly crept out of her mouth. "Rex, I know."

His head shot up. "You knew? You didn't tell me?" His eyes narrowed as he focused in on her.

"I, I, my father, I swore . . ."

"You are my wife! You kept this from me?" His hand stretched back, then met her face with a force that almost caused her to fall back on the bed.

She fell down and hid her face in shame. Her tears soon saturated the bed.

Soon he realized what he'd done. He sat back down on the bed and touched her shoulder. "Baby, I'm sorry. I don't know what's gotten into me. But Jermane, please tell me you have an explanation. Please," he said.

She looked up at him, still stunned by what he'd done. Through tears she said, "Rex, I went to my father myself years ago because of the rumors I heard. He admitted it to me. I mean he is not proud of what he did, but he said he did what he had to do to start his business. But I swear to you, it's over. That was at least twenty years ago. He's run a legitimate practice since then. I don't blame you if you want to resign. But before you do, I want you to go to God, because my father has. No he's not perfect, but he's confessed all his sins to God. God has forgiven him so maybe you can too. Rex, above all things, you are my husband. I will respect whatever you want to do. But all I ask is that you go to God first." She touched her husband's arm.

"Forgiveness, that's a good word. Yeah." He looked up, "I feel really confused right now. But forgiveness is a really good word. I don't even know who you are. I'm not sure

who I married. I love you, but I just need time to think,"
he said as he took a deep breath. He stared past her out
the window. He could see the backyard garden in the distance. For a minute it provided some sense of serenity and
peace. He was almost in a daze.

"Rex, I understand." She waited for a cue from her
husband to know what to do next. "I'm going to leave you
alone for awhile. But before I go, you said you had a few
things to talk about. We might as well get everything out.
What else were you going to tell me?"

"Never mind. Don't worry about it," he said still facing the window.

CHAPTER FORTY-SEVEN

Godmother Connection

"*H*ello."

"Hey, how are you feeling? This is God-mother Two. Are we going to look for your baby furniture this weekend or what?"

I rolled my eyes. "Jewel, I'm in the middle of drafting a petition. Can we talk about this later?"

"The shower's set for the end of September. But I'm a planner, so you know I like to stay on schedule. I'm trying to come up with shower ideas too. I know, I know, nothing over the top. No live storks and no shower games—how boring."

"It's my shower, Jewel. Anyway, this is Fourth of July weekend. I need to rest. But then again, I can probably catch some good sales. I'm just looking for that one layette. I guess we can go to a couple of places this weekend. I just have so much work to do. All of a sudden we've been getting a lot of business. I've even had to refer some business elsewhere."

"It could be worse."

"Yeah, you're right about that. It'll be nice to get together at Capri's Saturday night."

"Oh yeah, that's right. Boy, everybody seems so lovey-dovey since that Las Vegas trip. I haven't heard any complaints," Jewel said.

"Girl, I'm not gonna ask any questions. Chris has been wonderful and he tells me how beautiful I am every day. Boy do I need it, I feel like a boat. To be five months pregnant in the summer in Houston? It's torture. Chris has been working extra jobs so we can prepare for my time off work. At least I can do some things at home and we've hired a law clerk from Thurgood."

"That's smart. I wish some of that planning would rub off on Kevin's ex. I can say she's been a little more low key even though the child's father wants nothing more to do with her or the baby. She has cut back on the damsel in distress syndrome."

"So, I guess she is finally getting a life of her own. Are you doing her shower too?"

"Lexi, let's not get ridiculous. I still think Kevin is a little too concerned about her. I don't argue anymore, but when I do mention it, he says we just need to be 'Christ-like' and have empathy for others. I think that's a bunch of crap. I guess I feel left out a little sometimes," Jewel said.

"Well, unless he's really giving you a reason to worry, I suppose you have to let it go. They always will have a connection, but I think he's gotten the message."

"I've been praying on it and God must be doing something with me. I've never been this nice to her. I notice, the more I let go of that resentment, the less of a problem it is."

"Maybe God was waiting for you to change."

"Um, maybe. I'm just tired of being the one who always has to change."

"You know, Jewel, I think the sooner we stop looking at it that way, the easier it is for God to work. It's all about obedience."

"Lexi, why do you always have to say the right thing? Can't you just let me be selfish in peace?"

"Nope. I have to let you know what the Lord drops in my Spirit."

"I guess that's why I love you, girl. Okay . . . Godmother Two out."

"Oh brother."

Fireworks

Everyone except Jermane and Rex had made it to Capri and Anthony's Fourth of July barbecue. Capri and Anthony had a pretty big turnout because Anthony had invited some of his teammates. Still, I missed Jermane. I was worried about those two. I knew they were having problems. The last several times I called Jermane she'd rushed me off the phone, and Rex was just as anti-social. I kept them in my prayers, feeling this was just something God would have to work out.

On another note, I knew I was going to pay later for all the sausage I was eating, but I couldn't seem to help myself.

"Girl, you getting big," Kevin said as he saw me walking across the room with my plate.

"Shut up, boy. You know you don't say that to a pregnant woman," I said as I slowly eased into my chair and wrapped my bread around my sausage.

"Yeah, don't talk about my baby like that." Chris came over, sat on the arm of the chair, and kissed the top of my head. "My wife is still fine."

We finished playing just about every board game in the house and ended with a round of Taboo.

"So, when are y'all going to find out the sex of the baby?" Jewel asked, then stuffed a mouthful of potato salad in Kevin's mouth. She slapped her thigh as she adjusted herself on his lap.

"I told you, we aren't. We want a surprise."

"That is *so* boring. There are absolutely no cute yellow outfits out there. I guess we can do the mint green . . . I'll go by Chase's Closet this weekend."

"Baby," Kevin said. "Can you please let Chris and Lexi do what they want. It's their baby. You just focus on the shower." Then he opened his mouth for another bite of potato salad.

Chris and I laughed. Soon the fireworks were lighting up Anthony and Capri's backyard. After watching the sky light up for a few minutes the men, as usual, went off to the game room and the women went to the kitchen.

"Lexi, you relax, we'll start cleaning up this mess," Capri said.

"Oh, don't worry, I wasn't trying to help. I'm just putting away my plate," I said as I sat down at the kitchen table. "It looks like Mr. Anthony is all up on Ms. Capri. Y'all might be getting a visit from the stork soon," I said as I grabbed a piece of cake.

"Girl, please. I can barely take care of the big baby I have," she said and started to laugh. "But I have to tell you something . . . and you better promise not to say anything." She looked around to make sure her husband wasn't anywhere around. "We had some issues before he left for Vegas. Do you all know Anthony was almost addicted to pain killers?"

"What?" I said. "How did you know?"

"Well, I found a bottle of Vicodin almost half full and I knew the doctor only prescribed them during the time when he hurt his back. I'd found them before his last game of the season. He denied having a problem. But when he came back from Vegas, he finally told the truth. It explained why he was tired all the time and, well, why we hadn't made love in a while and Anthony never had a problem in that area. I don't know, I guess Vegas did him some good. We had a long talk and we both realized we had gotten away from our prayer time. Ever since he got back from Vegas we've been making more time for fellowship and devotion together."

"Wow, that's deep," Jewel said with her elbows propped on the table and her chin resting on her fists.

"Yeah, we've been talking a lot and yes, we want to start a family soon. But, I will say, when he was in Vegas, I did lay down some prayer! I woke up in the middle of the night the Saturday they were there and Anthony was heavy in my Spirit. The Lord put it on my heart to fall on my face and pray. Even before he left that weekend, Anthony was not himself. The enemy was really stalking him. I prayed until I felt something lift, until I felt a peace."

All the ladies were silent.

"Hey, I think we all need to take a trip, because after they went out of town they all came back like new men," Jewel said, breaking the silence. "Well, he isn't taking those pills anymore is he? I mean, he doesn't have to go to Club Promise, or whatever that place is where Britney Spears and Lindsay Lohan went."

I pinched her leg under the table.

"What? I'm sure he's fine. Isn't he, Capri?"

"Well, we've been going to a few counseling sessions. He was really depressed after the playoffs and it could have become a major problem. But God has a way of exposing things. We're also going to go to a class Angel recommended at Lakewood. Honestly ladies, I'd rather not talk about it. I'd rather talk about a girls' getaway. I think we all could use one. We need to head to a Spa Retreat!"

"Sounds good to me," Angel said quickly as she raised her fork after shoving a piece of cake in her mouth. "So what's the date of the baby shower? I need to put it on my calendar."

"Um, the third weekend of September."

"Are you sure that won't cut it too close?" Angel said.

"No, it'll be okay. I'll have several weeks to spare," I said as I felt my belly.

"Girl, I am so glad we took you shopping for maternity clothes," Jewel said. "You are looking awfully cute in that sundress. We couldn't have you walking around here looking like you don't care."

"It's about all I can fit now. Especially going to work. It's tough trying to look professional when you're as big as

a beached whale. I had to go out and get new shoes, my
feet are so swollen. It's a good thing we can get away with
sandals in Houston," I said.

"Speaking of work, how's that going?" Angel asked.

"It's getting rough, girl. Capri and I have been holding it down and we've been getting a lot more business."

"Well, I don't want to put you guys on the spot, but I
can help," Angel offered.

"Girl, they keep you busy enough at your job," I said.

"Not anymore. I've been praying really hard on this.
I'm leaving the legal department at the oil company."

"What?" Capri and I both said at once.

"Yeah, I'm just not fulfilled. I'm taking my 401(k) and
I'm gonna run. I have enough savings until I figure out
what to do. I can step in and help you all."

Capri and I looked at each other.

"I'm thinking this is answered prayer," Capri said.

"Yeah, Angel. Don't you want to join Reynolds and
Stanton?"

"You know, I was sort of feeling that in my Spirit, but
I'm gonna pray on it and make sure that's God's will for
my life right now. But I feel a peace about it. In the meantime, I'm at your service!"

"Oh, thank you, girl . . ." I tried to stand up to hug her.

"That's okay, Lexi, don't try to get up. It's gonna take
you all day to get out of that chair." Angel reached down
to hug me around the neck, as everyone laughed.

"Okay, y'all. Since I'm doing you a favor, I want you all
to keep Octavio in prayer." She lowered her voice, although she knew the men were way at the other end of the
house in the game room. "He still hasn't been back to see

his father and I believe this man is holding on until he sees his son. I've never seen Octavio so stubborn about anything. He has such a good heart. He must be in so much pain."

"Definitely, as a matter of fact, we can pray right now. We got a lot of power in this room," I said. We all grabbed hands and I led the prayer. Before it was over, so many other things in addition to Octavio came up in my Spirit. Sitting in the kitchen praying with my friends, I was convinced more than ever how special our bond was. I realized all the love that would surround my child. *I am truly blessed,* I thought. The next thing I knew, I had broken down in tears and everybody was hugging me. They thought something was wrong, but I was just so full of joy. "I'm just so blessed to have you all as friends."

CHAPTER FORTY-NINE

Obedience Is Better Than Sacrifice

"I had a good time tonight," Octavio said, his eyes glued to the road as he and Angel drove home from the Fourth of July barbecue.

"Yeah, me too," said Angel as she turned on the radio. The smooth sounds of jazz on radio station 95.7 filled up the car.

A few moments passed. "Angel, you know family and friends are so important. You do know I want to have children one day and I want to be a really good father."

Angel didn't say anything. She let him talk.

"Yeah, family is important." She wanted to talk about her decision regarding Lexi and Capri's law firm but didn't want to interrupt the moment. She sensed he really needed to talk.

"Angel, I think I'm ready," he said.

Ready for what?

"I think this whole issue with my father is really holding me back from a lot of things. I'm going to see him,
this weekend. I know I need to go, and I just feel like I
need to let God have His way. Besides, it's making me mis-
erable. I just needed to get strong enough," he said quietly.

She didn't speak for a couple of seconds. She was smiling on the inside, knowing their prayer in Capri's kitchen
had had a lot to do with it. *Thank you God. You are so faithful.*
"Baby?"

"Yeah, sweetie."

"I'm so proud of you." She leaned over to kiss him on
the cheek. He grabbed her hand and rubbed it. "Do you
want me to go with you?"

"Yeah. Yes, I would really like that."

She took a deep breath. *He's finally going to be free from all
that bondage.* Her heart rejoiced at what she knew God was
doing.

As soon as he arrived at the hospital Octavio started
shaking. As he walked closer to his father's room he
turned into a little boy all over again, and when he walked
into the room, he was terrified. Angel was about to head
for the waiting room, but he held her hand and said, "No,
I want you to come with me."

When he walked up to his father's bed, his father's eyes
remained closed. His breathing was shallow and he had
shriveled up to almost nothing. All the hate Octavio had
refused to let go was instantly released at the sight of this
feeble man. He was drawn up into a tiny ball, frail and

barely able to speak. Soon his eyes slightly opened, barely resembling two slits. Angel walked over to the window. She felt like she was intruding, but Octavio insisted she stay. The least she could do was turn away so Octavio could have a moment.

He reached down and rubbed his father's hand, feeling the protruding veins with his fingers. His father's eyes opened a little more. His father's mouth opened a little and all he saw was his gums moving slightly. Then he closed his eyes again.

"He's been waiting for you." The priest standing in the doorway said, "Hi, I'm Father Stevens. You must be his son."

"Yeah, I mean yes, I am." Octavio was a bit puzzled. He squinted as he shook his hand. "He can barely speak. What makes you think he's been waiting for me?"

"He didn't say it with his voice. He said it with his eyes. When your mother comes to visit, she says your name and his eyes open and he smiles a little."

"Oh," Octavio said, almost disappointed.

"But we're glad you are here now, my son," he said and patted Octavio on the back.

Octavio sat back down and grabbed his father's hand again. Soon an avalanche of tears flowed out of his Spirit and down his face. He cried without shame. His mother came into the room and grabbed her son. *"Mi hijo,"* she said quietly as she cried too.

Angel tried quietly to leave, but Octavio got up and grabbed her hand. He walked her over to his mom and placed her hand in his mother's. After a little hesitation, she grabbed and held Angel's hand. All three of them stood and prayed. Angel finally decided to leave the room. She kept on praying because she knew his father wouldn't make it much longer. She walked down the hall and back again. Finally she peeked in the room. She saw Octavio holding a Bible. Then she heard him say, speaking softly:

"Papa, do you believe Jesus died and rose from the dead? Do you know and confess that you are a sinner and lost without him? Do you wish Him to forgive you of your sins and come into your heart? Do you give your life to Him and want to live for Him the rest of your life?"

Octavio placed the Bible on the bed and watched his father nod his head ever so slightly at his words. His father finally opened his eyes and he could see gray and blue surrounding his dark brown pupils. A single tear trailed down his wrinkled face. Octavio placed his head on the bed as his father took his last breath. His father lightly touched Octavio's arm and closed his eyes.

"Okay, Angel, hold it together," she whispered to herself as she stood right outside the doorway. She placed her hand over her mouth to keep from breaking down. The next thing she heard was Octavio's mother crying. He came out of the room a few minutes later. Octavio grabbed Angel and held her.

"You okay?" she said when he let her go.

He looked into her eyes. "Yeah, I really am." He smiled at her and she smiled back.

CHAPTER FIFTY

Rain on My Parade

Dear Jesus:

You KNOW how much I hate showers; baby showers, bridal showers, any kind at all—to me, going to a shower is like taking medicine. But I'm going to make the best of this. Lord, the baby is kicking a lot and I feel as though I'm ready to burst. For the most part I've been calm, but every time I look down at my stomach I'm still in disbelief. At first I was really scared. Then I felt overwhelmed with all the advice everyone's been giving me. I decided to ignore everybody. I mean millions of women have given birth before me right? One thing's for sure, this baby will be surrounded by love. Father, I'm believing for an easy delivery. All that extra pain really isn't necessary. Nothing's too hard for You. Lord, and one last thing, thank God someone had the sense to make some cute maternity clothes. I think I'd be even more depressed if I had to walk around wearing a tent and looking like

a beached whale. If I do say so myself I've looked pretty cute
during my pregnancy. Well, I better head over to the baby
shower. Lord, You know Jewel gets an anxiety attack when her
events don't start on time.

Love you, Lexi.

"Girl, are you alright?" Capri said as she walked in front of me. I was sitting in a rocker waiting for this baby shower shindig to start.

"Yeah, girl, just a little uncomfortable. I looked at myself in the mirror and it looked like my nose has spread all over Houston."

Capri tried not to laugh. Over the next several minutes the doorbell rang again and again, as women poured into the room. All the physical discomfort I felt left when I saw Jewel's mom walk in.

"My baby, my baby," she said, almost pulling me out of my chair. She kissed me all over my face.

"Mom, Mom, chill out," Jewel said.

"Excuse me?"

"I mean, you are going to make Lexi fall out of the chair."

"So what names have you picked out?" Jewel's mother asked.

"It's going to be a surprise. But of course if it's a boy it will be Christopher Blake Reynolds II." I didn't even have to look to know his mother Mrs. Reynolds was over in the corner beaming.

"Well, Rex said Chris has been on cloud nine about the baby," Jermane said.

"Yeah, but I'm glad his friends decided to come get him. I had to put him out, he was getting on my nerves," I said.

"What has he done to get on your nerves?" Angel asked.

"I don't know. Just his presence."

"Girl, you're being silly now," Jewel said and brought me some tea.

"I'm just ready for this baby to come out."

The doorbell rang again and in walked Jermane. My face burst into a smile. I was trying to get up, but she quickly walked over to me and reached down to hug me.

"Hey girl, I'm so glad you made it," I said as she held on to my neck. She didn't want to let go.

"I missed you girl, I know you've been praying for me," she whispered. When Jermane finally let go she kissed me on the cheek. "We'll talk later," she mouthed as she walked over to put her gift on the table.

We played only one shower game—*thank you, Jesus*—and shortly after we were finished Capri's cellphone rang.

She went to the kitchen. The next thing I heard was "Oh no, he didn't! Oh no, they didn't! Girl, thank you. I appreciate it." She was so loud that by the time she came back everyone was trying to figure out what the heck was going on.

"Oh, uh, just a little issue going on. You know, I know Lexi is tired, so it's been nice of you all to share this moment. Lexi, you want to say a few words before we start cleaning up?" Jewel said.

I was looking at her, completely baffled. "Jewel, what in the world is going on? That's rude."

"Oh, yeah, um . . . it's personal. I apologize, but I

really need to take care of something and so do you." She tried to grab my hand but I pulled it back.

"What? Ladies, can you excuse us for a minute?" After the five minutes it took me to get up from the chair I went in the back with Jewel to hear what she had to say. Of course Angel, Jermane, and Capri followed me.

"They'll be back soon," Jewel's mother said, trying to be ever so gracious to the remaining guests. She slapped on a fake smile, knowing something wasn't right.

When we all came back in with our purses, everyone else started to grab their own. "I apologize, ladies, we have a little personal emergency that we have to attend to." We waited for all our guests to leave accept for Chris's and Jewel's moms.

"You want to tell us what's going on?" Jewel's mother insisted.

"Not now, Mama," Jewel said.

Her mother walked over to the door and would not move until we told her where we were going.

"Okay, okay. Mama, Kevin, Octavio, Rex, Anthony, and Chris, of all people, are at a strip club right now! We have to go."

"Lawd, chile," my mother said. "Is that all? You all need to set right down and wait for the men to come home. Yeah, I'd be mad too. But that is not the way to handle it. You can do what you want, but that's not gonna solve anything. You need to act like you don't know and when they come home, let them have it!"

"Oh my . . . not my Christopher," my mother-in-law said. "What in heaven's earth has gotten into him?" She started to fan herself and dropped down on the couch.

"Mom, you are from the old school. This is the new school and we are going down to that strip club."

"By the way, who called to tell you they were there?" she asked Jewel's mom, her hand on her wide hip.

"Missy, a friend of Capri's. She has a husband in the NBA and she goes with him everywhere."

Jewel's mother rolled her eyes, moved out of the way, and opened the door for them. As she watched them march past, she grabbed a piece of cake, sat down on the couch, and put her feet up. Chris's mother was almost hyperventilating. "Don't worry darling, it's gonna be fine. I can't wait for this. Sometimes you just gotta let things flow. They'll learn. They have a long way to go."

"Lexi, can't you drive any faster?" Jermane said. "I knew we should have taken those keys from you."

I clutched the steering wheel and had my pedal to the metal. The music in the car was loud and we were getting pumped up.

"Lexi, you need to pull over and let me drive," Capri said.

"Capri, touch me and you die." My eyes were fixed on the road.

"You give them an inch and they take a mile," Jewel said.

"Yeah, I don't know who they think they're messin' with. I'm not trying to be made a fool out of," Capri said. "They must have lost their minds."

When we whipped around the corner to that hole in the wall we all jumped out like the SWAT team. Well, everyone except me. I sort of slid out. We valet parked. So you know it had to be serious, because I rarely pay for valet parking.

As soon as we walked in, I saw security pick up his radio.

"What are you looking at?" I said as we walked by him.

"Hey baby, you look good," a man to my left said.

I was horrified. "Can't you see I'm about to give birth?" *I swear to God, if I have this baby here I will never let Chris live it down.*

As we walked by, the security officer was yelling, "Code W, Code W." Finally he yelled, "Another wife ambush!"

In two minutes we found them and dragged them outside.

"Where's Chris?" I said. After a few minutes he came out of the bathroom.

"Honey, I was in the back. I was working with security," he said.

I grabbed him by the ear and started to drag him out. Once outside, I felt something wet pouring on my shoe. "Oh no!"

"What's going on?" Angel looked down. "Lexi's water broke! Her water broke! This package is coming early."

Chris threw his arms around me. "Oh, honey, I'm so sorry."

"Get off me. Get off me." I started to cry and finally stopped fighting him. Within seconds everybody was in their cars and we took off, racing for the hospital. I went from angry to scared. In the car, Capri held my hand and Angel prayed all the way.

"Angel, pray louder and harder," I said as I closed my eyes.

Before I knew it, I was sitting in a hospital bed. I was in too much pain to be mad. Chris sat across from me. "What in the world possessed you to go to a strip club? Do you do this all the time? Do you know how embarrassed— ouch!" I could barely form a complete sentence in between huffing. "I'm not due for a few weeks, how could this happen? It's all your fault." I closed my eyes tight.

"Honey, honey calm down. Save your strength. I didn't want to go to the club but I wasn't driving, Rex was. It was out of my hands. I was outnumbered."

Sweat was pouring from what seemed like every pore of my body. "Just shut up. I want drugs, just give me drugs."

Chris ran to the doorway, "Angel! Capri! I mean, nurse! Please help me!"

"I don't know anything about this. Angel, you go!" Capri said.

Angel came in the room. Her presence alone calmed me down. Soon my dad arrived. Angel just prayed over me and sang little hymns. I felt like I was going into a deep sleep. The next thing I saw was a really bright light, and then I saw my mother's face. She was smiling. The light was so bright and warm. She told me she was proud of me and she kissed and hugged me. At her touch I opened my eyes.

"Honey, push," I heard Chris say.

"What?"

"Push, one good push," the doctor said. "Yes, that's it. One more—and make it a good one."

"You said one more push, not two." I pushed one last time and the baby eased out. I was breathing really hard. "Oh my, oh my God." I fell back.

"It's a boy," the doctor yelled.

"Good, honey, you did so good. You were only in labor for a few minutes," Chris said.

"Chris, is he okay? Five fingers, five toes? Chris, five fingers, five toes, talk to me." Then I heard the most beautiful cry, and I saw this little tiny body lying on my chest, all wrinkled, with a head full of hair. "A boy. Chris, we have a boy."

I started crying and so did he.

"I did it."

"Yeah, you did it, babe. I love you. I'm sorry for . . ."

I didn't hear anything else. I held my baby, *my* baby.

Over the next day the pain came and went, but I still managed to sleep a lot. Although I was still weak, excitement took over each time they brought me the baby. I had just gotten finished feeding him when the phone rang. I struggled to reach over and finally picked it up. "Hello."

"Lexi, how are you feeling?"

"Girl, good. You coming over here?"

"Yeah, I'm already here. I just wanted to see if you were up."

I adjusted my body a little. The nursed walked in, grabbed the baby, and put him in the crib next to me. "Thank you," I whispered.

"Yeah, I just fed Christopher. I'm wide awake," I said to Jewel.

A few minutes later both she and Angel came in. I expected them to be excited but they both looked so serious.

They must have realized how they looked because Angel

came right over to kiss me on the cheek. "How are you feeling?"

"I'm good. What's wrong?"

Jewel took a deep breath. "Lexi, shortly after you came to the hospital, they rushed Stacy in."

"Yeah, is she okay? What did she have?"

"She had a little boy."

"Oh, that's wonderful!" I realized that I was the only one excited.

"Lex, she's not doing too well. She, um, she had a stroke during the delivery and they're not sure she's gonna make it."

My stomach dropped and I immediately looked at my little one. "How did this happen, I mean, was it the doctor's fault?" I started to feel guilty already. How was I so blessed? What made Stacy's situation turn out to be such a nightmare?

"Lex, she evidently had high blood pressure and, well, there were some complications. She wasn't supposed to get pregnant again. The doctors warned her she'd have a high-risk pregnancy."

I was still in shock. I couldn't say anything. My heart started to literally hurt. "How's Kevin?" I said.

"Well, he's not taking it too well. Chris, Anthony, and Octavio are with him now. Rex had to be in court, so he's coming later."

"Wow, talk about a bittersweet moment. I feel awful," I said.

"Sweetie, we still have to celebrate and be thankful for your blessing," Angel said as she stroked my hair. I rolled over on my side and felt this overwhelming feeling of sadness. I was quiet for the next five minutes. Angel and Jewel looked at each other.

"Um, I'm going to be with Kevin," Jewel said. "I need to go get Aja soon. She needs to see her mother."

"Yeah, you go ahead, I'll stay here with Lexi."

Chris brought me home two days later. As soon as I walked in, I was so happy to see my dad sitting in the living room. Having him around gave me so much comfort. There was still no change in Stacy's condition. We took turns doing a prayer chain over the phone. When I finally went to bed I was exhausted. Just before I drifted off I got this strange feeling in the pit of my stomach.

I had strange dreams all night. The last dream I had, I remembered seeing my mother at the end of the bed. She was smiling. Then she looked next to her and held her arms out, like someone was walking toward her. I jumped, then woke up. Two minutes later the phone rang, and I knew.

Jewel confirmed what I'd already sensed in my spirit— Stacy had passed away. Jewel and Kevin were caring for Stacy's baby. When I hung up the phone it was time to feed Christopher. Before dozing back to sleep I felt led to write. I needed to get out what was on my heart.

Dear God:

Some things I will never understand. I guess I'm not supposed to. Staring at my baby, I see what a miracle he is. He's perfect, from the shape of his head to his fingers to his toes. Just perfect. Then again, I suppose that's what every new mother thinks. Sometimes he just laughs for no reason and when that

happens, I believe he's being kissed by an angel—or that my
mother is visiting her grandson. Lord, I've barely stopped smiling
or crying since he was born. Now, I just can't believe Stacy is
gone. I'm not going to question anything. The Bible tells us in all
things give him praise. I have to admit, this one's tough.

Lord, we prayed so hard for Stacy. I know prayer can make
a difference, but I have to accept this as Your will. How can I
celebrate my wonderful blessing under these circumstances? Am I
being selfish? Well, I guess that's what You mean when You say
we should praise You at all times.

I love You, God, and I praise You,
Lexi

CHAPTER FIFTY-ONE

Double Blessings

"Behold, sons are a heritage from the Lord, children a reward from him. Like arrows in the hands of a warrior are sons born in one's youth. Blessed is the man whose quiver is full of them. They will not be put to shame when they contend with their enemies in the gate." The pastor quoted Psalm 127, then looked at us and smiled. "We have double blessings today." He stepped down from the podium.

"For all of you who are here to witness this baby blessing today, you are also responsible for the future of these little ones. Christopher Blake Reynolds II and Kevin Elijah Eastland II, may they have the blessings and favor of the Lord. I anoint them to live long lives and declare the works of the Lord. May they be covered in the blood of Jesus Christ. May they be surrounded by love. Let love greet them wherever they go."

None of us were prepared for Stacy's passing. I never want to question God, but for a mother to die two days after giving birth, that's really a tough one. Chris put his arm around me because he knew I was about to lose it. Tears were creeping down my face. I looked at Jewel and she could barely stand up. Kevin held Aja's hand. Aja, surprisingly, was the strongest of us all. After Pastor dedicated the babies we headed over to the reception. On the way we stopped at the cemetery for a special prayer at Stacy's grave site.

Kevin tried to stay strong. When he looked over at Aja, he lost it as he watched her place a flower on her mother's grave. Baby Kevin started to cry.

"Daddy, it's okay. Can I read now?" Aja said.

MISS ME, BUT LET ME GO

When I come to the end of the road,
And the sun is set for me . . .
Why cry for a soul set free?

. . . So when you are lonely and sad at heart,
Go to the friends we know,
Bury your sorrows in doing your deeds,
Miss me, but let me go.

AUTHOR UNKNOWN

Kevin cried a little more. But then he reached out and wrapped his arms around Aja and Jewel, who held their new son. He leaned down as Aja kissed the baby and whispered to Jewel, "I love you, you know that?"

"Yes, Kevin, I know."

Epilogue

I could not wait to start writing in my journal again.
It had been a while. The baby was fast asleep and I
went and sat on the porch.

Dear Jesus:

*I am truly blessed. This has been another year filled with lots
of highs and lows. Each year presents its different set of
challenges: victories, tragedies, old and new beginnings. I guess if
I didn't have You to trust or believe in, I'm not sure what I'd do.
It's funny how things happen. We search for answers and
sometimes we just have to accept the fact that You are God and
You owe us no explanations. We must enter into Your presence
through praise and worship and it is only there that we find rest.
I just have to trust that it will all make sense . . . one day. I'm
finally learning that death is a part of life. We all have to go
sometime. For now, I will celebrate every day. I'll try to*

encourage myself during the hard times and be open to whatever instructions You have for me. God, I want only Your will for my life. I've stopped believing that every day has to be problem free. I'm still growing, still trying to be that Proverbs 31 woman. She left some big shoes to fill and I'm beginning to doubt if she ever really existed. Lord, I'm sure it was You who gave Stacy the wisdom to make that will. It's amazing, as much as she and Jewel used to fight, Jewel was the very person Stacy trusted with little Kevin. It was You who knew Angel was supposed to be the third partner in our firm. She's still praying about it, but I know in my Spirit it will happen. It was You, Father, that caught Rex just in time before he fell into pornographic addiction. He'd been sneaking off to those strip clubs all this time and none of us knew it. If I had to practically give birth there to expose it, then so be it. Continue to use me, Lord. But I would have rather have had a different story to tell my child. Anyway, I'm glad that You love us so much. You allow us to fall, but You help us back up to learn a lesson. Father, I know I get angry with You at times, but You always welcome me back to Your arms. It's me who's always the stubborn one. I can't wait to hear Angel's first sermon. I'm glad she finally said yes to Octavio and it's a blessing to attend their couple's ministry. Wow, a lot has happened, but I know this is all a part of Your divine plan. I love You and praise You for it. I'm thankful to sit at Your feet, if only for a moment. Uh-oh. Gotta go, I think the little one's awake!

I love You.

Your daughter,
Lexi

1. What adjustments do you believe Lexi had to make once she went from being single to married life? Do you think marriage changes the dynamics of married and single friendships?

2. When Angel explained her reasons for changing her membership to Lakewood Church, why do you think Jewel wasn't so accepting? When and under what circumstances do you think it is appropriate to consider changing your church membership?

3. When a person acquires more responsibility in her life, how does she continue to make God a priority? How does a person maintain that balance?

4. Do you think men are less likely to forgive a hurtful pass than women? Why or why not?

5. How do you think Kevin should have handled the issues between Jewel and his ex-wife? Do you think Jewel had a fair assessment of the circumstances?

6. Why do you think Anthony Stanton had such a strong re-action to his championship loss?

7. Why do you think the men did not openly demonstrate their prayer life until their trip to Las Vegas?

8. What do you think are the spiritual benefits of keeping a journal?

9. Do you think Rex should have remained with the law firm after finding out the impropriety of his father-in-law's business?

10. Are there any prayers in *The Sunday Brunch Diaries* that af-fected you personally?

11. How do you believe couples in this century can improve communication?

12. What are some of the most common issues facing couples of this generation that would threaten their union?

13. Do you think many married men go to strip clubs? What do you think prompts such behavior? Do most people view that as an addiction or do they excuse it away?

14. What Scriptures do you rely on during a time of crisis?

About the Author

Norma L. Jarrett is a speaker and author of the novels *Sunday Brunch* and *Sweet Magnolia*, which was an *Essence* national book club selection. She is a graduate of the Thurgood Marshall School of Law and North Carolina A&T State University. Her work has garnered praise in *Ebony, Essence, Upscale, USA Today, Gospel Truth, Publishers Weekly*, and other publications. Among her honors, Jarrett has been awarded a Certificate of Congressional Recognition for her literary work. She attends Lakewood Church in Houston, where Joel Osteen is the pastor.

Also by Norma L. Jarrett

Waiting to *Exhale* meets *Church Folk* as Lexi, Capri, Jermane, Angel, and Jewel start doing brunch each week to trade tales of their love lives, law firms, and the Lord!

"How fun and rare is this— that once in a 'famished' while, sistas are able to gorge on the 'delicious morsels' of such fine literary cuisine...Enjoy!"
—VIVICA A. FOX

When a New Orleans wedding reunites two feuding sisters, will their faith be strong enough to heal the rift between them?

"Norma Jarrett has crafted a beautifully written, soul-stirring story that touches the heart."
—RESHONDA TATE BILLINGSLEY, author of *I Know I've Been Changed*